HOUSEHOLD SAINTS

HOUSEHOLD SAINTS

A NOVEL

FRANCINE PROSE

OPEN ROAD

INTEGRATED MEDIA

NEW YORK

Cover design by Jason Gabbert

978-1-4804-4543-7

This edition published in 2016 by Open Road Integrated Media, Inc.
180 Maiden Lane
New York, NY 10038
www.openroadmedia.com

For Howie

HOUSEHOLD SAINTS

Lord of all pots and pans and things,
Since I've not time to be a saint
By doing lovely things
Or watching late with Thee
Or dreaming in the dawn light
Or storming heaven's gates
Make me a saint by getting
Meals and washing up the plates.

"Kitchen Prayer"
FROM A HOLY CARD SOLD
AT THE SHRINE OF THE VIRGIN,
KNOCK, IRELAND

1

SAUSAGE AND PINOCHLE

IT HAPPENED BY THE GRACE OF GOD that Joseph Santangelo won his wife in a card game. This fateful game of pinochle took place in the back room of Santangelo's Sausage Shop, on Mulberry Street, in New York City, on the last night of the record-breaking heat wave of September 1949.

That summer, each day dawned hotter than the day before, and the nights were worse than the days. All night, pregnant women draped wet washcloths over their faces, begged the Madonna for a good night's sleep, and thought how lucky Mary was that her baby was born in December. Children, three and four to a bed, squirmed to escape each other's sweaty skin until their fathers' curses hissed through the dark and they dozed off only to wake, moments later, stuck together like jelly apples.

Downstairs, the streets belonged to the young men who gathered on the corners, smoking, tapping their feet as if the sidewalk were too hot for them to stand still, and especially to the sort of old people who claimed they never slept anyway.

From the doorsteps and fire escapes, they kept watch through the humid night—grandmothers cooing like pigeons and picking their black cotton stockings, grandfathers with their eyes shut, their chairs tipped back, dreaming out loud of that legendary summer in the old country when all the grapes shriveled on the vine, when the trout boiled alive in Lake Maggiore and floated belly up so that the whole lake shone in the moonlight like this: And here the old men would reach in their pockets for a nickel or a shiny dime.

This summer, they said, was a hundred times worse. Compared to Mulberry Street, Lake Maggiore smelled like a rose garden. At this, their wives nodded, even the ones who could usually be counted on to remember another time, in another place, when everything was bigger and better and more extreme.

Each morning, the papers ran photos of pretty girls in bathing suits frying eggs on midtown sidewalks. Each morning, some desperate mother asked her children: If I cooked on the pavement, would you eat? But her grumpy children only shook their heads, and even the best eaters would touch nothing but a slice of melon, a glass of milk, a peach. By noon, the bakeries were like steam baths, the bread like hot towels. Frank Manzone, the vegetable man, took to burying his wilted spinach beneath the last fresh leaves and stuffing it into paper bags, quick, so the housewives wouldn't see. The women knew that the spinach was wilted and bought it anyhow, because it was so hot that no one could stand to eat meat.

No one knew this better than Joseph Santangelo, the butcher, whose cash register hadn't rung since early June. Beads of oily sweat collected on the sausage, and the beef began to shine with the delicate fluorescence of butterfly wings. Eventually Santangelo transferred his stock to the refrigerator room at the back of the store, and spent August alone in his shop. Tired of staring at the empty cases, he'd make quick trips to the meat locker, like dips into a cool pond.

Labor Day came, summer's end, but the only thing that stopped was the air, which simply quit moving and would not budge no matter how the grandmothers fanned it with rolled-up newspaper and prayed to the Virgin for a breeze. Well into September, the temperature rose so steadily that even the young men got worried and repeated the solemn rumor that all this had something to do with the A-bomb. Among the old women, alarmists were predicting the end of the world: Hadn't God promised the fire next time? What if He'd meant this low steady roasting? So saying, the women fell silent and, from the habits of a lifetime, waited for their husbands to tease them out of their fears.

"Lord, turn me over!" cried the husbands, as the martyr San Lorenzo was supposed to have screamed from his agony on the hot griddle. "Cook me on the other side!"

Nervous joking, because it was the kind of heat wave which made the most sensible people think about doom. Even Joseph Santangelo began to wonder how his life would change if it just got hotter and hotter, and no one ever bought sausage again.

The night that Joseph won his wife at pinochle was the final night of the feast of San Gennaro. But for the first time that anyone could remember, it was too hot to celebrate. All week, the cotton candy had refused to spin. Giant ice blocks melted into lukewarm puddles for the beer kegs. At the start of the feast, crowds gathered near the ferris wheel to see if its turning might stir up a breeze; but the rickety wheel revolved in slow motion, and up in the high cars children could be seen getting sick from swinging in the heat. One by one, the food stands closed for lack of business; among the first to go was the sausage concession run by Joseph Santangelo and his mother.

And so it happened that Joseph was free to play cards.

That night, every light in the sausage shop was blazing, and the smell of blood clung to the damp sawdust. Yet there was no meat, no sausage to be seen, and the cases had been empty for so long that the place had the ghostly air of a ruin—precipitously abandoned, unchanged. Except for the four men drinking and playing cards, it could have been the butcher shop at Pompeii.

Among the relics of this lost time was a growing collection of empty wine bottles. By ten o'clock, six bottles had circled the table and fallen, as if passed out, on the floor. By that time, the four players were approaching the same condition, but some were closer to it than others.

The soberest was Joseph Santangelo. A tight bantam rooster of a man, the youngest and strongest, he was physically best able to hold his liquor. Also he was the host, and like many experienced hosts, believed in staying sober enough to keep an eye on his property. This was no problem, for Joseph was one of those men who can drink twice as much as his friends and never get half as drunk. Consequently he had a reputation for being lucky at cards.

Across the table sat his regular partner, Frank "Midas" Manzone, so nicknamed because everything he touched turned to gold. His wife was the best cook on Mulberry Street, his daughters were as lovely as princesses, his sons had already captured every debating prize and sports trophy at St. Anthony's. The wine he made in his cellar was not only the tastiest in Little Italy, but abundant enough for a full year of lunch and dinner, holiday feasts and nightly pinochle games. The day that it matured was a neighborhood holiday; shopkeepers were drunk by noon, and women turned out for the bargains. His vegetable stand, next door to the sausage shop, was a gold mine. His brother's New Jersey farm grew cabbage in the midst of blizzards, and the housewives bought his spinach even in this heat wave. At cards, he was considered even luckier than Santangelo, for Frank Manzone could drink as much as he pleased, and somehow his card game improved with every drink.

Joseph and Frank poured their wine into glasses. Their opponents, Lino Falconetti and his son Nicky from Falconetti's Radio Repair across the street, drank directly from the bottle.

If for no other reason, it was an uneven match—but of course there were other reasons.

For Lino and Nicky came from an ill-starred line, a family history of Falconettis wiped out by locusts which alighted nowhere else, Falconettis decimated by plagues which spread no further than their own front yards. Except for a few "good" years, when the wartime hunger for overseas news had made people need their radios like food, Lino's business had never done more than survive. Now, Lino saw the rising spectre of television (for which he had no talent) as yet another example of Falconetti luck—the same malevolent destiny which had wrecked his family life. His wife had died young, of diphtheria, a baby disease from which the two babies recovered. As the father of an infant daughter, Lino had prepared himself to defend her honor; seventeen years later, his Catherine was such a runt, such a smart aleck that her honor had never been challenged. And Nicky, his pinochle partner, his only son and heir? Nearsighted, overweight, pale, Nicky was not exactly slow, but his mind seemed to wander off like a toddler stumbling away from its mama in the park, and the simplest details slipped through his grasp like goldfish through the child's cupped hands.

At cards, the Falconettis lost so consistently that they had learned to bring no more than the few dollars they could ill afford to lose. When this was gone, the game ended, despite Lino's attempts to prolong it by swearing on his sainted wife's soul and scribbling huge IOUs which neither Santangelo nor Manzone would accept—except perhaps as a sign that it was time to quit and go home.

But on that September night, it was too hot to quit. No one had the strength to stand up. The game went on as seven, then eight empty bottles fell beneath the table. Even Santangelo was having trouble telling jacks from kings, and everyone bid out of turn. The scorekeeping broke down, which was just as well, because the Falconettis had long since lost their money, and the betting had gone wild.

Frank Manzone put up four pounds of wilted spinach and won a newly reconditioned Stromberg-Carlson from Nicky. When at last Lino produced a coral rosary and swore, with tears in his eyes, that it had come from his sainted wife on her death-bed, Frank Manzone took a deep breath and somehow found the strength to say, "Okay, gentlemen, once more around from me and we call it a night."

It was during the final round that Joseph Santangelo took one look at his cards and bet the North Pole.

"The North Pole?" said Lino Falconetti. "Since when can you bet the North Pole?"

"Since right here behind me," said Joseph.

Rocking back in his chair, Joseph reached over, shot the bolt on the refrigerator room door and flung it open wide.

"Jesus," said Frank Manzone.

A cold blast hit the players like a punch in the face. They gasped, gulping the chilly air, and threw back their heads to let the sweat dry off their faces. Outside, the ferris wheel played music-box tarantellas, a vendor sang "zeppoli zeppoli" in a melancholy voice. But for the men in Santangelo's shop, the world fell silent. For, like a punch in the face, the icy blast had taken them out of themselves and made them forget their daily cares. Though not as intense as a vision of Our Lady, or an evening in bed with Rita Hayworth, it was the closest they would come to ecstasy on that hot night.

Santangelo shut the door. Immediately the cool wind stopped blowing, and the humid air flowed in like water. Sweating again, the men stared toward the meat locker, their faces slack with longing and regret.

"Christ," said Lino Falconetti. "Do that again."

"Win it off me," said Joseph.

"You're on."

"Not so fast, Falconetti. What'll you put up to see it?"

"My life savings," said Lino.

"Terrific," said Santangelo.

"All right, listen. I'll kick in the shop." At this, Lino glanced at his son, but Nicky was still contemplating the meat locker with a lovesick gaze.

"Do me a favor," said Joseph. "Keep the shop."

Lino pulled a handkerchief from his hatband, mopped his face, then sighed and bowed his head as if in prayer.

"God help me," he said. "Here's what I'll do. I'll put up my daughter—my only daughter. I win this hand—you open that door and keep it open till I say quit. I lose—you can have my daughter, my beautiful daughter, Catherine Agnes Falconetti."

"In that case, I'll take the shop," said Joseph, then caught himself. You could joke about a man's business—but not about his daughter.

"Ha ha," he said. "Just kidding. Sure I'll take your daughter, Falconetti. What have I got to lose?"

Then very slowly, pleased and smug as a magician completing a trick, Joseph fanned his cards and smacked them onto the table.

Nicky Falconetti whistled.

"Mama," said Frank Manzone.

"Am I seeing things?" said Lino. "Or is that the kings, queens, jacks, tens *and* nines of hearts?"

Joseph Santangelo smiled.

"Hearts is trump," he said.

The next day was so humid that the copper wires stuck to Lino Falconetti's fingers and came out in his hands like clumps of red hair. Lino cursed the wires, the radio, the weather and his many misfortunes, among them the fact that, after a lifetime of hard drinking, he still suffered the exquisite hangovers of a novice drunk. His eyes felt cottony, pressure clamped the bridge of his nose. All he knew was that he needed something and didn't know what it was.

Outside the gritty windows, scraps of tinsel and crepe paper clogged the sewer; festival garbage stewed in the gutter. An old woman in a man's winter jacket shuffled by on swollen legs wrapped with layers of crew socks and nylon stockings and stuffed into open sandals. She was preaching at the top of her lungs, something about Jesus dying on the cross and dogshit on the sidewalks of Sodom and Gomorrah.

"Ever notice?" said Lino. "It's always these gray cloudy days brings every cuckoo out of the clock."

Any normal son would have nodded, even if he weren't listening. But Nicky was off somewhere, in one of his operas, where even the crazy women wore satin, sang wild arias and never, never mentioned dogshit.

"Lost in a dream," said Lino, and took it as proof that Nicky didn't deny it.

Nicky was listening, but his father's voice had a watery echo, like conversations in dreams or shouts ricocheted off the tile walls of the Carmine Street pool. All his life, Nicky had heard this echo and felt the peculiar detachment of observing his life in a dream. Other people's earliest memories were sensual, immediate: The smell of Mama's clean apron, a flash of gold from Papa's Sunday watch. But Nicky's first recollection was a flat and distant image of himself in his baby tender, eating something (he couldn't remember what). The war had been a three-year dream set in an army radio shop in Germany, and now he had come home to a similar dream of losing his way inside radios—labyrinthine, eerily lit, cobwebbed and musty as attics. Evenings at Santangelo's, he watched himself draw one nightmare pinochle hand after another.

At twenty-four, Nicky felt so tired from all this watching that he could barely stay awake—except for those few hours on Saturday afternoons when he sat in his room with his radio blasting Milton Cross, Live from the Metropolitan Opera. For Nicky listened to opera the way other men read pornography: He put himself in the scene, imagined that Mimi and Carmen were trilling exclusively for him. Twice, he'd actually attended Saturday matinees; both times, he was disappointed. The gaudy, strapping divas bore no resemblance to the fragile creatures of his fantasies, and the shock of seeing Madame Butterfly sung by a German lady wrestler in a geisha wig made his heart literally hurt.

The pain was particularly sharp in that *Madame Butterfly* was Nicky's favorite opera. Often, as the days dragged on in his father's shop, he escaped by picturing himself as Lieutenant Pinkerton, enthroned like an emperor amid chrysanthemums and paper screens as his Oriental mistress waited on him hand and foot. He worked so hard at this that the smell of solder and hot wire was transformed into jasmine incense, and he could move himself to tears by imagining the guilt of discovering that his geisha had sung "Un Bel Di" and plunged a samurai sword into her breast for love of him.

On the day after the pinochle game, Nicky was grieving over the carnage in his Japanese love nest when he heard a loud click, then the squawk of an announcer's voice raving that the heat wave was about to break.

"Thank God," said Lino. It was unclear whether he meant the weather forecast or the fact that the radio was working.

"For what?"

"Rain by late afternoon."

"You need a radio to tell you that?" Nicky pointed a thumb at the window, the overcast sky.

"Bread and butter is what I need it for. Otherwise I don't need it for a thing." To illustrate, Lino turned off the radio, for the truth was that he had no interest in anything which might have come over it. Lino's own English was fluent, but after twenty years, radio English was yet another foreign language. Music only reminded him of those afternoons when Nicky's opera took over the apartment and he felt excluded, embarrassed, as if he were overhearing a neighbor couple in bed. The only thing he liked about radios was fixing them, and even that (he hated tinkering) was limited to the moment when he turned on a "broken" set and heard the Bakelite hum.

In the exhilaration of the wartime boom, Lino had joked about being a better mechanic than God: It didn't take *him* three days to bring a radio back from the dead. But the armistice (and its companion, television) had put a stop to his joking. When Nicky came home from the service, Lino began to suspect that the only pleasure which God had ever gotten from Jesus was the momentary thrill of resurrecting Him—and even that was more than *he* had ever gotten from *his* son.

"I need something," groaned Lino. "Wish to God I knew what it was."

"What you need," said Nicky, "is a hair of the dog that bit you."

"The hell," said Lino, infuriated by how proudly his son suggested this, like a doctor coming up with some brilliant diagnosis. Then, if for no other reason than to keep from cursing his own flesh and blood, Lino cursed the poison which Frank Manzone passed off as wine, cursed his bad luck in general and would have gone on to curse every hand he'd been dealt the night before—except that Lino was one of those drinkers who can never remember the night before.

Now, for example, he had a vague recollection of losing some money, then making his way home past a few tired revelers and zeppole vendors consuming the last of their unsold pastries. . . .

"That's it!" Lino pointed straight up like a witness at the Ascension. "That's what I need—a bite to eat."

Later, Lino would blame this selective amnesia for all his subsequent misfortunes. If only, he would say, if only he had remembered the terms of the previous night's betting, he would never have yelled upstairs and ordered Catherine to go buy some sausage at Joseph Santangelo's shop.

Later, Catherine would blame it on the weather. If it hadn't been so hot, Joseph would have been selling sausage instead of playing pinochle. If not for the heat wave, her father would never have bet her for a breath of cold air. But by then, the extraordinary course of their daughter's life had led Joseph to see deeper reasons for everything. And he would urge his wife to look beyond the heat to the hand turning up the flame—the same hand which timed the cloudburst for the next afternoon, for the instant that Catherine stepped out to buy sausage.

Catherine had just left her father's shop when the sky cracked open, releasing a low boom of thunder and a hail of raindrops so fat, they struck the pavement and bounced. Sheets of water flapped in the wind; streams washed through the gutters.

Released ten minutes early, the children came tearing out of St. Boniface and started shrieking and slamming one another with their lunch boxes. Watching from the doorways, their mothers fought the long-forgotten urge to run out and dance around with their heads tipped back and raindrops falling into their open mouths. They had to remind themselves that full-grown women didn't go out and get drenched for no reason—until, one by one, they came up with a reason to go out. For the cool air had made them imagine how nice it would be: The whole family gathered around platters of veal chops steaming in tomato sauce and cheese, sausage fried with onions and peppers, the good hot food they hadn't had the appetite for all summer—everyone eating, talking, laughing while the rain pattered softly outside. Even the ones who would eventually go home to a dinner table in hell, meals soured by rancor and arguments, imagined as they hurried through the rain that they were rushing to buy food for an ideal family, a cozy dinnertime paradise.

By the time the women reached Santangelo's, they were giddier than their children. Breathless from running and laughing, they shook their heads, streaming droplets onto the sawdust.

"Sweetheart!" Joseph greeted each one. "Lover, where have you been?"

The women blushed, as if he were really their lover, and perhaps that was why they felt so unself-conscious, though their wet dresses clung to them, revealing intimate details. All they could think of was how much they'd missed him. Crowding into

15

the shop, each was reminded of some long-ago wedding when she'd danced past midnight like Cinderella, one night when the rules which governed the rest of her life were suspended. Now, in that same way, the women dispensed with the rules of normal butcher shop behavior, and giggled and gossiped without the usual itchy awareness of whose turn was next. Even the thriftiest forgot to watch Joseph's thumb, but it didn't matter; that day, in celebration of the heat wave's end, Joseph refrained from sneaking it onto the scale.

Ordinarily, Joseph was a master of dishonesty. Like his father before him, Joseph knew exactly when and how to tip the scales, knew which housewives would notice the short weight and which were so oblivious, they could cook and carve a roast with the meat hook still inside it.

And yet, like countless generations of Santangelos, Joseph never thought of himself as a dishonest butcher but rather as a leveler, an instrument of primitive justice like the legendary outlaws of the old country. In this tradition, he sold to widows at cost and sent rich matrons home with a pound of pancetta that was half a pound of paper. Like all great bandits, Santangelo men delighted in playing cat-and-mouse with the law, and indeed the housewives' strategies equalled those of the cagiest detectives. Fed up, the women ordered Joseph to write his computations on the brown paper bags, and they reweighed their purchases on the scales in other shops. Always the sums totalled, the weights checked out, and still the women knew that they hadn't received what they'd paid for.

Of course there were other butchers in Little Italy, and nothing prevented Joseph's customers from taking their business elsewhere. But their families would have missed his special sausage, made by old Mrs. Santangelo from a secret family recipe which they could never quite duplicate. And they themselves would have missed Joseph.

In part it was the cheating itself which won their loyalty. They enjoyed the perpetual challenge of trying to catch him and couldn't help admiring a man who could lie to their faces and get away with it. But why didn't they feel the same thrill when other merchants shortchanged them? Why had they wasted no love on Joseph's father Zio, a sour-faced man who never took his cigar out of his mouth long enough to talk?

The answer was that Joseph liked women, and they knew it. As he strutted behind the counter—slicing, grinning, saluting them with his knives—his customers felt such warmth in their hearts that his petty dishonesties flattered them like secret signs of attention, and the energy he put into cheating them made them feel as lovely and desirable as brides.

On that rainy September afternoon, Joseph's dashes to the meat locker made the women think of a lover running for that special bottle of chilled champagne awaiting his mistress's return. Like women reunited with their lovers, they felt that there was nowhere else they would rather be, no way they would rather celebrate this God-sent break in the weather.

Yet this celebration, like so many others, included one determined holdout, one teenage girl leaning into a corner with the folded arms and put-upon expression of someone who's not enjoying herself and doesn't care who knows, someone so unable to get into the swing of things that she forgets completely where she is and winds up being the last one to leave.

And so the shop was empty again when Catherine Falconetti remembered what she was doing there, stepped up to the counter and said, "Two pounds of sausage."

"Hot or sweet?" Joseph's sly grin suggested a choice between two delicious and obscene alternatives.

"Mixed." Catherine didn't smile back.

"Half and half it is." Reaching into the display case, Joseph bent till his eyes were level with Catherine's chest, then straightened up and said, "Two pounds of sausage for a shrimp like you?"

Catherine looked as if she were eyeing a silverfish in the bathtub.

"Not just for me."

"Too bad. If you don't mind my saying so, you could use the extra meat."

"Spare me the beauty advice and let's have the sausage so I can get home and start cooking. Lino's hungover from your card game last night and he's hungry."

"Right," murmured Joseph. "Two pounds of special sausage for my good friend Lino Falconetti."

Unlike Lino, Joseph was blessed with a memory which no amount of alcohol could impair. He awoke in the morning with perfect recall and no intention of holding his drinking companions to the stupid things they did and said the night before. A spiteful man could have used such a memory to ruin half the businesses and marriages on Mulberry Street. But Joseph kept his neighbor's confidences to himself, for his own amusement—just as it amused him now to think that little Catherine Falconetti belonged to him. He would never collect on the bet, no more than Frank Manzone would dream of claiming poor Nicky's reconditioned Stromberg-Carlson. For one thing, Lino wouldn't remember staking his daughter. For another, Joseph didn't want her.

Idly, he took another look at his prize—built like a ten-year-old boy and about as attractive as she stood there, chewing gum like a kid who imagines that toughness is a matter of how sullenly you can chew. Rain dripped from her spiky dark hair and shone in the pebbles of her black, old lady's cardigan. Like his other customers, Catherine was soaked, but she was the only one with hunched shoulders, arms folded in on herself—as if, thought Joseph, she had something to hide.

What would he do with her if he had her? No father, no matter how drunk, would gamble away his daughter's honor—and that automatically left marriage. But Joseph wasn't ready to marry; and if he were, Catherine wasn't the wife he would choose.

Still, she was a female. In honor of that fact, and for the sake of form, Joseph tossed the coiled sausage up into the air and caught it on his knife blade in such a way that it fell to the counter with six links neatly separated from the rest. The elegance of this gesture was wasted on Catherine, who was gazing over his head at the poster of a cow divided into cuts of meat.

No longer amused, Joseph slammed the sausage onto the scale and was suddenly overcome by the disappointment which so often follows near-disasters, catastrophes survived. The heat wave was over, people were buying sausage again. Just yesterday, he'd wondered how his life would change in some slow, hot, vegetarian end of the world—but now he knew that it would never change at all. And what did that leave him? Forty, maybe fifty years of cheating housewives out of their precious pennies, of drinking his way through dull pinochle games and winning uncollectible bets from the Falconettis. At this, Joseph's melancholy changed to anger—directed, for want of a better object, at Lino Falconetti. The old man owed him something—if not a daughter, then something to redeem a lifetime of worthless IOUs.

Joseph decided to make the Falconettis pay in the only way he knew. Pressing his thumb into the sausage, he leaned ever so lightly on the weighing pan.

"A couple ounces over. Dollar fifteen."

"Don't think I didn't see that," said Catherine. "Weigh it again."

"See what?"

"I saw you weigh your thumb along with that sausage."

"You saw that, did you?" Joseph raised his thumb, clenched his fist, and thrust it inches from her nose. "See this thumb?"

"Sure."

"You know where I can put this thumb if I want to?"

"No." Catherine popped her gum and stared off into the distance beyond his left shoulder.

Joseph wheeled around. Sometimes his mother came downstairs from the apartment and stood at the back of the store to see how her sausage was selling. But now, thank God, there was no one there.

He grabbed a link of sausage and shoved it toward Catherine. Slowly he rubbed his thumb along the casing, pulling till the skin stretched.

"Now," he said. "Now do you know what I mean?"

"No." Catherine's black eyes were serious and innocent, so wide open that Joseph realized: She didn't know.

"Jesus Christ," he said.

Ten years behind the counter had given Joseph plenty of chances to study his taste in women. He liked them all, but the ones he loved best were the plump ones, so eager to get home and eat that they bounced in and out of his shop; the pretty ones with fast reputations; and the married ones who had borne ten children without losing the will to sparkle for an appreciative man. What moved him was how sweetly they examined their purchases, checking for gristle as if it were human flesh, probing with a practiced gentleness which Joseph had always associated with women of experience. Only now, after all this time, did Joseph understand the fuss men made over virgins, the longing for that startled grace which vanishes with experience. Only now did he feel the urge to watch a girl cross over; and now, as he thought of his customers, he felt that he would never know them because he hadn't been the one to watch them cross. Now, staring back at Catherine Falconetti, he began to imagine what he would do with her if he had her. First he'd dress her in a white communion outfit which he'd peel off, petticoat by petticoat, like the outer leaves of an artichoke. And then he would show her exactly where he could put his thumb.

Right then, Joseph decided that Catherine was kind of pretty: No Rita Hayworth, maybe, but delicate. And it was then that he made up his mind to collect on Lino's bet.

"Dollar even," he mumbled. "My mistake."

He stuffed the sausage into a bag, took Catherine's money, graced her with one final sexy smile and said, "Go ask Lino. Go home and ask your father where Joseph Santangelo can put his thumb."

He was so delighted with this parting shot that Catherine was long gone before he noticed: She'd only given him eighty-five cents.

By that time, the sausage was browning in the pan. Stepping back to avoid the sputtering fat, Catherine heard coins jingling in her cardigan and thanked God that they were in her pocket and not in Joseph Santangelo's. Theoretically the change was Lino's, but Catherine had worked so hard to keep it that she felt as if she'd earned it and had every right to make plans for the money she'd saved.

Tomorrow morning, she'd leave the breakfast dishes in the sink, the laundry in the hamper. She'd walk up Sixth Avenue to the Woolworth's and treat herself to a slip of begonia or a few strands of ivy in a cardboard pot. Edgy and alert as a mother taking her newborn on its first outing, she would hurry back downtown, stopping only once, at the newsstand, to buy the September *Silver Screen*.

All month, its red banner headline had shouted to her from the magazine rack, loud as a voice crying: What is Loretta Young's Tragic Secret? All month, she'd speculated, like someone trying to outguess the detective in a mystery. But tomorrow, she would put off finding out till she'd repotted and watered her new plant. This she did immediately, with an urgency which was part of the pleasure; it was the only time when Catherine felt she was doing something which couldn't wait.

Catherine's plant collection dated from a trip to the five-and-dime years before. On her way to buy darning thread for Lino's socks, she'd paused in the houseplant section. There, amid the sacks of dried-out potting soil and peat containers, she'd found herself thinking of some photos of Italian war orphans which the nuns had passed around at school. The class had been instructed to say ten additional Hail Marys for their less fortunate brothers and sisters, but Catherine had forgotten till the pitiful plants reminded her of those children—starving, abandoned, calling out to be taken home and loved. This maternal sense stayed with her; as the plants sprouted new leaves and flowered, Catherine felt as proud as any adoptive mother, watching her skinny foundling polish off a meal.

Tomorrow, dozens of healthy plants would be shifted so the newest addition could bask in that brief spot of morning sun by the kitchen window. Only then would Catherine open her *Silver Screen* and learn Loretta Young's secret.

So far, Catherine's guesses included a failed marriage, a broken contract, a retarded little sister, a boyfriend killed in the war. Whatever it was, it couldn't be worse than the story of that distant cousin of Lino's who'd once been a movie actress. According to family legend, a certain Maria Falconetti had appeared in a silent movie about Joan of Arc, made somewhere in Europe in the twenties. With typical Falconetti luck, the picture was a total flop. But the worst of it was that Saint Joan's part was nothing but crying and crying; the director made Maria cry so hard that she couldn't stop when the movie was finished, and wound up crying in a mental hospital for the rest of her life. Catherine had never seen the film, nor was it mentioned in any of her movie magazines. She wondered if the story were true.

It wasn't that Catherine accepted *Silver Screen* as the gospel truth, but she did believe that the truth could be learned by comparing its gossip with the facts she observed on Mulberry Street. In this way, she had come to two conclusions which made her life easier to bear.

The first was that fate had no respect for celebrity. Gene Tierney and Judy Garland were living proof that famous stars could draw unluckier hands than the most obscure Falconettis. The second was that work was work. To hear Myrna Loy tell it, waiting around soundstages and slaving under hot lights was as bad as ironing Lino and Nicky's shirts. The only difference was that Myrna Loy got paid a lot better than Catherine Falconetti, because no matter how you fooled yourself, life was not the movies. Hollywood had its Leslie Howards, its Charles Boyers; Mulberry Street had its Joseph Santangelos, shoving their thumbs in your face.

Catherine turned the sausage and put Santangelo out of her mind. She had a talent for suppressing unpleasant thoughts, a knack which allowed her to think she'd been switched in her cradle and left with a family known for dwelling on its own misfortunes. Most days, she tried to forget about her mother dying so young and leaving her responsible for two men who would never say thank you in their lives, about the fact that she was seventeen and had never had a boyfriend or any sign of male attention but a butcher's grimy thumb. To check herself, she concentrated on immediate realities—the popping sausage and, beyond that, the clamor of her father and brothers homecoming, their wordless racket directed at the kitchen, as if even the scraping chairs and rattling silver were demanding to be fed.

Yet when Catherine set out the food, the room fell so silent that she could hear the sound of chewing and the rain outside. She thought of the other women at Santangelo's shop and wondered how many of them were hearing these discouraging noises, so unlike the warm appreciative buzz which the rain had tricked them into imagining.

"Sausage," said Lino, and that was all. No one spoke again till Lino put down his fork, tossed his balled-up napkin onto his plate and said, "Okay, Nicky, finish up. Let's go play some pinochle. Must be the weather, I feel like this could be my lucky night."

Somehow Lino sensed from the start that tonight's game would be different. Maybe it *was* the weather. All summer, they'd smacked their cards on the table as if trying to rouse each other from some hot weather stupor. Yet tonight, thought Lino, the cards would slip and slap, gentle as the tapping rain. Though Lino knew better than to hope for luck, what he felt tonight was so close to hope that he could hardly wait to pick up the cards and deal.

But when he did so, the only slap he heard was the one which Joseph Santangelo gave him on the back of his hand. The deck flew across the table.

"Christ, Santangelo." Lino leaned over to retrieve the scattered cards. "What's eating you?"

"Hang on," said Joseph. "Nobody's dealing till we settle from last night."

"Settle?" repeated Lino. What was there to settle? He never bet more than he had in his pocket. And though the others teased him about forgetting himself and staking his dearest possessions, he trusted them, as gentlemen, to sympathize when a gentleman got carried away. Besides, what use would Santangelo or Manzone have for his late wife's rosary?

"Settle what?" said Lino.

"You mean you don't know?"

"So help me God." Lino kissed his fingertips and crossed his heart. "I don't remember."

"Maybe I can refresh your memory," said Joseph.

"Maybe you can." Lino faked a laugh.

"Your daughter."

"My daughter?" Lino looked from Joseph to Nicky to Frank Manzone. "What about her?"

"You bet her on the last hand. And you lost."

"I bet *Catherine*?"

"For a blast of cold air. From the meat locker."

"That's crazy." Lino twirled a finger at his temple. "I must have been out of my mind." Again he appealed to Frank Manzone for confirmation, but Frank—who believed in safe-guarding his good luck by minding his own business—only nodded, took the deck and said, "Whose deal?"

"Nobody's!" Jumping up, Joseph grabbed a cleaver and flicked at its blade, a gesture which would have conveyed more menace if he hadn't been trying so hard not to laugh. "Not till we settle."

"I knew it," said Lino, with an edgy smile. "He's kidding. What a joker. Listen, Santangelo, you don't want my Catherine." Yawning, Lino forced up a belch. "That sausage she cooked tonight, it's still coming back on me."

"Shut your mouth, Falconetti. She bought that sausage in this shop." Glaring at Lino, Joseph's eyes looked steelier than the cleaver, sharp enough to cut meat. Lino realized that he wasn't joking.

"Now *you* listen." Joseph rapped the chopping block. "You know what it means to be a man? A man means you pay up."

"Come on now." Lino struck his forehead with the heel of his palm. "What kind of man bets his daughter in a pinochle game?"

"I give up," said Joseph. "You tell me."

"A man doesn't . . ."

"Have it your way," said Joseph. "You're not a man. And from now on you can forget about pinochle. You can go play canasta with the women—*if* you can find women dumb enough to deal a well-known deadbeat into their game."

Lino imagined himself going crazy for a taste of Frank Manzone's wine while the women sipped hot chocolate and exchanged recipes, household hints, the details of their latest operations.

"Catherine?" he said. "I bet Catherine? You know anything about this, Nick?"

"What?" said Nicky.

"Where have you been?" demanded Lino.

"Right here," said Nicky, though in fact he'd been lost in the final act of Gluck's *Iphigenia,* watching Agamemnon sacrifice his beloved daughter for the good of his navy, and longing to stay there, where he would never have to face the fact that *his* father had lost Catherine in a pinochle game.

"It's not so terrible." Joseph replaced the cleaver and slid back into his chair. "I'm talking about marriage, a regular church wedding, everything on the up-and-up. No one will ever have to know what happened. The story will stop at that door. Let's drink to it."

Lino took a sorrowful pull on his wine bottle.

"All right," he said. "We'll discuss it later. Tomorrow night, Santangelo, you and your mother come to the house for dinner. We'll work it out. Tonight, let's play pinochle."

That night, as always, the Falconettis lost every hand. And yet as Lino had sensed from the start, things were different. That night, for the first time anyone could remember, Lino made no attempt to prolong the game. When his pockets were empty, he threw in his hand and walked home through the rain.

Despite her intention to wait till tomorrow, Catherine had run out to the newsstand just before it closed. Now, curled on her bed, she was reading about how Loretta Young's father was killed in a freak tractor accident on the family dairy farm. Because of this early tragedy, Loretta had problems with men, and a "perfect" marriage had ended in divorce.

Just then, Catherine heard Lino coming upstairs and wondered if Loretta Young had been raised to listen for the menfolk at the end of the day, for the sounds which stopped conversations like an angel passing and cut through daydreams like the tolling of a knell. Could Loretta tell how the cows were milking from the rhythm of her father's footsteps in the hall? Listening to Lino, and Nicky behind him, Catherine could almost count the radios which had come into the shop and the money gambled away at pinochle. Ordinarily the wine propelled Lino up, two steps at a time, like a much younger man. But tonight he waited on every rung. He was drunker than usual, or had lost more at cards. Something was different.

But she didn't know how different it was till the footsteps stopped outside her room. At the first hesitant knock, Catherine slipped the *Silver Screen* into her nightstand and opened the door, as if it were perfectly normal for her father to knock on it late at night.

Swaying slightly from side to side, Lino blinked at her, his face expectant, slightly skeptical, as if she were the one who had knocked on *his* door. After a while he remembered his purpose, at least enough to say, "You cooking tomorrow? Company's coming to eat."

"Company?" In fifteen years, Catherine and Lino and Nicky had never had company to dinner. For among the Falconetti misfortunes was not just a lack of family closeness, but a positive horror of other Falconettis, who only seemed to remind each other of their genetic bad luck. "Who?"

"Joseph Santangelo and his mother."

"Oh no. Anyone but."

"Don't you like him?" asked Lino, his voice insinuating, like a poke in the ribs.

"Not especially."

"That's too bad. He likes you."

The way Lino said "likes" reminded Catherine of certain boys in the seventh grade who would trap you into saying simple words with secret dirty meanings. This time she was wary.

"What does that mean?"

"It means he and his mother are coming to eat. It means my Catherine's going to cook up a storm. And you know what *that* means."

Catherine shook her head.

"Meat. Tomorrow night, we'll show the Santangelos how the Falconettis cook a piece of meat. A roast, a veal roast. I'll pick it up tomorrow when I go tell Santangelo what time to come."

Of all the night's surprises, this, to Catherine, was the most unexpected: Until that night, she had never once heard her father express a preference about his food. Who would have thought that Lino knew veal from liver? The shock of this was so great that it diminished her amazement when, moments later, Lino said, "I want this meal to be so good, a man would get married to eat like that every night."

Suddenly Catherine remembered Joseph Santangelo telling her to ask her father where he could put his thumb. And now she understood what he'd meant as she imagined it, swollen to monstrous proportions, squashing the Falconettis like ants.

"I've got news for you," she said. "No one gets married for the food."

Catherine awoke at three in the morning with a vague sense of something wrong. She checked back over the previous day, imagined into tomorrow, got as far as Joseph Santangelo and stopped right there. By dawn, she was in no shape to cook up a storm. Long before she started cooking, she knew that it was going to be one of those days when everything goes wrong in the kitchen.

Yesterday's rain, slowed now to a steamy drizzle, had refreshed the neighborhood, but the produce in its markets had yet to recover. The mozzarella in Passaglio's dairy was yellowed and rubbery; the ricotta rose in grainy islands from seas of its own whey. At the Grand Street Market, olives were up ten cents a pound and specked with coarse dry salt. Frank Manzone's tomatoes showed patches of fuzz, soft spots like circles of pudding; his spinach was so slimy that Catherine wondered how she could have bought it a few days before. The only items which weren't overripe were the rock-hard pears and the acidy Gorgonzola.

Catherine complained to the storekeepers, who told her not to blame the weather on them and reminded her that no one was twisting her arm. But people rarely said that, she'd noticed, unless your arm was already twisted. She had to buy what the merchants offered, just as she had to cook it for Joseph Santangelo and his mother. If she struggled, her whole life would snap like a bone.

Upstairs, she concentrated on cooking to keep her mind off the upcoming dinner. But real concentration would have kept her from burning the butter, from scorching the cast-iron pan so badly that she had to scour and reseason it. Meanwhile she forgot the escarole soaking in the sink—which overflowed, strewing greens like beached seaweed on the floor. She broke three eggs into a bowl and the fourth was rotten, so she threw them out and started again. No matter how she experimented with the manicotti batter, the pancakes came out leathery, pocked with blisters and holes. The iodine smell of boiling shrimp mingled with that of burned butter and permeated the apartment.

At one, Lino came home with a roast which was brownish-purple, marbled with gristle and splintered bone.

"What's this?" demanded Catherine. "Something the cats killed and left out in the alley?"

"Ha ha," said Lino. "Santangelo swore up and down, it's the best veal roast he had."

"Ha ha," said Catherine. "The best shoe leather."

"Now why," said Lino, "why would Santangelo sell me shoe leather when he's the one that's going to eat it?"

"Because he's such a crook. When there's no one else around to steal from, he'll cheat himself."

"Shut up and cook it," said Lino.

Catherine tried, she tried. She hacked through sinew and fat till the roast was half its original size, then lowered the flame under the tomato sauce and ran out for some eels to replace the brackish shrimp. On her return she was greeted by the smell of scorched tomatoes. She dumped the eels into the sink and prodded them with long-handled tines; they sloshed in the cold water, too moribund to squirm.

She mixed together some stuffing, crammed it into the veal, then slid it into the oven and waited for the comforting pop of juices and fat. She waved her hand inside the stove—it was luke-warm. She turned up the heat, and the gravy began to burn.

Even the plants on the shelves seemed to shrink from the acrid smoke. But Catherine was glad when it watered her eyes, priming them for a good cry. Crying helped relieve the tension, and she let the tears fall until, she imagined, they had salted and further thinned the runny zabaglione. So she gave up on a sweet dessert and resigned herself to serving the Gorgonzola and pears.

At six, when Joseph and his mother arrived, Catherine was on her knees by the oven, mourning over the underdone roast. She missed their knock on the door and the spectacle of Lino greeting them with the somber formality of a mortician.

"Good evening," said Mrs. Santangelo, in an appropriately funereal tone. Then, looking stricken, she sniffed the air.

"Mister Falconetti, is something burning?"

Catherine emerged from the kitchen just in time to see Mrs. Santangelo's face fall like a stalk of overcooked broccoli.

"Mrs. Santangelo," said Lino. "My daughter Catherine."

"I know your daughter," said Mrs. Santangelo.

Somehow Catherine got the first course onto the table. Somehow they found their places.

"Great antipasto," said Joseph. "Delicious."

"Thanks," mumbled Catherine, so grateful that she couldn't look at him and stared into her plate.

God is merciful, she thought. People understand. Even Mrs. Santangelo—she was a woman, she knew. If the celery was a little limp, she'd realize that it was the crispest Frank Manzone had. If the roasted peppers were a shade too black, she'd know that there were days when everything went wrong in the kitchen. Besides, why worry so about a meal for two strangers she didn't particularly like?

"Not much you can do to ruin cold antipasto," said Mrs. Santangelo. Then, as if to prove herself wrong, she picked a dark hair off a tomato and gingerly rubbed her fingertips till the hair dropped to the floor.

Catherine jumped up to clear the dishes and bring on the next course.

Though Lino and Joseph had arranged this meal to discuss the wedding, they each took one bite of the eels, looked at each other and silently agreed that this was no time to talk of marriage. With this subject excluded, there was little else to say.

"Thank God the hot weather's over," said Joseph.

"Thank God is right," said Catherine. Then, with a plead-ing look at Mrs. Santangelo, she added, "You couldn't cook a decent meal with the stuff they had in the stores—"

Mrs. Santangelo cut her off: "When I first came over from the old country, me and Zio were so poor, I had to pick shells out of the garbage can by Umberto's Clam House. And believe me, I made a delicious soup."

"When?" said Joseph. "When did you cook clam shells out of the garbage?"

The meal continued in silence, punctuated by the noise of silverware picked up and put down, food being scraped to the sides of plates, forks chasing recalcitrant strings of cheese, knives grating against china—all to a background of chewing and chewing and chewing.

No second helpings were offered, none requested. No one asked anyone to pass anything. No one looked up from their plates when a chunk of gristle flew out from under Nicky's knife and landed by Mrs. Santangelo's forearm. The men attacked their portions bravely enough, but their courage deserted them after one taste. Mrs. Santangelo sampled everything served her, then very deliberately pushed back her chair, folded her hands in her lap and stared into space. After each course, Catherine cleared the table, her work compounded by the extra clumsiness of stacking full plates.

At last Mrs. Santangelo nibbled at a crunchy pear, then stood, extended one regal hand to her son and said, "Thank you kindly, Mister Falconetti, Catherine, Nicky. Joseph, let's go. I got sausage to make for tomorrow."

On the way out, Joseph shook Lino's hand.

"Falconetti," he said. "We'll talk." Then he turned to Cath-erine, smiled, and said, "Thanks. The food was great."

Catherine listened for sarcasm in his voice, heard none.

"Don't thank *me*," she mumbled, too pleased and embarrassed to acknowledge the first such compliment she had ever received.

No sooner had Lino shut the door behind them then he spun around and slapped Catherine's face.

"What was that for?" Catherine, who'd been raised to decipher the occult meanings of men's insults and slaps, now had the distinct impression that Lino was actually pleased with her. Perhaps this was what he'd meant when he'd told her to show the Santangelos how the Falconettis could cook a piece of meat. Perhaps, for some perverse reason of his own, he'd wanted her to serve a meal bad enough to scare off the Santangelos.

"For putting crap like that on the table."

"Crap? You heard your friend Santangelo. The food was great."

"Great," mimicked Lino. "Since when has love got taste buds?"

"Love? What's this got to do with love?"

"What else do you think this meal was about? The good-neighbor policy? You're marrying that guy. It's settled. I've given my word."

"*Your* word? Papa, this isn't the old country. It's America."

"It's my house," said Lino, but Catherine had already left it. Pushing past him, she ran down the stairs and didn't stop till she reached the ticket booth of the Essex theater.

The Heiress was almost over, and Catherine was glad. Tonight, Olivia de Havilland and Montgomery Clift depressed her. She sat through the second feature, *To Have and Have Not,* which she'd missed in its first run, years before.

By the time she left the theater, the temperature and humidity had dropped; it was a crisp autumn night. All the way home, Catherine kept thinking of Bogart and Bacall—their teasing and fencing and falling in love. Somehow these thoughts led to Joseph Santangelo—how tough he'd acted in his shop, how sweet he'd been in her apartment, smiling and telling her that the food was great.

That night, as Catherine got into bed, she found herself think-ing that life was more like the movies than she'd ever dreamed.

Long ago, when an erupting volcano threatened Mrs. Santan-gelo's ancestral home, a teenage boy named Gennaro waited till the last possible moment, then ran up to the smoldering crater, arms outstretched as if to greet a long-lost friend. Down below, the Neapolitans watched him catch the flowing lava in his arms and prayed for Gennaro's soul. But their newfound patron saint survived to turn and wave, leaving his impression in the hissing rock, a fossil of two open arms preserved to this day in the hill-side above Mrs. Santangelo's birthplace.

If San Gennaro could do that, thought Mrs. Santangelo, he could tell her what her Joseph saw in a girl like Catherine Fal-conetti.

She lit a votive candle in a beveled glass holder and set it on the mantelpiece which served as the family altar: a plaster Madonna, a statuette of Gennaro with his arms spread wide, and a photo of her husband Zio, framed in gold and matted with black crepe.

"Holy Saint," whispered Mrs. Santangelo, easing herself down on her knees. "I'm not praying for a miracle. Just a simple explanation."

After a while she got up and slid the candle over in front of the photo.

"Zio," she said. "How about it? How could a smart boy like our son marry a Falconetti?"

It was not a rhetorical question; Carmela Santangelo fully expected an answer. Every few weeks, she was visited by the ghost of her late husband.

The first time, not long after his death, she was roused from a deep sleep by the smell of cigars.

"God help me, I'll kill you!" she screamed, forgetting he was dead. "Are you smoking in bed again?"

Only later, when she saw him hovering in the corner and realized the truth, did she think how fitting it was that the presence of a man's ghost should be announced by his worst habit. Much of Carmela Santangelo's life had been a struggle against Zio's cigars; in the end, the cigars had won. Yet that night, relieved of all responsibility for her husband's physical body, she was delighted by the cigar-smoking spirit and even by the stogie smoldering unchanged beyond death.

Zio, however, had changed a great deal. In life he'd been a down-to-earth man who wasted no more words than it took to tell her how many pounds of sausage were needed for the next day's customers. But his ghost was given to the vague, the philosophical, the cryptic; often, Carmela had no idea what he meant. She forgave him for this, for it seemed only reasonable that the company of angels might make a man flighty.

But she couldn't forgive him that night when he came to her room and refused to answer the question she'd been asking San Gennaro all day.

"Why Catherine Falconetti?" she asked. "Zio, why her?"

"Man deals," was all Zio's ghost would say. "And God stacks the deck."

The task of illuminating Mrs. Santangelo fell to her daughter-in-law Evelyn, who so relished this mission that the very next morning she drove all the way in from Long Island to perform it.

Evelyn waited till Joseph stepped out of the shop, then flounced in, opened her big orange mouth and said, "So, Mama. How do you like our Joey winning his bride-to-be in a pinochle game?"

Mrs. Santangelo suffered occasional palpitations and shortness of breath; now she felt as if her heart were being lanced with a hot needle. But the pain was bearable compared to her distrust of Evelyn's big mouth. So Mrs. Santangelo put one hand on her chest to contain it, shrugged nonchalantly and said, "Better pinochle than bingo." This was a dig at Evelyn, who had met Augie at a prewar bingo game in the basement of Our Lady of Victory.

"Mama." Evelyn gave the air a playful slap. "That's ancient history."

"What do *you* know about ancient history?" snarled Mrs. Santangelo, under her breath.

For Evelyn cared only for the newest, the latest, the most American. Under her spell, Augie had been lured away from Mulberry Street. He'd deeded the family business to Joseph, then moved to Long Island, where he'd started a truck rental firm and fathered twins names Stacey and Scott. ("And who will protect them?" Mrs. Santangelo had demanded at the christening. "Saint Stacey and Saint Scott?") Invited to her daughter-in-law's home, Mrs. Santangelo was served a barbaric concoction of fried pork and celery in a briny sauce which Evelyn said was Chinese. (The children, Mrs. Santangelo thought, the poor children.) But the truth was that she had no great love for her freckled, suntanned grandchildren, who didn't even look Italian. On that same visit, when she'd hugged them and asked when they were coming to her house, little Scott had wrinkled his nose and said, "Never. Your apartment smells funny."

Now, as if to atone for such ungrandmotherly thoughts, Mrs. Santangelo stuffed a bag full of sausage and passed it over the counter.

"Here. For Augie and the kids. Fry it up with a couple onions and peppers."

"Mama!" Evelyn made a show of being affronted, though Mrs. Santangelo had found her to be virtually uninsultable. "I know how to cook sausage."

Mrs. Santangelo let it pass. She paused and then, struck by an afterthought, said, "Oh, and by the way. About that pinochle game. I wouldn't tell anyone, would you?"

"*I* certainly wouldn't!" exclaimed Evelyn, her smile betraying the fact that there was no one left to tell.

Mrs. Santangelo had no choice but to draw herself up to

her full five-three and practice the line she knew she'd be called upon to deliver many times in the coming days: "If my Joseph won a horse and wanted to marry it, I'd feed it hay off my wedding china and love it like a daughter."

"Your daughter," muttered Evelyn. It was hard to imagine. For the general consensus was that Mrs. Santangelo was the kind of woman who never had daughters, only sons; the kind who would have been happier in another century, when the times required them to pick up rifles alongside their men and defend the family compound from marauders; the kind who worked themselves harder than mules, then outlived the mules and the men by thirty years.

"That's what you say *now*," sang Evelyn, and pecked a goodbye kiss in her mother-in-law's direction.

Evelyn was closer to the truth than she knew. For that same evening, when Mrs. Santangelo confronted Joseph over the dinner table, she said nothing about feeding a horse off her wedding china. Instead she ticked the facts off on her fingers.

"One." She started at the pinky. "The Falconettis haven't got a pot to pee in. Two: The girl's no beauty, that you can see yourself. And number three"—she waited for Joseph to stop chewing—"You don't win your wife in a pinochle game."

"What's number four?"

"Number four is: How could you bring children into this world with that lousy Falconetti luck?"

If there was one thing Carmela Santangelo knew about, it was luck. An expert on good and bad fortune, on benign and malicious influences, she knew precisely where to look for the Evil Eye and how to prevent it from looking back. No one was more conscious of hunchbacks, albinos, suspicious configurations of liver spots and moles. Mrs. Santangelo could spit three times and make the sign of the horns so discreetly that someone could be standing inches away and never notice.

Stronger even than her faith in God was Mrs. Santangelo's passion for serving and protecting her family. And though she

36

had lost her battle with Zio's cigars, she never stopped fighting the mischievous and invisible forces which threatened her boys. From birth, her sons wore silver *cornuti* around their necks and were forbidden to remove them even in the shower. When Augie was an infant, his mother cured him of pneumonia by hanging a lamb's hoof from his crib. Superstition had turned her mind into an adding machine, perpetually counting sneezes, steps, pigeons, potato eyes, orange pits—and reading portents in the totals.

"Number five: The meal that girl cooked. Raw meat, sandy greens, a hair on the tomato—every one of those things is a bad omen."

"Don't worry," said Joseph. "The kids will be half Santangelo."

"Joseph. Take some more sausage."

Of all Mrs. Santangelo's arcane information, perhaps the most magical was the recipe for her homemade sausage which, like some powerful magnet, drew customers from upstate New York and the eastern tip of Long Island. This formula—passed down, like the augury, through generations of women—was the mainstay of the family business, and included the specification that the cook must work rapidly, crossing herself often and trying not to think of the exact proportions lest someone read her mind.

That morning, as soon as Evelyn gave her the bad news, Mrs. Santangelo had started a fresh batch of sausage. With every pound of pork, every pinch of pepper, fennel and paprika, she had willed her son to change his mind about Catherine. Calling in a passing schoolboy, she'd sent three pounds across the street to thank the Falconettis for their hospitality. Then she'd gone back upstairs to fry some for Joseph's dinner.

Now, waiting for her sausage to work its magic, Mrs. Santangelo decided to help it along.

"And number six." She flexed the fingers of her left hand and held her right thumb beside it. "You don't even know the girl."

This last point hit Joseph so hard that he forgot to swallow and inhaled his food. Hurrying over, his mother pounded his back and with every slap, Joseph thought: She's right. He didn't know Catherine Falconetti from the Blessed Virgin Mary. For all he knew, she could be stupid, insane, lazy in bed, a shrew and a nonstop talker. Or maybe *he* was the crazy one, marrying a total stranger to collect on some drunken old man's pinochle bet.

And then, for the first time that either of them could remember, his mother's own magic worked against her. For as Joseph stared down at his plate, he thought of the sausage he'd rubbed in front of Catherine's face, and of her serious wide eyes watching him. More than anything in the world, he wanted to see her look like that again.

Sensing the sudden change in him, Mrs. Santangelo resorted to her darkest tone, saying, "Joseph, if you marry that girl, your whole life will taste like that meal."

But Joseph's only reaction to this gloomy prophecy was a dreamy grin.

"As I remember," he said, "the antipasto was delicious."

Across the street, Mrs. Santangelo's plans were working no better. She had hoped that a peppery sausage meal might fire the Falconettis up to resist Joseph's claim on Catherine. But the sausage, perfectly cooked, put Lino in such an unusually good mood that he gave up struggling against his fate and embraced it as a blessing in disguise: He wasn't losing a daughter, he was gaining a lifetime supply of sausage.

"Nice of the old lady to send this over," he said.

"After that meal we served her," said Catherine, "it's a miracle." Then, knowing that neither her father nor brother would say it for her, she added, "It's delicious."

"Good thing you think so," said Nicky. "You'll be eating enough of it from now on."

"What's your problem?" said Lino.

Picking at his food, Nicky was wondering if Madame Butterfly had had a brother, and thinking: Lucky him. Other men's sisters were exquisite geishas who fell madly in love with dashing lieutenants and wound up singing arias with samurai swords in their chests. His sister married the butcher from across the street, on a pinochle bet. Most likely she'd get fat with the first kid and go on to have ten more. At sixty, she'd be able to pass for Mrs. Santangelo's twin, with mean little eyes and legs as swollen as the sausage she stuffed for the shop. This image ruined Nicky's appetite, and he pushed his plate away. The sausage, sent over for courage, so disheartened him that he felt a sinking sensation, forgot where he was, and spoke his private thoughts out loud: "Some guys, their life's like *Madame Butterfly*. But for guys like us, it's nothing but sausage and pinochle."

"What's wrong with sausage?" said Lino, and would have kicked Nicky under the table if he hadn't been afraid of startling him into deeper trouble. Why bring up pinochle? The last thing they needed was for Catherine to find out about that card game. But he needn't have worried. Catherine was busy enjoying her meal and was only half-listening.

She was thinking of how Bacall had told Bogart to whistle for her, of how Joseph Santangelo had told her that the food was great; she was considering this with one part of her mind and listening with the other. Yet perhaps the strains became confused, because now, in a gesture of tenderness so rare that it made Nicky jump, she reached out and took her brother's hand.

"Nicky," she said, "it could be worse. There's a lot worse in life than sausage and pinochle."

The neighborhood outdid itself for Joseph and Catherine's wedding; no one would have missed it for the world. Even hardboiled cynics were intrigued by the romance of this marriage, arranged not just in heaven, but in a pinochle game. Recluses made plans to emerge, and the bad boys who had to be dragged to their own sisters' weddings now imagined telling their grandchildren that they had witnessed this historic event. Only the children, with their love of parties and sugared almonds, didn't care whose wedding it was, but were glad for any excuse to stay up late, run around, and dance.

At the bars and cafes, a man couldn't pick up a pinochle deck without thinking of the upcoming wedding. Romantics were reminded of their own courtships, and couples married thirty years fell in love all over again. At night, the husbands said to their wives, "Isn't that how it was with us? I won you in a card game." And in the daytime, the women said to their friends, "Isn't that how it is? One way or another, you win your husband in a card game."

The days leading up to the wedding were like the week before Christmas. The caterer's assistant blanched and sugared fifty pounds of almonds. The bakers worked all night. The women skinned hundreds of tomatoes, diced thousands of onions, and slid them into vats of sauce which got richer and thicker all week. To make their work go faster, they took turns telling the story of how Joseph had won the Falconetti girl at pinochle for a blast of cold air. It was the best kind of gossip, juicy and bittersweet. Always they ended it by wishing the couple a dozen healthy children, then knocked on wood—not so much for protection from the spirits as from the presence of Mrs. Santangelo and the fact that Catherine didn't seem to know the story at all.

It was Catherine's impression that Mrs. Santangelo was arranging a small reception for relatives and close friends; it went without saying that the bride's family would never be able to manage it.

Actually Catherine wasn't thinking much about the wedding; she was too busy trying to keep her mind off the fact that she was getting married. She couldn't stop thinking about Joseph Santangelo, though in all this time she saw him only twice, both times at the shop. On the first occasion, she counted four quarters into his hand, then realized that two of them were nickels. He pressed the coins back on her as if they were performing some awkward secret handshake, and told her to keep her money; he didn't feel right about taking it. The other time, she was so self-conscious in front of the other customers that she waved them to go before her, which only shamed her more: Now they would think that she was stalling for extra time to watch Joseph. And she was watching him as he paced behind the counter—carving, weighing, flashing the ladies his smiles. She kept thinking, "Why does he want to marry me?" But even with her secondhand knowledge of men and women, she knew better than to ask. Did Ingrid Bergman ask Rossellini, "Why me?" That day, she ran out of the store without buying anything, went home and told Lino that *he* could do the meat shopping for a while because it was bad luck to see your fiancé too often before the wedding.

"Our luck's so bad already," said Lino. "I wouldn't worry."

Catherine's greatest worry—which reflected nothing so much as the limit she put on her fantasies—was that after the ceremony, when it was time for her and Joseph to kiss, they would miss each other's mouths. This preoccupation carried her though the last-minute preparations, up the aisle, and well into the service.

The kiss at the altar was on target, more or less, but so hasty that its accuracy didn't register. For all the passion in that first embrace, Joseph and Catherine might have been birds pecking water. By then, both had woken to the fact that all this was real, and both were in a panic. Somehow Joseph got his arm around Catherine's shoulders and steered her around; they leaned against each other, down the aisle. They emerged into the daylight, blinking at the crowd of onlookers cheering and pelting them with rice. By the time their eyes adjusted to the sun, they were halfway down the block, on the steps of the parish hall.

Joseph's arm dropped. They couldn't look at each other; neither could think of a word to say. They just stood there in the middle of the banquet room, feeling like two party crashers with the bad sense to arrive before any of the invited guests.

Then Catherine saw the tables, each with its bowl of yellow chrysanthemums, its baskets of sugared almonds, trays of cigars, magnums of champagne on ice, the buffet spread, the platters of sliced meats, cold shrimp, pickled mussels, cheeses and cakes, chafing dishes of fettuccine and chicken Marsala, gardens of parsley, carrot curls, radish roses growing from stalks of fresh asparagus.

"Joseph," she said, "who did this?"

"You'd be amazed what my mother can do when she puts her mind to it," said Joseph. God help me, he thought. The first thing I tell her after the wedding is a lie.

"Asparagus in November? Even your mother couldn't do that."

"Asparagus? That must be Frank Manzone. Let's get something to drink." Joseph jumped at the first loud pop, which he misheard as a gunshot.

"Champagne?"

"Sure." Catherine drank three glasses in quick succession.

The hall filled up with guests, a blur of eating and drinking, sitting down and standing up. Catherine found herself at a dozen different tables; as soon as she approached, they refilled her champagne glass. There were toasts which Catherine could never quite hear, followed by bursts of applause; then everyone turned toward her and she sensed that she was supposed to smile. Faces came into focus, congratulating her—always, she noticed, with the most peculiar expressions, as if they knew something she didn't.

Intermittently, people left her alone, as if by some private agreement she had become invisible. She was walking to stay conscious, lurching actually, around the perimeter of the room. On one of these slow revolutions, she passed Lino and Nicky— drinking all alone, in silence, at a corner table. She didn't stop, nor did they call out to her.

Never in all this walking did she once pass Joseph. In fact she fled from him, around and around the hall, without losing sight of him for a minute. She watched him kissing the ladies, hugging and slapping their husbands' backs, always with an envelope in his hand. He seemed to have forgotten her, which excited her; she knew that he hadn't forgotten.

It was an odd time to think of the Bible, but suddenly Catherine caught herself thinking of the marriage at Cana, the wedding at which Jesus changed the water into wine. This, she thought, is the same story: A poor couple gets married, expecting nothing. And wham, out of nowhere, there's music, wine: All you can drink.

A band (two guitars, a bass and a mandolin) struck up a tarantella. The first ones on the dance floor were children, who whirled around in circles till they got dizzy and fell down. Then three old women danced a graceful scarf dance, their heavy bodies lovely in rippling black taffeta.

Catherine had always imagined the people in the Bible as Italians, and now she pictured a big Italian wedding at Cana, with Jesus like somebody's great uncle crying, "Drink, drink! More wine, Cousin Leo, more wine!" Then she thought of the bride at this wedding and wondered, who was she? Was it possible that she resented it? After all, it was *her* wedding, but the star of the show was Jesus with His magic tricks, His water into wine. Most likely, no one had paid any attention to her.

Catherine wondered if this was how all brides felt on their wedding day—like spectators, or travelers who have stumbled in on the ceremonies of an alien religion. What a waste, she thought, what a pity to let such feelings spoil a wedding, when God Himself is providing the wine.

And she stopped at another table, where they refilled her glass.

2

WEDDING NIGHT

TWO DAYS BEFORE THE WEDDING, Augie Santangelo walked into Joseph's shop with a present for his brother. Inside a crisp manila envelope, which looked as if it should have contained a deed or a will, was a magazine called *Wedding Night*, a kind of comic book with photos instead of drawings. Joseph glanced at the title, thanked Augie, and slipped the magazine back inside the envelope. But on the afternoon of the ceremony, he rested up before the wedding by reading it from cover to cover a dozen times.

The first shots showed a '46 Buick, festooned with tin cans and streamers, pulling up to a rambling wooden structure marked "Honeymoon Hotel." The next page belonged to the groom—middle-aged, balding, with a greasy pencil moustache, mugging nervousness at the camera as he signs the hotel register. Then an elevator scene, the groom and the bellhop smirking, with the shy blonde bride half-disappeared into the woodwork; into the room, and a photo of the bride from the back, heading for the bathroom so fast that her train and veil are a white blur. Shots of the husband pacing the room, checking his watch, kneeling outside the bathroom door and talking through the keyhole—until the door opens and there on the very last page is his wife, pouting and licking her glossy lips, a tough, busty blonde in high heels and a sheer black nightie.

Now, on his wedding night, as Joseph lay in bed waiting for his own bride to return from the bathroom, it occurred to him that the couple in the magazine weren't staying in a small apartment with the groom's mother. Imagine Catherine sashaying down the hall in that get-up. The doorknob clicked, and while Joseph would not have been disappointed by the blonde in her push-up bra, he was more excited by the sight of Catherine in her little white dress, her white angora sweater trimmed with pearls.

Catherine closed the door and stood with her back against it. She had always reminded Joseph of an alley cat, and now, like a newly adopted stray, she seemed to be casing the room for a bed to dive beneath, a bureau to crawl behind.

Joseph raised himself up on one elbow.

"Nice dress."

"Thanks." Unable to look at him, Catherine searched the room for something to focus on. She passed over the faded gray and rose carpeting, the hard wooden chair, the obligatory crucifix on the wall, lingered briefly at the framed photo on the dresser: Joseph and Augie in bathing trunks, posed arm in arm before the parachute jump at Coney Island. Behind the photo was a mirror, and there in the mirror was Joseph in bed.

"You need something?" he asked.

"Someplace to change."

"What are you going to change into? Batman?" Joseph chuckled at his own joke, then instantly regretted it as Catherine turned white as her wedding dress and said, "Change my clothes."

"Right. Well, go ahead. I won't look, I promise."

"Here?"

"There's always the bathroom." Joseph shrugged.

"Your mother's in there now."

"Too bad. She'll be in there all night."

"In that case, I guess here's okay."

Reaching up to unfasten the clip of artificial feathers which held her veil in place, Catherine realized how tipsy she was; the effort nearly threw her off balance. The bobby pins caught in her hair, raising stiff hairsprayed points which stuck out from her head like antennae and defied her attempts to pat them down.

"Where's the cord?" she said.

"What cord?"

"To turn out the light."

Joseph pointed to a switch near his bed and said, "How about leaving it on?"

"Are you crazy? You start undressing with the lights on, there's fifty guys on the fire escape before you've got your top button undone. Little girls know that, little kids with nothing to show."

From the visible evidence, Catherine herself had nothing much to show. Yet Joseph had climbed a few fire escapes in his time, and he knew that what she had was enough. He rolled onto his stomach to hide himself, just as he'd done on those fire escapes, even when there was nothing to see. Yet now his excitement was only half sexual and half the thrill of finding himself a married man with a wife he was honor-bound to protect.

"What guys?" he said. "Tell me their names, I'll kill them."

"Those guys on the fire escape right now. Turn out the lights and you'll see."

"Okay, I'll make you a deal. I'll get the light, you undress and hop in."

"It's a deal." Quickly Catherine checked for her overnight bag, memorizing the arrangement of the room so she could change in the dark and find the bed.

Joseph leaned over and flipped the switch. The night lamp went out, but the ceiling fixture stayed on. The room was nearly as bright as before.

"You cheated," said Catherine.

"For a Santangelo, that's the greatest compliment there is. And now that you're part of the Santangelo family, I'll never cheat *on* you, just *for* you."

Too dizzy to understand the distinction, Catherine sighed and thought how much easier it was before she knew she was going to marry Joseph—how simple it had been to stick up for her rights and make sure that the butcher gave her a fair deal. Now what was hers was Joseph Santangelo's, and she no longer knew what her rights were.

So she turned resolutely, opened her suitcase, and fished out her pink flannel nightgown. In doing so, she recalled a photo of Rita Hayworth showing off her wedding trousseau—all lace and silk and pale filmy satin.

"*She* doesn't have to buy stuff to last all winter," Catherine said aloud, as if called upon to defend herself. "You marry Ali Khan, you can wear a nightgown once and throw it away."

"Huh?" said Joseph.

"Nothing." Catherine slid the nightgown over her head, smoothed it down in back and let it ruck up in front so she could undo the tiny buttons on her dress. Her dress and half-slip slid down in a circle around her feet. Stepping out of it, she tripped, then turned to face Joseph.

"Please," she said. "Please turn out the light."

She forced herself to watch as Joseph jumped out of bed, crossed the room in two steps and turned off the wall switch. Dressed in shorts and a T-shirt, he looked as natural and unashamed as he did in his butcher's coat in the shop. The ceiling light went out, and the springs creaked loudly as Joseph got back into bed. Catherine was left trying to figure out why the room was still so light.

From outside the window, a street lamp shone in through the

blue curtains, illuminating the room with the dusky glow of a grotto—soft, yet bright enough for Catherine to make out the photo of Joseph, bare-chested, one arm around Augie's shoulders, smiling the same cat-that-swallowed-the-canary smile he was smiling now.

"You win," said Catherine.

Revealing a minimum of flesh, she unfastened her stockings, garter belt and bra, eased the whole mass down beneath her nightgown, and stuck her arms into the sleeves. Then she lifted the blanket and lay down on her back, as far from Joseph as the narrow bed would permit.

Joseph rolled toward her and in one motion raised the hem of her nightgown to her chin. He slid one hand down the front of her body, grazing her skin.

"Scared?"

"No," said Catherine, though in fact she was shaking so hard, she had to hold her breath to keep from rocking the bed.

"Don't be scared." Then in a husky voice, Joseph said, "Hey, remember what I told you that day in the shop, that I'd show you where I could put my thumb?"

Catherine nodded.

"Well, here's what I meant." Joseph moved his thumb down her stomach. "Understand?"

Even before Catherine shook her head, Joseph realized that she didn't understand at all. So he took his thumb out from beneath the sheet and put it in his mouth till it was wet, then slid it very gently back between her legs.

"Now? Now do you understand?"

When her back arched forward, pressing her hips toward his hand, Joseph knew that she understood.

"Now look. Look what else I can put there."

He slipped down his shorts, knelt between her legs and entered her, thanking God for how easy it was, despite what he'd heard about virgins.

"Jesus," he said.

Catherine caught her breath, then slowly began to move against him.

"Santangelo," she said. "Santangelo, Santangelo."

She forgot where she was, forgot everything but his face in the underwater light, everything but the urgency (a million times sharper than the exigency of watering a new plant), the sweetness of doing something that absolutely cannot wait.

Then she remembered, and froze.

Joseph stopped.

"What's the matter? Am I hurting you?"

"The bedsprings. Listen, they're creaking like crazy. And your Mama's right there in the next room. . . ."

"No problem. She sleeps like a log."

This was a lie. And yet if God had taken Joseph Santangelo at that moment, He would not have sent him to that special circle of hell reserved for men who can lie to women in bed. For in his heart, Joseph was telling the truth—if not the truth on Mulberry Street, then the truth in some other world, some underwater-blue grotto where bedsprings creaked celestial music, where angels sang Santangelo Santangelo Santangelo, and mothers slept through it all like logs.

Catherine awoke in a circle of light, warm through the blue curtains. Alone in bed, she curled up and pulled the covers around her chin. After a while her thumb wandered to the place where Joseph's had been last night, but it was not at all like Joseph's, and even less like that other thing of his for which she still had no name, and which seemed to her now like some miracle she must have imagined. Then she heard footsteps in the hall, heavy reproachful steps which shamed her out of bed and into the kitchen to begin her new life as Mrs. Santangelo's daughter-in-law.

Mrs. Santangelo was standing at the sink, cutting up a chicken. The set of her back told the whole story.

"You sleep okay?" she said.

"Like a log."

"Not me. I slept terrible."

If at that moment an erupting volcano had threatened to bury Mulberry Street, Catherine would have welcomed it with open arms. With no volcano to rescue her, she sank into a chair by the kitchen table and prepared for the worst. But what followed was not quite the martyrdom of embarrassment she expected.

"It's my late husband Zio," said Mrs. Santangelo. "May he rest in peace."

"I guess you must miss him." Catherine felt a rush of sympathy for all the lovers in the world, even Mrs. Santangelo. She wondered how a woman could possibly survive the loss of her husband; after one night of marriage, she was already praying that Joseph would outlive her.

"Miss him?" Mrs. Santangelo laughed. "How can I miss him when he won't go away? Fact is, I don't know why I bother saying rest in peace. If my Zio was resting in peace, he wouldn't be coming back and pestering me. Right?"

"What?"

"Always he picks the worst nights. When I been working like a dog, or like last night, after the wedding and all that excitement, my chest was hurting so terrible, I had to take a pill. And I'm finally closing my eyes when I smell that rotten cigar smoke, and there's Zio.

"'Zio,' I say, 'What kind of hour is this for visiting?'

"'It's all God's time,' says Zio. That's how he talks.

"'Listen to you,' I say.

"'Carmela,' he says. 'What is more precious than rubies?' Up in heaven, my Zio has become a big Bible reader, always showing off and quizzing me.

"'I give up,' I say. 'What?'

"'A virtuous wife,' he tells me. 'A virtuous wife is more precious than rubies.' Then he says, 'But the most precious ruby of all is the blood.' I ask you: Would you understand, a man talks like that?"

Catherine shook her head.

"'Blood?' I say. 'What blood?'

"'The blood of a virgin on her wedding night,' he says. And I'll tell you, I blushed. I didn't think they talked about such things in heaven.

"'And tonight,' says Zio, 'there are no rubies in the Santangelo home.'"

After a dramatic pause, Mrs. Santangelo put down the chicken, rinsed her hands and turned to glare at Catherine.

"How about it? Was there blood on my Joseph's sheets?"

"I didn't look."

"Then *I'll* go look." Mrs. Santangelo was out the door and halfway down the hall before Catherine could catch up. By the time Catherine reached the bedroom, Mrs. Santangelo had stripped off the blanket to reveal a wrinkled bottom sheet, some dust specks, a few dark hairs and a number of yellowish stains. The sight of it made Catherine's knees weak.

"Disgrace," hissed Mrs. Santangelo. "Infamy."

She bustled out of the room and returned seconds later with a shot glass full of what looked like wine.

"You know what this is?" She shoved the glass under Catherine's nose. Catherine jerked her head back from the stinking liquid. Then she thought: It smells like Joseph, and it was all she could do to keep from sniffing it again.

"That's right!" cried Mrs. Santangelo. "Chicken blood!"

With one sharp pull, she had the bottom sheet in a heap on the floor. She gave the shot glass a quick, disdainful toss, and blood splashed across the center of the sheet.

"That's what it is! All your bouncing springs, your giggling and moaning, your Santangelo Santangelo Santangelo! It's nothing but chicken blood, a patch of chicken blood and nothing more! You understand?"

In her fury, Mrs. Santangelo seemed to puff up like an angry brood hen and flutter several inches off the ground. Catherine saw a giant vein pulsing in her mother-in-law's neck in an awesome galloping rhythm which so alarmed her that she forgot to be ashamed, forgot even to wonder why there wasn't any blood.

"If this was the old country," continued Mrs. Santangelo, "if this was anyplace decent, we'd go right now and hang this sheet from the kitchen window so everyone could see. But even here in America, there are ways. Ways to do what we have to do, when we have to do it. Steps that can be taken when the Santangelo family honor is at stake. You know what I'm talking about?"

"I haven't the foggiest." In her panic, Catherine wondered how Deborah Kerr would have acted in a similar situation.

"Don't talk fresh to me. What I'm saying is: Last night, just before my Zio left to go wherever he goes, he tells me one last thing: "'Carmela,' he says, and you know I'm telling you the truth, how could I make this up? 'Carmela,' he says, 'cover our Joseph's sheet with rubies and send it to the Chinese laundry.'"

It was obvious to Catherine that Mrs. Santangelo was crazy—but of course she would never say that to Joseph. Already, with her overnight knowledge of men and women, she realized that you don't go telling a man that his mother is crazy—not if you want more of what you got on your wedding night.

Pausing in the hallway, Catherine refolded the sheet so that the blood stain was hidden on the inside. Then she tucked it under her arm and headed for the Chinese laundry on the corner of Mott Street and Grand.

On the way, it occurred to her that the circumstances of your life could be deduced from the way you did your laundry. Movie stars, she imagined, had everything dry-cleaned. She recalled her father telling her of the unlucky Falconetti woman who fell into the Tiber while beating her clothes on its rocky banks. Catherine, who had always used her mother's hand-crank washer in the kitchen, pictured hell as an eternity of ironing shirts, a doom alleviated only slightly by the fact that Lino and Nicky weren't especially particular about their collars and cuffs. Still, she'd never in her life used the Chinese laundry. Who could afford such luxuries? And besides, the Falconettis weren't the sort of family who paid other people to do their dirty wash.

As soon as she got to the laundry, she realized that Mrs. Santangelo had never been there either. For if her mother-in-law imagined it as a public place and believed that sending her sheets there was the equivalent of hanging them from the window, she couldn't have been more wrong.

The laundry was as dim as a confessional, and the old Chinese man was as odd, distant, and private as any priest. In fact, thought Catherine, the laundry would keep her secrets better than a confessional. Priests had been known to gossip, but the Chinaman could barely speak English.

"Starch?" he said. The rattle and slam of the trouser press, which a young Chinese woman was operating in the back of the shop, made it nearly impossible to hear.

"Starch in the sheets?" said Catherine.

"No starch." The old man took the sheet from her and stuffed it into a hamper behind the counter.

"Tuesday," he said.

Only later, on the way home, did Catherine begin to wonder why there hadn't been blood on the sheets. Finally she decided that blood was for the old days, when families hung the nuptial linens from their balconies. This was America, in the twentieth century, where girls grew taller than their mothers and virgins didn't bleed. A million to one, she bet, there had been no blood on Rita Hayworth's satin sheets. Luckily, there was no one around to bet against, for she knew that no movie magazine on earth would settle such a bet. . . . Not that she wanted a movie magazine. All Catherine really wanted was to go home and sleep till Joseph woke her getting into bed.

Daydreaming, she overshot the Santangelos' door and was

passing the shop when its smell evoked the miracles of the previous night and made her knees go weak all over again. All night, the smell of meat and blood had clung to Joseph's warm skin; by dawn, Catherine had found herself hunting it on his body, rooting for the secret places where it lingered.

Joseph, who'd been chatting with Frank Manzone, fell silent when Catherine entered the store. She wondered, had they been talking about her? Too shaky to move, she nodded to him from the doorway.

For a few moments, the neon light seemed to flicker and dim to the glow of a street lamp filtering in through blue curtains. Everything stopped, as if frozen in time, and did not begin again till Frank Manzone laughed, slapped his friend on the shoulder, and said, "I got the feeling you and me won't be playing much pinochle tonight."

"You're crazy," said Joseph. "I'll see you later. Same time, same place."

But Joseph was no longer the same.

That night, he played two hands, then opened his mouth, yawned, rubbed his eyes and seemed so generally exhausted that it took all his energy to stand up and say, "Gentlemen, it's been a pleasure. Good night."

"What's the matter?" said Frank Manzone. "Something come up at home, ha ha?" And when Joseph wouldn't laugh, Frank turned to the Falconettis and said, "Boys, I got the feeling we won't be playing pinochle for a while."

There followed that uncomfortable interval when the host is ready for the evening to end and stands there impatiently, faking yawns while his guests gather their things and go. But who could blame Joseph for this breach of hospitality? Surely not Frank Manzone, who remembered the start of his own married life, when he'd lost all interest in cards and couldn't believe that he'd ever have time for pinochle again. Even the Falconettis weren't affronted, just a little surprised that Joseph would pick Cath-

54

erine over pinochle, when they had chosen the opposite way for so many years.

Joseph was more surprised than anyone. Earlier that evening, after dinner, he'd sat at the kitchen table watching the women wash and dry the dishes. When they finished, and his mother was holding the glasses up to the light, inspecting them for streaks, Catherine had reached back to untie her apron. The sight of the thin cotton apron tightening over her tiny breasts had excited him; later, just the thought of it was enough to throw off his pinochle game. Leaving the shop, he had only one regret: It was still too early for bed.

"Hey Catherine," he said, the minute he got home. "How about a little walk?"

"Where's there to go?" said Mrs. Santangelo, who had never known her son to take a stroll for no reason. "Nowhere."

"Nowhere and back." Joseph grabbed Catherine's elbow and steered her out the door.

There was nowhere to go, but neither of them noticed as they paced the streets, past the darkened shop windows in which there was nothing to see. Nor was there anything to say.

"Nice evening," ventured Joseph.

"Beautiful," said Catherine, thinking that she had never taken such a pleasant and interesting walk in her life.

Often Joseph had heard it said that you could tell if a woman was getting laid from the way she moved. Now he was relieved to see that this wasn't true of Catherine, who was walking the same as before. He was so busy studying her for signs of change that they were nearly run over by a big green Plymouth rounding the corner of Mulberry and Hester.

Joseph yanked Catherine back from the curb and hugged her against him so tight that she couldn't breathe.

"We better get off the streets," he said. "We're a menace to the public safety."

Upstairs, Mrs. Santangelo had gone to sleep. They went directly to the bedroom, where now it was Catherine's turn to be

FRANCINE PROSE

surprised. For how could she have imagined that the bedsprings could creak louder than the night before?

"Santangelo!" she cried, and had to bite the edge of the pillow to keep from calling his name again.

Like Joseph, Catherine was no longer the same. In twenty-four hours, she had become a married woman. And though this change was so subtle that it went unnoticed by her own husband, its principal symptom was this:

Several times during that night, she looked over at Joseph's bureau, its polished surface glinting in the street light, and she thought: How nice an African violet would look, right there.

Mrs. Santangelo didn't agree, but neither did she make a point of it. She tended to her sausage-making and kept quiet as Catherine moved her plants, one by one, from the Falconetti apartment. Frequently Catherine would turn from watering a plant to find her mother-in-law peering over her shoulder and glowering—just like Judith Anderson creeping up on Joan Fontaine in *Rebecca*. At such times, she felt sorry for Joan Fontaine, always wondering if the old lady and her husband were in cahoots. Catherine knew she could count on Joseph, knew from what happened between them every night in bed that he would defend her in anything—which is why she had the courage to move her plants over in the first place.

It was lucky that her plants had adapted to Lino's dark kitchen; here across the street, there was even less sun. And it was a miracle that they continued to survive under Mrs. Santangelo's withering eye.

One night at dinner, Joseph complimented his mother on the escarole fried in garlic.

"Escarole?" she said. "You think this is escarole?"

"Sure, it's escarole." Joseph helped himself to another portion. "It's delicious."

"It's African violets!" With a sweep of her arm. Mrs. Santangelo indicated every plant in the apartment, and her tone made the modest little violets sound like some barbaric head-hunting tribe which Catherine had invited in to live with them.

"What's this got to do with escarole?" said Joseph.

"Garbage!" cried his mother. "That's what it's got to do with! Garbage growing in those pots, breathing our air, stealing the oxygen out of your mouth when you're asleep in bed at night. . . ."

"Hold it," said Joseph. "Just hold it."

Mrs. Santangelo should never have mentioned the bed. Suddenly Joseph felt such affection for Catherine that he fell in love with her plants.

A green thumb! How could he have overlooked the ferns and ivy which—he saw now—had taken over much of his mother's counter space? How could he have missed this evidence of Catherine's tenderness and care, this clue to the life she led before they were together? Now as if to compensate, he paid special attention to each plant, particularly the latest addition—so recently arrived from across the street that even Mrs. Santangelo hadn't spotted it.

"Mama," he said. "Look at the altar."

Directly in front of the image of San Gennaro was a fuzzy-leafed plant in a small clay pot.

Mrs. Santangelo took one look and grabbed her chest.

"I'm dying!" she cried. Yet she was clearly alive enough to scream at the top of her lungs,

"Get that garbage off there!"

"It's not garbage," Catherine said quietly. "It's a geranium. And I can't take it back. I gave it to the saint."

"You aren't even Neapolitan," said Mrs. Santangelo. "Gennaro isn't even your saint."

"He's Joseph's family's saint," said Catherine, with such a sweet wifely smile that Joseph, feeling like a fool, smiled back. "So I guess now he's mine."

"Catherine's right," said Joseph. "You give something to a saint, you can't just change your mind and take it back."

Even Mrs. Santangelo couldn't argue with the logic of that, and so Catherine's plants gained a somewhat firmer foothold in the Santangelo apartment.

By the next morning, they had claimed it as their rightful territory.

Shortly before dawn, Mrs. Santangelo woke up choking from the lack of oxygen which the plants had stolen overnight. On her way to the kitchen, she shot a hateful look at the altar. Then, fearing that the saint might misunderstand, she lit a votive candle and carried it toward the mantel. She looked at Catherine's geranium, looked away, made the sign of the horns and looked again.

"Joseph!" she called. "Wake up! There's been a miracle!"

Last night's grubby and unpromising geranium had bloomed—two huge crimson blossoms cradled in San Gennaro's outstretched arms.

"It's a miracle." Mrs. Santangelo bobbed up and down and crossed herself as her son and daughter-in-law entered the room. "Last night that plant was a mess. And now?"

"Sure, Mama," Joseph agreed sleepily. Anything to keep peace in the family was a miracle. "Right, Catherine?"

"Right," said Catherine. "A miracle."

It wasn't a complete lie. There was always something miraculous about the flowering of a plant. But miracles, as Catherine understood them, were supposed to be surprises—God's way of shocking you into believing. And there was nothing surprising about those flowers. The geranium had been in bud, due to blossom any day. That was why she'd put it on the altar. Yet if Mrs. Santangelo wanted to believe it was a miracle, Catherine would not disillusion her. For she knew that she could trade on her new power as a worker of minor miracles for the one privilege which she had craved since the start of her married life:

That same day, Catherine asked Joseph if she could work in the shop.

Next to the bedroom, the shop was her favorite place, for it was only in those two places that she could find Joseph's smell. She loved to watch him work, loved most of all to think that those hands which sliced and boned so deftly were the same ones which would touch her so gently that night.

Joseph couldn't believe that she really liked the smell. Ignoring her protests, he took hot showers before coming to bed. When she walked into the store to find him elbow-deep in gristle and blood, he was horrified to think that she might recognize those arms as the same ones which held her in bed.

"What would you do in the shop?" he said. "It's a man's work, it takes muscles—"

"It takes two fingers to work the cash register," said Catherine.

And so the job of cashier was invented for her.

Mrs. Santangelo saw evil omens in every aspect of this arrangement.

"That's the end of the Santangelo business," she predicted. "My Zio is turning over in his grave so fast, he can't get up and visit me."

Mrs. Santangelo's prophecies had a disconcerting tendency to come true, and Joseph feared that this one had a better chance than most. It seemed inevitable that Catherine's help would hurt the business. How could he flirt with his customers if she were there? And more important, how could he cheat them with Catherine looking over his shoulder?

As it happened, there was no need for Joseph to abandon these practices. In fact, Catherine's presence made them easier. The saddest old women, the ones with no time or patience for flirting, were impressed by how nicely Joseph talked to Catherine—nicer than their husbands had ever talked to them. And there was nothing the others liked more than to catch a wink from Joseph when his pretty little wife's back was turned.

Of course Catherine's back was never completely turned, but she forgave Joseph the winks, just as his customers overlooked the short weights. For she knew that he was winking for her, cheating for her, and she felt that loyalty stronger even than love—the passionate bond of partners-in-crime.

Despite Mrs. Santangelo's predictions, the business flourished—and yet she was not convinced. She continued to oppose Catherine's working, if for no other reason than that her Zio had never let *her* work. And she took consolation in the old saying that God will never allow your wealth to multiply faster than the number of mouths at your table.

Soon enough, she predicted, the nightly creaking of bedsprings would put an end to Catherine's working career. And so, like a besieged and dethroned queen, she retreated to the heart of her fortress and waited for her kingdom to be restored.

The first sign came on a muggy Friday morning in September, almost a year after Joseph and Catherine were married. The store was crowded with women shopping for the weekend, each one with small talk for Catherine, a giggle for Joseph.

Suddenly Catherine felt as if the floor were sliding out from beneath her feet and the sawdust rising up to meet her.

As luck would have it, Evelyn Santangelo walked into the shop just as Catherine ran out.

"Hey!" called Evelyn. "How's the little cashier?"

"Fine," Catherine muttered through clenched teeth, then brushed past her sister-in-law and headed into the street for some air. By the time she returned, feeling only slightly better, half of Mulberry Street knew that she and Joseph were expecting a child—a fact which Catherine had yet to admit to herself.

"Congratulations!" said Evelyn. "You look a little green around the gills. Wait. It gets worse. With me it was gasoline. Every time I pulled into a gas station, I had to run straight to the Ladies'." She waved at the cars parked out on the street, to remind everyone that she was from the suburbs and drove a Chrysler.

"Congratulations!" chorused the younger women, Americans like Evelyn, while the older ones bit their lips because it was bad luck to offer congratulations so early in a pregnancy.

"What do you want?" Evelyn rattled on. "Boy or girl? How about a little boy cousin for my Stacey?"

"What's this?" Joseph was so surprised by the drift of things that he momentarily forgot the others' presence. "Catherine, is this the truth?"

"Could be," said Catherine.

"Isn't that typical?" said Evelyn. "Papa's always the last to know."

Until that morning, thought Catherine, there hadn't been anything to know; except for two missed periods, she'd felt no different. But as soon as Evelyn and her big mouth were turned loose on Mulberry Street, Catherine's pregnancy became an established fact. She had no physical symptoms; in the mirror, she looked exactly the same. But people talked to her, looked at her in a new way. It was, she thought, as if you knew you were Italian and everyone acted as if you were Chinese. Now, women she'd never spoken to felt free to offer advice, information, predictions of her baby's sex:

"Boys don't show till the sixth month—then they pop out like mushrooms."

"The way you can tell is: It's the girls make your gums bleed."

"You can't be sure till the last month. Then, if your fingers swell, you know for sure it's a boy."

But all the prophets agreed on two things. The first was that it made no difference, girl or boy, so long as the child was healthy. Which reminded them of the second: A woman in Catherine's condition shouldn't be working in a butcher shop.

Total strangers started warning her against working there. No one had hard evidence. Though everyone knew stories of mothers who brought forth gibbons after innocent trips to the zoo, children born with ghastly deformities because their fathers worked on Sant'Anielo's day, no one could cite specific instances of pregnant women harmed at the butcher's. Still, the women had a vague intuition: It didn't seem right.

"Doesn't it make you queasy?" asked Joseph's customers. "All this blood . . . the smell . . . in your state . . .?"

"You know how some women are about pickles and ice cream?" said Catherine. "That's how I am about this shop."

But she could never look them in the eye as she said this, for she knew that what she really craved was Joseph and the smell of Joseph's skin.

She and Joseph rarely discussed the baby, except to say that they couldn't believe it was really coming. Yet always now, in the midst of making love, Joseph would stop and say, "Is it safe? Are you sure it's all right?"

"I'm sure," said Catherine, urging him on. "If it isn't all right, what is?"

But once again, Mrs. Santangelo disagreed.

A counter of days, an observer of signs, Carmela Santangelo kept intimate track of her daughter-in-law's biological life, and thus was the first to know that she was pregnant. Thrilled by the prospect of another grandchild, Mrs. Santangelo waited till she was sure, then held a burning candle over a basin of water. The wax solidified—not in separate droplets, but in one long curlicue which floated to the top.

"A boy," whispered Mrs. Santangelo. "Baby Zio."

They would call him Zio, and she herself would wean him on milk, bread, and honey. She would feed him pasta and good cheese, not Chinese pork like her undernourished grandchildren on the Island, and little Zio would grow closer to her than her own sons had been before they grew up and left her.

Mrs. Santangelo took the candle, set it in front of San Gennaro and was just about to thank him for this blessing in her old age when a breeze gusted in the window and blew out the candle. She crossed herself.

"God help us," she said.

That evening, she located Zio's St. Anthony's horn, wrapped in tissue at the back of her bureau drawer.

"It was my husband's," she said, tying the cord around Catherine's neck. "It's not for you, it's for the baby."

But despite the good effects of Zio's *cornuto*, the bad omens continued: Blood streaks in the egg yolks. Three pigeons roosting on the portal of Our Lady of Mount Carmel. Rain on crucial feast days. Of course there was trouble, thought Mrs. Santangelo, what with those creaking bedsprings, those hours Catherine spent downstairs in the shop. But how to convince Joseph that such omens were proof of more than her ill will toward his wife?

Perhaps it would be wiser to concentrate on Catherine. Mrs. Santangelo knew that a pregnant woman could be persuaded of anything—provided you understood that she was temporarily out of her mind and that the only way to her brain was through her stomach.

And so Mrs. Santangelo devoted herself to cooking for the mother-to-be.

Every night, Catherine got sick on the meat. Usually she made it through the soup and bread, but could only force down a few mouthfuls of meat before stopping to excuse herself.

"I'm sorry," she'd say, back from the bathroom with cold water shining on her face. "It's not the food. It's me."

But it was the food.

"Mama," said Joseph, "this sausage taste all right to you?"

"All right? It's the best!"

"Maybe if you cooked it a little more . . ."

"And cook all the juice out of it? Eat up, Joseph. Anyone would think you were the pregnant one."

Little by little, her cooking worked its magic: Catherine lost her taste for meat. After gagging on enough of her mother-in-law's underdone stews, she could no longer stand the smell of it and finally told Joseph that it was time for her to quit working in the shop. She still loved the scent on Joseph's skin; but now when he took a shower before bed, she didn't argue.

"It's my mother's cooking making you sick," said Joseph. "We'll go out, get a hamburger, you'll be fine."

But Catherine was revolted by the idea of a hamburger, and for the first time felt like a different person, a pregnant woman nauseated by the food she had loved all her life. It was this difference which first made her conscious that the child inside her was real. Everything was changing—even the way she walked, cautiously now, hips turned inward, cradling her center, shielding something fragile as an egg. Gradually her habits changed as she homed, like any nesting creature, toward the comfortable and familiar. She took long naps, tended her plants, and in the afternoons walked uptown to buy this fragile secret thing an African violet and a movie magazine.

Two weeks before Thanksgiving, everything changed again. One Monday morning, a green panel truck pulled up in front of the shop. And by the time Joseph and the driver had unloaded it, the sights and sounds and smells of life were different.

It was as if there were nothing in the world but turkeys, as if the autumn days fell silent, as if Mulberry Street put a finger to its lips and listened to the squawking and gobbling. Even at night, turkey dust and pinfeathers swarmed around the street lights like clouds of gnats.

The counters in the shop were pushed back against the wall to make room for the stacked crates; beaks and necks protruded through the wooden slats, and wattles hung down like wilted flowers. Upstairs, the familiar meat smell was gone, replaced by the sticky sweetness of turkey blood.

"I turn my back for five minutes," said Mrs. Santangelo, "and you turn your father's shop into a chicken coop."

"It's Thanksgiving," said Joseph. "You know, the American holiday."

"In Italy, we had holidays for the saints, the Virgin. And here? They worship turkeys!" Then Joseph told his mother how much these turkeys were bringing in per pound and put an end to her grumbling.

Even Joseph's clientele was different. With nothing but con-
tempt for this godless, wild-Indian holiday, the grandmothers
fed their husbands fish and pasta, or took their business elsewhere. But their daughters drove in from Westchester and Long
Island to talk of yams and marshmallows, to chastise the old-
fashioned grocers for neglecting to stock enough cranberry
sauce. Ladies in fur coats came in, dragging toddlers in velveteen riding suits. Taxis double-parked while Irish maids ducked
into Santangelo's to fill their mistresses' orders.

All of them wanted the fattest, juiciest bird Santangelo had—
less of a meal than a monument to America and to the gran-
deur of their tables. Like the Plymouth pilgrims, they wanted
to eat so much that God would feel duly thanked for delivering
them through another year. And finally they wanted each member of their families to eat a double helping for all the wartime
Thanksgivings when they'd had nothing but Spam.

That was what they thought they wanted. But Joseph knew
that what they really wanted was blood. His regular customers,
the old ladies, had been wringing chickens' necks for so many
years that they were glad to have the butcher do it for them, off in
the back room where they didn't have to watch. But these American women, these city women, had never killed a chicken in
their lives. Not only did they want their turkey, but they wanted
its death, as if witnessing the slaughter would make them feel
nearer to the tall corn, the yams, the fruits of the harvest and the
sweet November earth.

Joseph gave them what they wanted. He let them take
their time picking over the live birds, choosing not merely
the choicest flesh but their destined sacrificial victims. While
they decided, he sharpened his knives so that the scraping of
the blade raised the hairs on the backs of the women's necks.
When they'd chosen, he opened the cages and grabbed the turkeys in a violent stranglehold, loosened his grasp just long
enough for one bone-chilling squawk, then snapped his wrist
so hard that the birds began to quiver. Finally he brandished

his knife in the air and slit the turkeys' throats with three neat slices.

"That's the Z that stands for Zorro," he said, and his customers shivered in the grip of an almost sexual thrill. For everyone knew that the movie-Zorro's sword had brought forth only ketchup. But this was real blood.

Joseph let them watch it soak the feathers. Then he lifted the lid of a huge oil drum and dropped the bird inside so that the death spasms would be amplified by the resonance of the metal.

"For your protection," he said, and the ladies would nod as if they were in dire need of protection from a dying bird. Arms crossed, Joseph stood before the oil drum, his face impassive, staring straight ahead until the pounding stopped. Then he picked the bird up by its feet. He let the ladies stare at the dangling head to their hearts' content, then said, "You want it plucked?"

When they nodded, speechless, Joseph gave it to the boy he'd hired to help till Thanksgiving. And when at last he handed over the turkeys, still warm in their paper bags, he knew that he could charge his customers anything. For they were paying not only for the meat, not only for the useless pounds of feathers, beak and blood, but also for a miracle, a spectacle which they imagined had brought them that much closer to the forgotten center of life.

Watching from her window, Catherine saw the women leave the shop with radiant faces, as if they'd been at church. If they could be there with Joseph, why couldn't she? Yet it was not exactly jealousy which moved her to go downstairs, but rather a deeper, more instinctive urge—like the impulse to suck her finger when she cut it, to gulp a glass of water she hadn't even known she'd wanted.

Entering the store, she nearly gagged on the feathers and dust. As the doorbell rang above her head, every turkey turned its neck to fix her with its piercing, opaque eyes. Only Joseph and his customer were too busy to notice her.

The customer—a middle-aged woman with marcelled black hair and a nip-waisted suit—was standing on tip-toe, peering into each cage and pushing her face toward the turkeys' beaks as if she meant to kiss them. Finally she stepped back, crooked one finger under her chin and tilted her head as if trying to judge if a picture were hung straight.

"I swear," she said in a Southern accent and a gravelly voice like Mae West's, "if that one don't remind me of a big tom lived one year on my daddy's plantation."

"Madam," said Joseph, "any turkey you could remember would be younger than that one there in the cage."

Giggling, the woman made a scissors of her fingers and pinched the crests of her waves.

"I should hope that bird isn't half as tough as me."

"Tender as a spring chicken," said Joseph. "So help me God."

"Then that's the one I'll have."

Crossing the store to unlatch the cage, Joseph saw Catherine standing near the door.

"Jesus Christ!" he shouted. "You shouldn't be here in your condition, breathing in these feathers, lice, God knows what these filthy birds—"

He caught himself. If Catherine were here, it was probably all right. She was a woman, she knew, just as she knew that it was still all right for him to climb on top of her in the dark. . . .

Quickly he opened the pen, grabbed the turkey and held it at arm's length. It was an enormous bird, pure white, with rosy wattles and a scarlet crest. It began to struggle, scattering feathers like a torn pillow. Joseph gripped it harder.

"It's a twenty-pound beauty," he told the woman. "You got lots of kids to eat all this turkey?"

"No children. Nephews. Lots and lots of cute nephews." She gave him a sly wink, as if there were something dirty about these nephews, something he didn't want her winking about in front of his wife. He glanced at Catherine, checking for damage, and was relieved to see that she wasn't paying attention.

Catherine was watching the turkey twitch in Joseph's grip like a hanged man in a Western. But those men were supposed to be dead, and the turkey was still very much alive. Its wings thrummed like a revving engine. Catherine stared at its eyes, expecting some intimation of fear; but fear would have been less horrifying than the absolute expressionlessness of those flat black discs.

Joseph loosened his hold on the turkey's throat, just long enough for it to scream—a tortured cry, more human than any-thing Catherine would have imagined in the barnyard.

"My God," said the woman. "Can't he fuss, though?"

Joseph nodded proudly, as if the turkey were his creation. Ordinarily he stepped on the tail feathers and bent over for the kill. Yet this time he held it in the crook of his arm, close to his body. It was a crazy way to slaughter a turkey, and Joseph prayed that he wouldn't slip and stab himself in the side. But if Cath-erine wanted to watch him work, he would risk an ignominious death to impress her.

The turkey fought him—beating its wings, twisting around and raking its claws. Joseph braced one elbow against his hip and jammed the heel of his palm into its backbone. He stretched its chest along his forearm and yanked back its head until its neck bowed out before him.

Joseph looked at Catherine. He turned and looked at his cus-tomer. Then he raised his arm, flicked the knife as if sharpening it on the air, and sliced through the throat—side to side, then down—a perfect cross.

What shocked Catherine most was how long it took for the blood to come. As soon as Joseph lifted his knife, she expected it to spurt halfway across the room. But for what seemed like an interminable interval, there was not even a crease to show where the blade had passed. Then very slowly it welled up and flowed down the turkey's breast, spraying away from its body in a narrow arc. Soon the white feathers were drenched, flattened and stuck together in pointed clumps, and its wings were spattered with red.

The customer clapped her hands like a child, and Joseph knew that this was exactly what she'd wanted. This brutal and inexplicably beautiful sight of pure white stained pure red was what she remembered from her daddy's plantation. There was something lovely about it, he thought proudly, and looked to Catherine for approval. But Catherine was flushed with another sort of pride.

"This," she thought, "this is what my husband does for me and our baby." And she rested one hand on her stomach as if to remind the child inside her to pay attention.

All Joseph knew was that Catherine was red in the face, holding her belly.

"Hey," he said. "Are you okay?"

Catherine didn't answer, but the customer looked at Joseph, Catherine, at the barely perceptible bulge beneath her black sweater, and cooed, "Ooh, are you expecting?"

"Jesus Christ, this thing's still kicking!" Joseph held the turkey away from him and let it jump, let its own weight spin it around so the women could see: Already it seemed to have shrunk to half its former size. When the turkey began to shudder, Joseph stuffed it into the oil drum, purposely fumbling to give the women one last impression of its power.

Catherine watched the drum as if she could see straight through it, wincing each time the turkey crashed against its walls—first high up, then lower, then up again, as if it were trying to fly. Its feet grated against the metal, and the beating of its wings echoed with a hollow ring. Joseph inspected his fingernails. Finally he lifted the lid and pulled out the lifeless turkey, but the women continued to stare at the drum as if the dying were still going on inside it.

"You want it plucked?" Turning to look for his helper, Joseph saw his mother—stolid and implacable as the angel guarding Eden—positioned at the back of the shop.

69

Mrs. Santangelo stormed across the room and stopped in front of Catherine. She took a deep breath, inflated her chest, and closed her eyes.

"Now you've done it," she said. "Now you've gone and done it."

"Done what?" said Joseph.

"I'm not talking to you. I'm talking to *her*." She took another step toward Catherine. "How was I to know you were down here? I was upstairs minding my own business, making the sausage, I didn't even hear you go out. So I'm standing there in the kitchen, I smell cigars . . . and there's my Zio.

"'Zio,' I say. 'What's this? Since when do they let you visit in the daytime?'

"'Carmela,' he says, 'it's an emergency. That girl our son married, she's downstairs killing turkeys!'"

"*I* was doing the killing," said Joseph. "She was just watching."

"So I ran down to see for myself," continued Mrs. Santangelo. "And it's true. Now you've gone and done it, now you've marked that child for life. Now, mark my words, you'll give birth to a chicken!"

"God!" shrieked the customer. "What a frightful thing to say. I shouldn't be intruding on y'all's private family business, so if you'll just wrap that turkey up, I believe I'll be . . ."

Joseph ignored her. He walked across the room and put his arm around Catherine's shoulders.

"Mama," he said, "there's no point scaring her."

But Catherine didn't seem scared—only amazed, as she looked down, touching her stomach.

"It moved," she said, laying both hands on the place where the child had just that moment shifted inside her with a flutter like the beating of wings.

The next morning, Catherine awoke with the wings beating in her stomach and Mrs. Santangelo's warning echoing in her ears. It was early, but her mother-in-law was already in the kitchen, stuffing scrap meat through the grinder. Without looking at Catherine, she said, "Your husband's breakfast dishes been in the sink two hours."

Catherine was washing dishes when the fluttering began again. Still facing away, Mrs. Santangelo said, "It's moving, the little chicken?"

"Don't call it that," said Catherine.

"Why not? You marked that child and now you're going to bear my son a chicken."

"That's superstition. You don't know."

"You'd be surprised what I know," said Mrs. Santangelo.

From then on, Catherine haunted the kitchen, watching her mother-in-law and trying to figure out how much she knew. She noticed how the old woman counted everything, how her lips moved constantly, producing an almost inaudible chant—part English, part Italian, part recipe, part incantation. And gradually, as the weeks went by and Catherine grew so big that she had to go back to her father's apartment and exhume her mother's long black dresses from the cedar trunk, she came to the conclusion that Mrs. Santangelo knew plenty.

Flattered by the attention, Mrs. Santangelo outdid herself in demonstrating the extent of her knowledge. She began with the simplest proofs:

One December morning, she bought some California artichokes at Frank Manzone's. Back home, she broke off the tough outer leaves and found a small slug nestled in the satiny interior.

"Catherine, look. It's going to snow."

That very night, the first light flurries fell on Mulberry Street.

Peeling potatoes for gnocchi, she said, "Eighteen eyes on this big potato. Within twenty-four hours, two beggars will come to the door."

"In Italy, beggars come to the door," said Catherine. "Not here in America."

But the next day, Catherine answered a knock on the door to

find two bedraggled old ladies selling raffle tickets for the San Gennaro Benevolent Society.

"If you can sell me one that ends with a thirty-seven," said Mrs. Santangelo, "count me in."

Obligingly, the ladies flipped through their booklets till they came up with a number to match Mrs. Santangelo's hunch. One week later, they returned with her prize—a scalloped cake plate in a rose pattern, with a metal hook for hanging on the wall.

One afternoon, Mrs. Santangelo looked out the front window and said, "Catherine. Guess who just walked into Violetta's Candy Store."

"I give up. Who?"

"Death. That's who."

By the end of that week, the candy store was closed, its window draped with black and purple bunting.

That night, Catherine snuggled close to Joseph, lay her head on his chest and said, "Listen, do you think your mother could be right?"

"About what?"

"About me marking the child, that day in the shop. About us having a kid like a chicken."

"Let me feel." Laughing, Joseph put his hand between her legs. "I'll tell you what's in there."

"No." Catherine pushed his hand away. "I'm serious. You think she really knows?"

"My mother knows sausage. That's what she knows. She's a superstitious old lady. She gets nasty. Don't let her frighten you."

But Catherine was already so frightened that she couldn't sleep and sat up half the night. Despite what Joseph thought, his mother knew a lot more than sausage . . . and she'd predicted the worst. The more Catherine brooded, the more it made sense. It was too miraculous that she and Joseph could go to bed one night and produce a perfect human being nine months later. It was too simple. There had to be a trick. Just before dawn, she understood that the trick was everything that could go wrong, the calamities that befell women and their unborn and newborn children. . . .

In the morning, Mrs. Santangelo made sure that these night-time fears survived the light of day. Soon after Catherine awoke, she called her to the window.

"That's poor Jimmy Leucci." She clicked her tongue and pointed to a blind man in a tartan cap, tapping his way down Mulberry Street. "His Papa, God rest his soul, was crazy for music. Colored people's music. So he drags his poor wife, six months along with Jimmy, up to a club in Harlem to hear some blind colored piano player. The blind man finishes his act, turns around and looks straight at Mrs. Leucci. And that's how come poor Jimmy . . ."

"If that's how come poor Jimmy, then how come you're call-ing me over here to look at *him.*"

"Your baby's already marked. You can't do any more harm than you've done already."

Catherine was silent for a long time. Then almost whisper-ing, she said,

"Isn't there *anything we* can do?"

Mrs. Santangelo turned to her with the satisfied smile of a deposed queen accepting the long-awaited invitation to reclaim her throne.

"Yes," she said. "There is."

Saint that he was, San Gennaro had not only the strength to catch volcanoes in his arms, but also the grace and humility to understand why, after so many years, his image should be moved toward the edge of the mantelpiece, why his favorite geranium should be taken from him and put in the kitchen, and why his accustomed place at the center of the altar should be usurped by a gilt medallion of Saint Anna, the Virgin's mother, protectress of pregnant women and their unborn children.

Following Mrs. Santangelo's instructions, Catherine walked to the libreria on Second Avenue where she bought the embossed medallion and a small painting of a cherubic Baby Jesus. On the way home, she noticed for the first time that her center of gravity had shifted. Her back ached, and the sidewalk hurt her feet. Pausing on every corner to catch her breath, she felt as if this short crosstown trip were a pilgrimage, and she thought of the penitents in Quebec, climbing the stone steps of Ste. Anne de Beaupre on their knees. She stopped in at Our Lady of Mount Carmel to say a dozen Hail Marys, sprinkle the Saint Anna medallion with holy water, and purchase three dozen votive candles.

Back at the apartment, she and Mrs. Santangelo arranged the altar, lit a candle, and asked Saint Anna to keep Catherine from giving birth to a chicken.

Yet no amount of prayer could quiet Catherine's fears. Secretly, she doubted that anyone was listening. The image on the medallion—Saint Anna, hands clasped in prayer, with a full-grown, fully clothed Madonna standing praying in her womb—what could she know about a husband who smelled of meat? When had desire ever driven her to the butcher shop to watch her man slit a turkey's throat? Saints were surrounded by an aura of brilliant light; Catherine lived in a dark apartment where even the plants had to struggle for life.

But Mrs. Santangelo—so unlike her normal self that everyone was astonished—was full of hope. Delighted by the change in Catherine, she was quite ready to reverse her former prediction.

"Now you'll see," she said cheerily, scraping paraffin off the candleholders. "The saint won't let anything happen."

Catherine nodded, but she wasn't convinced. For all her mother-in-law's reassurances and even the power of the saint seemed abstract and very distant compared to the fluttering inside her and the momentary hallucination, more and more frequent, of something flying past the corner of her eye, a blur of white wings soaring up past the saints and straight to God.

Soon after Saint Anna made her appearance on the Santangelo family altar, Joseph approached Lino and Nicky and asked if they would like to get together some night for a little pinochle. The men accepted graciously, having never for one moment imagined that the game would not eventually be resumed.

For this was the way of the world, the facts of life, as natural and inevitable as gray hair: A man gets married, he stops playing pinochle. A few months later, the wife is pregnant and he's ready to play again.

One evening, shortly before New Year's, Joseph was relaxing after dinner in his living room. Knees spread to accommodate her belly, Catherine sat across from him, reading a movie magazine. In the kitchen, his mother was rearranging her cupboards, clanging pans and rattling dishes to remind him that God didn't give *her* time to digest *her* food.

Joseph remembered a bottle of Strega which one of the meat wholesalers had given him for Christmas, and went down to get it from the shop. When he returned, Catherine was pointing at her magazine and saying, "Look, Mama, Judy Garland just gave birth to a gorgeous eight-pound baby girl."

"May God protect it from the Evil Eye," his mother called from the other room.

But the Evil Eye was just what she gave Joseph as he walked into the kitchen and, after much searching, took three liqueur glasses from the top shelf.

"How about a little drink for the New Year?" he said.

"New Year's isn't for three days," said his mother. "And these closets won't wait three days to get cleaned."

So he replaced one of the glasses, filled the other two and brought them out. Catherine reached for one, then hesitated. Right on cue, Mrs. Santangelo appeared in the doorway:

"Drink that, and the baby will be born the color of that Strega. That's *asking* for jaundice."

"Thanks, Joseph." Catherine's hand dropped into her lap. "I better not."

Sickened now by the thought of the sweet liqueur, Joseph

put down his glass. He needed something stronger. A whole bottle of Frank Manzone's wine might just begin to make him feel right.

"I should have known," he said. "When you started calling her 'Mama,' that's when I should have known."

Actually, he had known, weeks before, when he'd begun to catch Catherine and his mother whispering, head to head. In theory, he should have been delighted by this new closeness in the family; in fact, he couldn't help thinking that they were conspiring to exclude him from a private world which held no room for anyone but women and their unborn children.

The apartment smelled different, food smells mingled with the scented candles burning perpetually on the mantelpiece. Each night, Catherine knelt briefly at the altar before coming to bed.

"Since when are you so hot on the saints?" he'd asked her one night.

"For protection." She'd pointed at her stomach.

"What do you need protection from?" Joseph laughed. "Me?"

When Catherine turned away from him, he'd noticed that she smelled different too; the familiar aroma of her flesh was gone, replaced by the chaste cold scent of wintergreen soap. Right then, he'd known that their lovemaking was over till after the baby was born—just as he'd known that she wouldn't drink a glass of Strega for the New Year without consulting his mother.

"I'm going out. You want anything?" He left without waiting for an answer.

Outside, he picked his way across the icy asphalt and climbed the stairs to the Falconetti apartment, where he found Lino and Nicky drinking at the kitchen table. The house was a mess, but the only thing Joseph noticed was the pattern of circular rust stains on the bare shelves. He realized they'd been left there by Catherine's plants. This thought made him so unaccountably miserable that he felt as if she were dead, and had to remind himself that she was safe at home, reading about Judy Garland's new baby.

"You gentlemen care to play some pinochle?" he said.

"Sure," said Lino. "I'll talk to Manzone tomorrow. Your place?"

"Too cold." It depressed Joseph to think of playing in back of the shop.

"Then I'd be honored." Lino swung his arm to offer the comforts of his home.

The next night, Frank Manzone showed up with half a dozen bottles of wine. But now it was the Falconettis' responsibility, as hosts, to stay sober enough to keep an eye on things. Consequently their game improved, and the pinochle was no longer the nightly slaughter of before. Sometimes Joseph and Frank won, sometimes the Falconettis.

Unaccustomed to losing, Joseph took it badly. He drank himself into black, self-pitying moods and, at the end of the games, paid his debts so resentfully that often the Falconettis told him to keep his money, and he kept it. He knew a thousand ways of cheating, but for the first time in his life was afraid of getting caught.

One wet, chilly evening, early in March, Joseph lost every hand. He was down ten dollars when he stood and said, "That's it. I haven't seen a picture card all night. I feel like somebody's trying to tell me something."

"What's the matter, Santangelo?" said Lino. "You getting psychic?"

"On my mother's side," said Joseph, then shivered. Maybe he was getting psychic. Though Catherine wasn't due for another month, somehow he felt it was starting. . . . He looked out the window and up at his apartment. Every light was blazing.

"Jesus." He grabbed his overcoat and rushed out the door. "I'll see you guys later."

The living room was deserted, the door to his bedroom shut;

FRANCINE PROSE

from behind it came the muffled sound of his mother's footsteps. A dozen candles were burning on the altar. The place smelled of Lysol. Then he heard a moan so low and distant, it could have been the wind.

He ran down the hall toward the bedroom, but stopped halfway there. He'd heard it said that laboring women blame their husbands for every pain and swear between contractions that they'll never let a man touch them again. He retreated to the living room, where he tried unsuccessfully to make himself comfortable, but kept jumping up at every sound—his nervousness compounded by the embarrassment of acting like the old cliché, the comedian playing expectant father. All he really knew about childbirth was what he'd seen in the movies, the kindly country doc saying, "Don't just stand there! Heat up the water and get some towels!" With all his heart, Joseph wished that his mother would emerge from the bedroom and tell him to boil some water.

Mrs. Santangelo shot past the living room on her way to the kitchen.

"Hey!" yelled Joseph. "Is there anything I can do?"

"Pray," she said. "For once in your life, you can pray."

"Can I go in there? I want to see Catherine."

"See? What's there to see? What do you think this is, the movies? Stay right where you are and pray!"

She was gone so fast that Joseph forgot to see if she was carrying hot water and towels. He knelt awkwardly before the altar and began to pray—a Hail Mary, an Our Father. He had to grope for the words and recited them woodenly, like the poems he'd been forced to memorize in parochial school.

"Please let it be easy for her," he said, though it seemed to him that Saint Anna and San Gennaro were eyeing him as if he were a total stranger asking for a loan, or worse, a bum panhandling a dime. Why should they do him any favors?

He sat down on the couch and riffled through Catherine's magazine till he found the picture of Judy Garland and her fat

78

little baby. The accompanying article comforted him: With all the dope Judy Garland took, she'd done okay. Reading on, he learned that Judy's husband had converted one wing of their Beverly Hills mansion into a private maternity hospital; he imagined this man, in a smoking jacket, puffing his pipe in the den while a procession of nurses tiptoed in to announce that everything was going fine.

But when his mother came through, he had to jump up and trail her to the kitchen.

"How's it going?" he asked.

"Not so hot," she said, and was gone.

These three words provided Joseph with endless scenarios of tragedy and horror: Catherine would die. The baby would die. Catherine and the baby would die. How could he have overlooked these terrible possibilities, dismissing Catherine's fear as the crazy and perfectly normal delusions of a pregnant woman? *He* was the crazy one. Only now did he realize how badly he wanted the child, and he thought: This was some time to realize it.

He turned the radio on for distraction and heard Nat King Cole crooning faintly through a loud buzz of static. Got to get Lino to fix this, he thought. Then he imagined how painful it would be, seeing Lino and Nicky with Catherine and the baby dead.

Suddenly he felt as if the apartment were a mausoleum in which he and his mother and Catherine were walled up together, buried alive, the last three people on earth. He threw open the window. Was there anyone out there? His chest felt tight; he needed some air.

"I'm going out," he called. "Anything you want?"

There was no reply. What could they possibly need?

The drizzle had turned to sleet, and everything had a wavy, out-of-focus look, as if the sidewalks and street lights had melted, then frozen again in a slightly different place. Just as Joseph had feared, there was no one else in the world—not one drunk walking it off, not one poor slob escaping a fight with his wife. Everyone was safe inside, asleep or dead, and he was the only survivor.

Upstairs, he found his mother standing in front of the altar. At first he assumed she was praying . . . but why was she making those odd noises?

"Mama," he said, "what—?"

His mother glared at him, then, without a word, grabbed the Saint Anna medallion off the mantel. He followed her into the kitchen, where she lit a burner on the stove, grasped the medallion with a pair of tongs and held it over the flame.

The gilt blistered; the metal began to buckle, releasing a stream of smoke. The edges curled, the medallion bubbled, but Mrs. Santangelo kept it in the flame until it was a tarry lump, fused with the tongs. Only then did she fill the sink and drop the medallion into the water, where it landed with a hiss.

Mrs. Santangelo didn't flinch from the smoke, though her eyes turned red and watered. Joseph realized that he hadn't seen her cry since his father's death.

"Mama," he said.

"This is what Saint Anna has done for the Santangelos," she said. "And this is what Saint Anna deserves."

"Catherine?"

"Catherine's fine. The baby didn't have a chance. It lived three seconds, just long enough for me to splash some water on it and pray for God to accept it as a proper baptism. Go in now, go in and see your wife." Then her eyes narrowed and she said, "Go in and see what you won in that pinochle game."

Catherine was lying in bed beneath a clean sheet. She was staring at the far wall and did not turn when Joseph entered. On the bed near the footboard was a pile of sheets, and in the center, a parcel wrapped in a white pillowcase. Slowly Joseph unfolded it, and saw the tiny corpse—shrunken and discarded-looking, like something meant to be thrown out with the garbage or into the laundry with the bloodstained sheets.

He reached for Catherine's hand, but she pulled back. He gazed at the child for as long as he could stand it. Crying, he turned away, but not before the thought had crossed his mind that the infant resembled nothing so much as a plucked and freshly slaughtered baby chicken.

3

MIRACLES

THERE WAS A FUNERAL which Catherine was discouraged from attending, and a tiny white coffin like a toy boat. As the priest intoned the rites, Joseph imagined limbo as an endless Central Park Lake, with the souls of unbaptized infants skimming over the water in their miniature caskets, white sails rigged to catch the breeze.

When Joseph and his mother got home, the first thing Mrs. Santangelo did was slide the statuette of San Gennaro back to the center of the altar.

"That's the last time I move you," she promised the saint. "I swear to God."

Three days after the delivery, Catherine could hardly walk, but Mrs. Santangelo herded her and Joseph in front of the mantel and suggested that they pray:

"If he can catch a volcano in his bare hands, he can help us get over this."

"If I kneel down," said Catherine, "I'll never get up."

So Mrs. Santangelo prayed for them all. Still wearing her bulky coat, she knelt with the slow clumsy dignity of a circus elephant: "Holy Saint, help us accept God's will. And while you're at it, help us remember: Life goes on.

"Speaking of life goes on . . ." She stood up. "Catherine, that plant you used to have up here, we put it in the kitchen? Anyhow, it looks a little dry, maybe you could water it, we'll put it back up. . . ."

"I don't know why you bother." Catherine nodded at the altar. "I don't know why the hell you bother." And she shuffled back to bed.

"She's going to be okay," Mrs. Santangelo reassured Joseph. "It takes time, but you'll see. There'll be another baby, everything will be fine. I know, I've been seeing signs everywhere. And you, Joseph? You and the boys going to play a little pinochle?"

"What's it to you?" Joseph was still bitter about the way his mother had acted on the night of the baby's death, bringing up how he'd won Catherine at pinochle, as if it were all his fault. "Since when do you care?"

"Since now." Mrs. Santangelo held her ground. "You could use to step out, enjoy yourself, get your mind off your troubles. It would be good for you *and* Catherine."

"Sorry," said Joseph. "I don't have the heart." But what could be more disheartening than the prospect of spending another evening with a wife who wouldn't talk to him, wouldn't look at him, wouldn't get out of bed?

That night, Joseph and Frank Manzone called on Lino Falconetti.

"Three-handed pinochle?" said Lino. "I never heard of such a thing."

"Where's Nicky?" said Frank.

"Flew the coop." After two bottles of wine, Lino wasn't upset, simply stating a fact. "Bright and early this morning. Go look in his room."

The perfect neatness and anonymity of Nicky's room heightened the oddness of its single incongruity—a sheet draped over what appeared to be an enormous . . .

"Holy Christ," said Joseph. "A tombstone."

"Ha ha," said Lino. "A tombstone, that's terrific. It's his radio."

"I guess I've got tombstones on the brain," said Joseph.

"Look." Lino pointed to a postcard propped up against the radio. He passed it to Joseph and Frank and then, in case they'd missed the message, read it aloud:

"'Re-enlisting. Nicky.' Re-enlisting." Lino snorted. "A patriot."

"I don't get it," said Frank. "What's in it for him?"

Lino turned over the card. On the other side was a tinted photo of fluffy pink trees and the legend: Japanese Cherry Blossoms. Springtime, Washington, D.C.

"Madame Butterfly," said Lino. "That's what's in it for him."

"Run that by me again," said Frank.

"I'll tell you a story," said Lino. "The last time Nicky came home from the service—it was right after VJ Day, you remember—he says hello and doesn't say another word for two weeks. Okay, I figure, the guy doesn't want to talk about it. Then one night we're sitting out here after supper, Catherine's in her room, Nicky opens up.

"'The whole thing was like a bad dream,' he says.

"'Jesus,' I say. 'That bad, huh?'

"'Except for one night,' he says, and I know from the tone of his voice it's got something to do with a girl.

"'Ah hah,' I say. 'Some poor little fraulein's crying her eyes out for Nicky Falconetti.'

"He looks at me like I'm crazy.

"'It was a USO show,' he says. 'Except for that, it was like I was dreaming the whole time. The fighting, the blood, then they had me working on radio communications for the high command . . . it was like I was watching myself, I just couldn't wake up. And then one night—it was at the base in Landstuhl—I went to the USO show. Risë Stevens came on, she was singing "Un Bel Di" from *Madame Butterfly*. It was so beautiful, I couldn't believe it. All of a sudden I woke up and listened. Then she quit singing, the guys applauded—they were waiting for Bob Hope the whole time—and I fell asleep again. . . .'"

Lino looked at Joseph and Frank.

"I still don't get it," said Frank. "What's that got to do with re-enlisting?"

"Use your head." Lino tapped his skull. "Where's the action these days?"

"Korea."

"Exactly," said Lino. "Mark my words. Nicky's going to come home with Madame Butterfly and a couple of slanty-eyed babies."

Though Joseph couldn't follow Lino's logic, one thing was clear:

"Well, looks like that's the end of the pinochle game."

"How about Augie?" said Frank. "We could ask him to sit in. He'd be flattered."

"Fat chance," said Joseph. "You think Augie's dumb enough to commute in from the Island for a pinochle game?"

Augie Santangelo wasn't stupid, just extremely good-natured and eager to help Joseph get over his loss. He pretended to be flattered, and drove in the next night.

Despite Augie's hereditary addiction to cheap cigars, his presence seemed to bring a breath of fresh Long Island sea air into Lino's musty apartment. Determined to help Augie maintain his high spirits, Frank Manzone threw the first few hands his way. But Augie's geniality was no match for Joseph's unhappiness, and his enthusiasm only irritated Lino, who'd grown accustomed to Nicky's listlessness. Vaguely distrustful of his bright new partner, Lino felt the sting of his son's defection.

The game dragged on for an hour until Augie laughed and said, "Gentlemen, correct me if I'm wrong, but I thought the point of pinochle was, you play to win."

"We're playing," said Frank Manzone. "We're playing. Anyhow, what are you complaining about? You're winning, it's me and Joey that are down."

"That's what I'm complaining about," said Augie. "How does it look, me cleaning out my own baby brother? Well, thanks a million. I guess I'll be getting home, maybe catch a little television with Evelyn and the kids."

"Television!" cried Lino. "Don't mention that word in this house."

"See you, Augie," said Joseph. "Tell Evelyn to come around, pick up some of Mama's sausage. Give the twins a big kiss for me."

"Sure," said Augie. "Take it easy."

Joseph went home, undressed in the dark and eased into bed. Asleep on her back, lit through the blue curtains, Catherine looked like a statue on a tombstone. When Joseph brushed against her, she rolled onto her side and curled away from him. He'd learned to sleep without moving, as if he were lying beside her on the same stone slab. This particular tomb, he noticed, smelled of chicken soup with escarole, beef broth with pastina, the baby food which his mother cooked specially for Catherine and which Catherine refused to touch. Also there was the pungent odor of dying plants—Catherine's treasures dying from neglect because no one had the energy to water them or the heart to throw them out.

It was the end of everything which Joseph had taken for granted—not only the joys of married life, but the milder and more dependable pleasures of his mother's cooking. Each night, he ate dinner with his mother, as he had in his bachelor days. Back then, she could really pack the food away, though she spent the whole meal on her feet, running to the kitchen, boasting that God didn't give her time to eat. But now she sat opposite him, chewing the soft part of her bread and leaving the crust.

"Eat," she urged him. "Your Mama won't be around to cook for you forever."

Meanwhile she entertained him with the neighborhood news. Mrs. Santangelo had always had a fine ear for gossip, but now it was tuned to only one frequency:

"Guess what? Mrs. Imperato's Daniel, a young man, fifty-four years old. Cancer of the colon. And old Mrs. Tessatore, yesterday morning her son goes to take her some groceries—thank God he's got a key—the old lady's dead on the bathroom floor. So little Ronnie DeFalco, he's starting the barbeque in his brother-in-law's backyard, one squirt of lighter fluid—whoosh! Burns over sixty percent of his body."

"Jeez," said Joseph. "That's awful. But how come nobody's getting married anymore, having babies? To hear you talk, everybody's dying. Nobody's getting born."

"Nothing's beginning. Everything's coming to an end. Eat."

Joseph couldn't eat. It was not just the litany of death and horror ruining his appetite, but also a physical problem: he could barely swallow. The gluey pasta stuck to the roof of his mouth. The watery tomato sauce was so overseasoned that the pepper bit his throat. Everything tasted slightly spoiled.

Pushing the food around his plate, Joseph recalled that travesty of a meal which Catherine served them in her father's house. And now, he thought, his mother's prophecy was coming true. He had married Catherine, and his life tasted like that meal—worse, in fact, because he really did remember the antipasto with pleasure. Now there was no pleasure anywhere, and his future looked as gloomy as one of his mother's stories.

"Either it's the end of me," Joseph thought, "or it's the end of my mother's cooking."

It was almost the end of Joseph's business.

One Saturday morning, Evelyn came into the shop, so solicitous and subdued, so brimming with concern that Joseph, who'd given her ten pounds of sausage two days before, assumed she was ashamed to be coming back for more so soon.

"Gee, the kids must have liked that sausage."

"Joseph," said Evelyn, "how's Mama?"

"Fine," lied Joseph.

"Joseph." Evelyn affected a stage whisper. "Me and Augie and the kids were throwing up all night."

"That's terrible. You do look a little green. . . ."

"I know what you're thinking. So I'm not the best cook in the world. I'll admit it, I've ruined a meal or two in my time. But never *that* bad. Joseph, the sausage . . . My Stacey says, 'Mommy, this sausage tastes like dog food.'"

"Smart kid, that Stacey."

"Joseph." This was too important for Evelyn to be distracted by compliments. "I said to Augie, 'Augie, your Mama doesn't cook like this. Something's wrong.' Joseph, I wouldn't be telling you this . . ."

"I know you wouldn't," said Joseph. "I know all about it. So just don't go telling anybody else."

But Joseph's customers didn't need Evelyn to tell them that the sausage was inedible—for reasons which varied from batch to batch. Sometimes Mrs. Santangelo went crazy with the spices, adding so much fennel that the links were like licorice sticks, so much pepper that every ulcer in the neighborhood erupted anew: Sometimes she was careless with the grinder, and mothers lost years off their lives fishing bone fragments from their children's throats.

"That's how it goes," said the neighborhood women. "One day you're cooking for the king. And the next day pigs won't touch your table scraps."

Crowds no longer formed in the store on Mondays and Fridays, when Mrs. Santangelo was known to make a fresh batch. No matter how charmingly Joseph flirted, his best customers couldn't be tempted to round out their orders with a couple of links. Business limped along on chicken, beef, and veal, on the loyalty of faithful customers who kept the Santangelos' recent misfortunes in mind and forgave them this lapse. Eventually Joseph began to feel so grateful for their patronage that he couldn't bring himself to cheat them; it was then that he decided to talk things over with his mother.

One night at dinner, she provided him with an opening by tearing the center out of her bread and throwing away the rest.

"At my age," she said, "who's got teeth for crust? Old Mrs. Casserta, she's younger than me, she eats nothing but ricotta and a little cream of wheat."

"Mama," said Joseph, "face it. You're not as young as you used to be. Maybe you're working too hard."

"Who else? Who else is going to stuff forty pounds of sausage a week? Your wife? Guess again. Your wife won't get up to water her plants. It looks like the Sahara Desert in here."

"Who's to stop you from watering them?" Joseph pointed at the pots of dirt and twigs. "It's depressing."

"*Me* water them?" Mrs. Santangelo charged an imaginary jury to judge the outrageousness of this. "Already I'm the cook and the maid and now he wants me to be the gardener."

"Forget it. Catherine will take care of it when she gets better."

"Gets better? How long do you think it takes? Three days after you and Augie were born, I was up on my feet, washing diapers. Your wife's been flat on her back eight months!"

"It takes time. . . ."

"Time? It takes a miracle. A miracle's what it will take to get her out of bed."

Joseph didn't answer. After a while his mother said, "You look a little pale."

"I'm fine. Just thinking."

He'd been thinking of something Catherine had said the night before.

By now, it had become a nightly ritual, a regular mating dance in reverse. As soon as Joseph got into bed, Catherine scooted to the far edge and pretended to be asleep. Last night, though, Joseph had been too upset to play along.

"Listen," he said, "I'm worried about Mama. It's the sausage, the customers are complaining . . . I think she's losing her marbles."

"So what?" said Catherine. "She could stuff those casings with rat poison, what difference would it make?"

Joseph didn't often cross himself, but now he did, and kissed his fingertips for good measure.

"You know what difference it would make."

"Maybe. And maybe I don't."

"Catherine, it's not the end of the world. The last hand hasn't been dealt yet, the chips haven't been cashed in. We're young, we can still have a family." Then he paused and said, "Not at this rate."

"I wish it *was* the end of the world."

"Maybe you should see a doctor, maybe he could give you a little something to help you get out of bed."

"Which doctor? The one that showed up six hours after the baby was dead?"

"How about a priest?"

"The only priest you'll see in this house is the one who comes in to give me the last rites."

"This can't go on. You're nuts, and you're driving me nuts too." Then suddenly it occurred to Joseph that Catherine's problem might, after all, be sexual—as simple and magical as that. Maybe she needed it as much as he did, but, being a woman, was too shy to say. Actually, this theory had crossed his mind before; Catherine had never given him the chance to test it. Now, despite the near-certainty of failure, Joseph reached out for Catherine's thigh.

Catherine slapped his hand away.

"No thanks," she said. "None of that."

"That's what you said when we first got married." Joseph forced a laugh. "And look how much fun we had."

"Look how we paid for that fun."

"Paid for what? We didn't do anything wrong. We're married, we've got rights."

"That was then. And this is now."

"Okay, you win." Joseph rolled away from her. "I've got the patience of Job. I can wait. I know these things take time."

"Joseph." Catherine's voice was hollow. "It takes more than time. Believe me, Joseph. It would take a miracle to make me do that with you again."

It was not a time for miracles or even small wonders. Sadness lingered in the house, together with the smell of scorched metal. Mrs. Santangelo couldn't seem to make tea without letting the water boil out of the pot; it was almost as if the smoke from that Saint Anna medallion had never left the apartment. Catherine's dead plants sat on the shelves, like the skulls which the saints kept around as constant reminders of mortality.

Mrs. Santangelo had given up hope. What was there to hope for? A child, of course, a child to carry on the line and restore their luck. But the sound of Joseph's bedsprings suggested that a child was unlikely. These nights, she heard only the erratic shiftings of restlessness, tossing and turning, ill will between husband and wife, and she found herself longing for the squeaks and bounces which used to infuriate her. But how could she ask San Gennaro to make the bedsprings creak like before?

"What will become of us?" she asked aloud. No one answered; even Zio's spirit had abandoned her in this trying time. "What will become of us?" she repeated, if only to keep from hearing Joseph's bed and the morbid noises which rose up to her window from Mulberry Street.

All night, the muffled conversations reminded Mrs. Santangelo of whispering mourners, and the hoofbeats of the knife grinder's horse sounded like those of an animal being led to slaughter. The street was never quiet for more than a second, and during those seconds, she panicked: Everyone was dead. The noises of life would never resume.

The days were no better. Now, when she walked through

the neighborhood, the only building she saw was Castellano's Funeral Home; she imagined her own body laid out among the lilies, viewed as if from a great height. Was it any wonder that the shortest walks left her out of breath, with black spots dancing in front of her eyes?

"Zio," she said, not daring to hope that he was listening. "If you're coming, you'd better come quick. If you wait too long, I won't recognize you."

Her memory was fading; her knowledge of signs and portents was going first. Two pigeons perched on the windowsill—what did that mean? How could she count the eyes on a potato when she couldn't remember how many potatoes went into the gnocchi? She forgot the reason for wearing the *cornuto* she'd worn all her life, forgot that hopelessness was a sin, forgot where to find the priest she was supposed to confess it to.

The only thing she never forgot was her prayers, and eventually they were answered.

Late one night, anise-scented cigar smoke filled her room. Despite her failing memory, she had no trouble recognizing Zio's brand.

"Zio, help me." Mrs. Santangelo had waited too long to waste time on pleasantries. "Tell me: What will become of us? What's there to hope for?"

"Hope for a miracle," said Zio.

"What kind of miracle?" she asked, forgetting that Zio, in his spiritual state, resisted direct questions.

"The only miracle we can hope for," he said.

It was not a time for miracles. In all those months, the strangest thing that happened was that Nicky showed up—unannounced, still in uniform and apparently unhurt—at Lino's door.

Lino reached out to shake his son's hand, but Nicky just stood there, encumbered by the heavy duffel bag he was carrying in one hand, the thin, lacquered sword case in the other. It was this sword case, this samurai souvenir, which reminded

Lino of all the missed pinochle games, the hours of pleasure sacrificed to Nicky's idiotic dreams, and so irritated him that he said, "Where's Madame Butterfly?"

Nicky squeezed past him through the door. How could he have explained that until seventy-two hours ago, when the troop plane took off from the air base near Yokohama, Madame Butterfly had been everywhere, always but never quite within reach?

For the truth was as Lino had suspected, that Nicky had reenlisted in search of a Japanese wife. He imagined her in a kimono, white socks and those high wooden sandals, fluttering from room to room in his Mulberry Street apartment. His geisha-wife would light incense, pour tea, set bowls of formally arranged flowers in the places where Catherine's ugly houseplants used to be; she would blush and vanish behind a rice paper screen whenever a stranger entered the house.

Admittedly it was an incongruous vision, but the very incongruity of it struck Nicky with a piercing beauty which only made him desire it more. Their lives would smell of joss sticks and not of garlic and frying sausage; their days would be scored to a delicate blend of opera and koto music. Instead of pinochle, they'd play go and those coy games the geishas played with sake cups and disappearing shells.

On enlisting, he extracted a promise from the recruiting officer which the army honored: He was sent to Japan. There, he saw other men living out his dreams, half the company sleeping with Japanese girls, the other half boasting about it. A few were even marrying war brides, braving bureaucratic hell and high water to bring them back home.

The soldiers were generous with advice on how to meet girls, and Nicky did what they said. They told him to eat in local restaurants—he haunted every sushi bar and noodle parlor in Kyoto. They suggested public transportation—he took trams for short distances he could have walked. Dutifully, he accompanied his bunkmates to off-limits nightclubs and drank huge quantities of watered scotch. Still, somehow, he could never seem to find the proper approach; even the B-girls shied away from him. Besides, it seemed impossible that Madame Butterfly would be working in one of those sleazy, neon-lit bars; and the pimps who hissed at him from the doorways of the red-light district were nothing like Goro, Puccini's little "marriage-broker."

Recalling that Lieutenant Pinkerton had leased an apartment, and that the bride had come along with the place, Nicky thought briefly of renting a room in town. But all the houses with rooms to let belonged to war widows and families who'd lost sons in the fighting; their bitter, reproachful faces made the barracks seem homey and inviting.

Even as the plane took off, and Nicky watched the gray city, the bright green rice fields disappear beneath him, he never stopped praying for the miracle which would transform his life into *Madame Butterfly*. Only now, as he noticed that Lino's apartment hadn't changed since his departure and realized that it would probably stay the same till both he and his father were dead, did he finally accept the fact that his miracle would never come. He went straight to his room, turned on the radio and lay down on his bed.

Dreading this homecoming, he had timed it to coincide with the opera broadcast. Now, as the sounds of the orchestra tuning up and Milton Cross's hushed, pompous whisper filled the apartment, Lino put his fingers in his ears and kept them there, on and off, till four, when the program ended.

Nicky went out and returned a few minutes later with a bottle in a paper bag. Back in his room, he drained the bottle in one gulp and passed out through Saturday night and much of Sunday.

Monday morning, Nicky stumbled down to the shop, where Lino soon discovered that a second stint in the army had done nothing for his mechanical sense. Not that it mattered, for business was slower than ever. Everyone was buying televisions, and the radios that broke were left broken. All week, Nicky toyed with a battered Emerson, a hopeless case which had lain in the shop nearly two years. On Friday evening, Lino paused in the midst of closing up to examine his son's work, and found that Nicky had eviscerated the radio and abandoned it, an empty Bakelite shell.

That same weekend, Mrs. Santangelo got it into her head to invite the Falconettis to dinner, as a way of formally welcoming Nicky home.

"I don't know," said Lino. "I haven't seen much of your sister since before you left. If you ask me, she's not doing so hot, and the old lady isn't much better. Anyhow, don't you think it's a little peculiar? She's never invited us before. . . ."

Lino caught himself. Who was Nicky to ask about 'peculiar'?

The party got off to an inauspicious start as Nicky and Mrs. Santangelo greeted each other with rigid, almost theatrical formality. Like two inmates in a nuthouse, thought Joseph. Joseph shook his brother-in-law's hand and Catherine kissed the air in his direction.

"I won't hug you," she said. "I've got a cold."

"Sit," said Mrs. Santangelo. "The food's all ready."

Nothing could have been further from the truth. The melon was crispy and green, the pasta stuck together in clumps. Up and down the table, forks pierced the sausage and undercooked meat oozed out like toothpaste from a tube.

Joseph, who'd expected as much, thanked God that Augie, Evelyn, and the twins hadn't been able to come. He looked around the table and didn't bother putting any sausage on his plate. His mother was shredding a hunk of bread.

"At my age," she said, "who's got teeth for crust?" Then she noticed that the guest of honor had stopped eating.

"What's the matter?" She glared at Nicky. "They don't eat sausage in Uncle Sam's army?"

"Mama, I bought some seafood salad yesterday," said Joseph, who'd not only predicted, but prepared for, calamity.

"Five pounds. Maybe the Falconettis would like some with their sausage."

"Seafood salad with their sausage?" Mrs. Santangelo still had a sense—however dim—of the proper order of things.

"Sure, why not?"

"Where is it?"

"The refrigerator. You know."

Mrs. Santangelo was gone a long time before returning with the salad, still in its cardboard container. She set the carton on the table and motioned for her guests to pass it around. No one took much except Nicky, who loaded his plate with the marinated squid. The family sat in silence, watching him eat.

"In Japan," Nicky spoke with his mouth full, "they live on this stuff. Seafood and noodles, it's all they eat."

"What kind of country is that," Mrs. Santangelo leaned forward and scrutinized him, "where the women can't cook anything but seafood and pasta?"

"I didn't say *can't*." Bristling, Nicky rose to defend Madame Butterfly's honor. "I meant, it's all they can get. It's been rough for them since the war, you don't know. They can't get meat, sugar, ordinary ingredients—"

"Ingredients?" repeated Mrs. Santangelo. "What ingredients? When I first came over from the old country, me and Zio were so poor, I had to pick clam shells out of the garbage. And believe me, I made a delicious soup. If a woman can't cook what God gives her, she can't cook."

"You're a great one to talk." Nicky pointed at the untouched food on his plate.

"At least my son married an Italian girl." Mrs. Santangelo snapped her lips together like a turtle. "Instead of chasing after the Japanese."

"Right," said Nicky. "An Italian girl he won in a pinochle game."

"That's my wife you're talking about." Joseph slammed the blunt end of his knife on the table. "And your sister."

There was a silence. Finally Catherine said, "What pinochle game?"

"What pinochle game?" mimicked Mrs. Santangelo.

"*You* know." Ignoring his sister, Nicky addressed Mrs. Santangelo.

"I *don't* know," said Mrs. Santangelo. "I don't remember."

The subject was dropped. The meal ended. The Falconettis went home. Catherine cleared the table and went to her room, leaving her mother-in-law to do the dishes. Joseph paced the living room, feeling like a guest who has outstayed his welcome so long that his hosts have abandoned the pretence of courtesy and gone off to clean up or sleep. But where could he go? He couldn't bear the sight of his mother transferring the leftover sausage into refrigerator dishes, nor could he face Catherine, who'd be curious about that pinochle game. A grown man, he thought, afraid to go into his own bedroom.

Just as he was getting up the nerve to confront Catherine, his mother appeared from the kitchen, drying her hands on her apron.

"Joseph, I got a question. That boy that was here tonight—who was he?"

"That was my brother-in-law." Joseph couldn't look at her. "Catherine's brother Nicky."

"You mean, we're related to *that*?" said Mrs. Santangelo, but Joseph had already left the room.

The bedroom light was out, and Catherine lay on her back—so still that Joseph had to fight the urge to pinch her for some sign of life. Shamed by the thought, he undressed and got under the covers.

Catherine didn't speak; perhaps she was planning to ignore the whole thing. Joseph's relief was soon dissipated as he realized that it was not about to be ignored. Now that the pinochle game had been mentioned, it lay between them like another gloomy presence in the bed.

"You know what that dinner tonight reminded me of?"

Joseph decided to broach the subject in a roundabout way. "It reminded me of that meal you cooked before we were married, that first night I went to your father's apartment."

Often, in the early months of their marriage, they'd joked about that meal, about how nervous Catherine was, how good the ruined food had tasted to Joseph. It was part of their history, the private history which lovers construct around the beginnings of their love. And now, as Joseph prayed for this memory to ignite some long-extinguished spark of affection, Catherine turned toward him.

"What meal?" she said. "What dinner at my father's house?"

On Easter morning, Catherine woke up knowing that something was different. As she lay in bed trying to figure out what it was, she realized that the bedroom smelled of flowers. Easter lilies? The scent was lighter and less cloying than the fragrance of lilies. Seeking its source, Catherine looked around the room.

It was then that she noticed the violets on her dresser.

Last night, when she'd gone to bed, those plants were dead: crisp leaves curled up on dry stalks.

This morning they were in full bloom.

"Joseph," she said. But Joseph was asleep. Climbing over him, she picked up one of the pots and touched the purple blossoms. It was impossible. She didn't understand and didn't try. For by then, she had realized that the perfume wasn't coming from the violets, but seemed to be wafting in beneath the bedroom door. She put on her robe and went out into the hall.

The apartment looked like a garden, and the air was moist with an earthy greenhouse smell. Healthy plants, perfect as pictures in a seed catalogue, grew everywhere. Curtains of ivy hung from the kitchen shelves; asparagus ferns grew matted as birds' nests and overflowed their pots; spider plants sprouted tendrils tipped with star-like white blossoms. On the mantel, two geraniums climbed up toward San Gennaro, offering scarlet flowers which the saint received with outstretched arms.

This time Catherine knew she hadn't put them there.

She ran back to the bedroom.

"Joseph!" she cried. "Wake up, there's been a miracle!"

To Joseph, this meant only one thing: The miracle he'd been praying for, the miracle it would take to make Catherine go to bed with him again.

"You want to see a miracle?" Laughing, he reached out and pulled her down on top of him. "I'll show you a miracle."

"Why not?" said Catherine.

After so long, Joseph's kisses seemed so sweet that Catherine began to think she was experiencing a second miracle. She wound her arms around his back, feeling not only the physical pleasure, but also the rare and more complicated exaltation known to those chosen few who are lucky enough to make love after witnessing a miracle.

Afterwards, as she lay with her head on Joseph's chest, Catherine thought of the men and women, side by side in their tents on the night Moses led them across the Red Sea. She thought of the women at the well, going back to their husbands after seeing Jesus risen. She thought of the bride at Cana and smiled as she tried to imagine *her* wedding night.

"Was that enough of a miracle for you?" asked Joseph. "Or do you want more?"

"It's enough." Catherine turned to kiss his shoulder. "But there's more."

"More?"

"The plants. They're alive. All over the apartment . . ."

"Damn right they're alive. I thought you'd never notice. I've been watering them for weeks. Somebody had to take care of them, it was getting depressing around here."

"You?"

"Yours truly. The Italian gardener."

"Wait a minute." Catherine shook her head. "Water or no water, those plants were dead when we went to bed last night. And now they're—"

"They were fine last night, same as they are now. You've just been out of it for so long, you didn't pay attention."

"Not so out of it that I don't know: You can't bring dead things back to life."

"What kind of thing is that for a Catholic girl to say?"

"Joseph, I'm serious."

"Okay, okay. The ones that didn't recover, I bought new ones at the florist. What's the big deal?"

"You cheated. I thought it was a miracle."

"What a believer." Joseph laughed. "I pour a little water on your houseplants, you think you've seen a miracle. Well, try some of this"—he took her hand and put it on his thigh—"next thing, you'll be saying I'm a saint."

It was almost noon when they got dressed. Out in the hall, the smell of flowers was gone, obliterated by metallic smoke.

"Come on." Joseph grabbed Catherine's hand. "Mama's burning the teapot again."

They ran to the kitchen, where they found a blackened saucepan smoking on the stove and Mrs. Santangelo sitting on the floor—one cheek pressed against the bottom of the sink, like a child grown tired in the midst of playing, overtaken by a nap. Her eyes were shut, her skin gray. There was a purplish stain around her lips, as if death had caught her eating blueberries.

"Mama." Joseph gave her a gentle shake, and she slumped forward. "Holy Christ. This isn't the miracle you meant, is it?"

"God no." Catherine crossed herself. "I didn't know. . . ."

And then as she looked at her mother-in-law, surrounded by all those leafy and blossoming plants, Catherine began to think that maybe it was a miracle: How nice of God and His saints to send Mrs. Santangelo flowers.

When the first thud of dirt hit Mrs. Santangelo's coffin, Joseph and Augie hugged each other and wept. But theirs were the only tears. The old people grieved less for Mrs. Santangelo than for themselves, and for the end of that part of their lives. Carmela

Santangelo's existence was something they'd taken for granted, like the sidewalk under their feet; and now the sidewalk had vanished. At the chapel, the younger mourners spoke of God's kindness, of blessings in disguise, as if the death were some kind of divine mercy killing ("Face it," said Evelyn, "she was getting on"), until Joseph almost believed it.

As he reached for Augie's handkerchief, a curious numbness overcame him, blunting the realization that his mother, however crazy, was the only mother he would ever have; he had loved her and now she was gone. At the cemetery, on Long Island, it was a sunny spring day; birds were singing in the bare branches. His mother's grave was side by side with his father's, and it was comforting to think of them bickering about Zio's cigars for eternity.

But when the family went back to Augie and Evelyn's for a spread of supermarket bologna, white rolls, and processed cheese, Joseph couldn't eat for thinking what his mother would have said about the food. And when he and Catherine returned home, his mother's presence was standing at the stove, kneeling by the altar, settled in her favorite chair. Joseph needed to use the bathroom, but couldn't bring himself to walk past her room. He felt like crying again, but it was easier at the graveyard with Augie for company; alone with Catherine, he would have been ashamed.

Catherine seemed unaffected, or perhaps she was showing it differently: The first thing she did on arriving home was to put on one of his mother's old aprons and haul out the sausage grinder.

"Do me a favor," she said. "Go down to the shop and get me a small side of pork."

"Now?"

"It's what your Mama would have wanted." Even as she said it, Catherine knew that it was and wasn't true. Mrs. Santangelo would have wanted the family business to continue, the sausage to be made. But she didn't want anyone else to make it.

Joseph was glad to have something to do. The smell of saw-dust soothed him, and he could use the toilet downstairs. When he got back, Catherine was dicing garlic with his mother's paring knife and speaking of her new respect for Mrs. Santangelo: "If anyone could come back as a ghost and ruin things in the kitchen, it's your mother. But the fact is, Joseph, I can practically hear her mumbling the recipe."

Only this time, Catherine could understand every word; from this remove, she could appreciate her mother-in-law's forbearance. The whole process went so smoothly that in two hours the kitchen was clean, and there was fresh sausage and pasta on the table.

They sat down to a meal which consoled Joseph more than all the talk of blessings in disguise. For the food allowed him to remember his mother without her superstitious and passionate meanness, but simply as a wonderful cook. Her spirit was with them in the food and he ate three helpings, which is just what his mother would have wanted.

The smell of fried sausage drifted out through the neighborhood until even the old women—depressed by Mrs. Santangelo's mortality and their own—couldn't wait to get up the next morning and compare Catherine's work with her mother-in-law's.

The first batch sold out by noon. By dinnertime, the word had spread: Catherine's sausage was Mrs. Santangelo's at its best. That night, husbands got up from the table with tears in their eyes, as if they'd actually eaten that something special which Mama used to make.

"Life goes on," said their wives. "An old lady dies and the next day her daughter-in-law's making sausage good as ever."

One morning, nearly six weeks later, Catherine was stuffing sausage when she felt a sinking in her stomach, like dropping in an elevator, only more evocative, like something recalled from another life—or, more specifically, from her first pregnancy. It was on her mind: She'd skipped an entire period. But until that morning, she'd blamed the delay on overwork and nerves. What else could it be? After Easter, she and Joseph had quit making love again—first out of respect for Mrs. Santangelo, and then because the sudden demand for sausage left them little time for married life. Either Catherine stayed up working hours after Joseph went to bed, or collapsed hours before.

If she were pregnant—and suddenly Catherine knew she was—the child had been conceived on that Easter morning when Mrs. Santangelo died and the houseplants came back to life. Catherine shuddered. Just last month, *Photoplay* had queried fifty Hollywood stars for their views on reincarnation, and most of them seemed to believe. . . .

This child, Catherine promised herself, would not be suffocated in her womb by the weight of all that ignorance and superstition. This baby would be carried and born like an American. This time there was work to do—pork to grind, peppercorns to crush, fennel and parsley to chop—and not one minute to waste lighting candles.

It was the end of May, the kind of weather which usually starts women thinking of seafood and salads. But the shop was full of waiting customers.

Catherine greeted them, looking each one in the eye, daring them to guess she was pregnant.

"You're all dressed up," said Joseph. "Where you going?"

"For a walk. Uptown."

Catherine walked uptown to St. Vincent's Hospital where, like a true American woman, she submitted to a complicated series of indignities to confirm what she already knew. She undressed with her eyes shut and kept them shut until at last she opened them to find herself fully clothed, sitting in a cubicle with a young red-headed intern who was filling out a form.

"Can you remember the exact date of your last menstrual period?" he asked, coloring slightly, as if he secretly knew that it was none of his business.

"Two weeks before Easter," said Catherine.

On the way home, she stopped at a bookstore and spent a week's household money on three books. At the cash register, she put them down so that *The Mother's Medical Encyclopedia* was on top. Beneath it was *The First Nine Months of Life* and beneath that, *Childbirth Without Fear.*

It was an impulsive purchase, and later she regretted her haste. She opened the childbirth book at random and got so scared that she had to put it away. *The Mother's Encyclopedia* turned out to be packed with information about bedwetting, orthodontia, and chicken pox.

But *The First Nine Months of Life* was just what she'd wanted.

Afternoons, Catherine lay on her bed and studied the diagrams, compared the lists of symptoms and sensations with her own, and forced herself to look at the line drawings of embryos—half-tadpole, half-baby, with their swollen heads, their clawed hands and feet. Always she paid particular attention to the section entitled "Old Wives' Tales." It is not true, she read, that a baby will strangle on its cord if you raise your arms above your head. It is not true that a child born in the seventh month has a better chance of survival than one born in the eighth. It is not true that you can make your baby musical by listening to music, nor can you mark it by exposing yourself to bad influences.

Each time Catherine read these paragraphs, she embraced science for the most superstitious of reasons and vowed anew that this child would be born scientifically.

Occasionally this promise proved difficult to keep. When Catherine felt the baby's first quivering practice kick, she was on her bed, reading her book. This time, she knew what it was: There was life inside her, and she thought, "It's a miracle." Then she turned straight to the chapter on "quickening" and read the medical explanation till she had it memorized. When Joseph, reaching for her in bed, felt the change in her shape and said, "Hey, are you—," Catherine clapped a hand over his mouth.

"Shush," she whispered. "The walls have ears." Then she said, "Yes!" very loud, angry at herself for having made such an unscientific remark.

That weekend she talked Joseph into accompanying her to Klein's where, in defiance of every age-old warning against flying in the face of God, they purchased a complete baby layette, in yellow. And early Monday morning, as soon as Joseph left for the shop, Catherine—armed with a dry mop, rags, and a stack of cardboard boxes—invaded Mrs. Santangelo's bedroom.

Since her mother-in-law's death, Catherine had not had the time, and Joseph had not had the heart, to deal with her possessions. Yet now she went at it with the optimistic, impersonal efficiency of someone moving into an apartment, staking claim by scrubbing away every trace of its previous occupant. First the crucifix came down from the wall and went into the bottom of the largest box. On top of it went Mrs. Santangelo's clothes, forming a sort of nest on which Catherine laid the rosaries, the pictures of Zio, San Gennaro, the Holy Family. The knowledge that no one would ever use these things again gave her packing a certain carefreeness; and yet without thinking she wrapped the statuettes of the Virgin and Child in Mrs. Santangelo's aprons, so they wouldn't break. Likewise it never occurred to her to throw or give the boxes away; she stacked them in back of the hall closet.

Returning to the room, she hung the yellow organdy curtains, soaked the decals of bunnies and frolicking lambs, and pasted them over the bare white spot where the crucifix had hung. She set up the changing table, the bassinet, the crib, then stepped back to contemplate the gleaming, cheerful, sexless nursery, equally suitable for a girl or boy.

For Catherine refused to predict or even speculate about the baby's sex, nor was she anxious to hear such predictions from anyone else. She told no one but Joseph about her pregnancy; the most old-fashioned grandmother could not have taken greater pains to foil the Evil Eye than Catherine took to evade her neighbors' curiosity. By Thanksgiving, she had stopped leaving the house, and instructed Joseph to tell people that she was allergic to turkey feathers. Around this time, Evelyn marched upstairs and knocked on her door, but Catherine wouldn't answer.

Determined that everything be perfectly normal, Catherine spent an abnormal amount of time on her housework. Her plants doubled in size; new ones grew from cuttings. The hidden spots behind the canisters and spice jars shone, like trees falling in the forest where no one would ever know.

Early in December, she was unpinning clean clothes from a line strung across the kitchen when she felt the first cramp travel from her back across her stomach. Folding the laundry, she had two more contractions, then three more as she wiped down the burners and the refrigerator door. She was intent on leaving the house so spotless that if she died in the hospital and never came home, its condition would not shame her memory. She worked till the spasms were coming so regularly that she had to stop. Then she called downstairs to Joseph and asked him to get a cab.

The next day, Joseph's customers were astounded by his announcement that a seven-pound, eight-ounce baby girl, Theresa Carmela Santangelo, had been born to Catherine in St. Vincent's Hospital after a brief, uncomplicated labor.

"A baby?" cried the women. "Where did you find it, in the cabbage patch?"

Joseph took advantage of these pleasant exchanges to tip the scales. And though his customers knew it, they felt so selflessly happy for the proud new father that they wrote the extra pennies off as their baby gift.

Every evening, Joseph rushed uptown to visit Catherine and to stare through the nursery window at his daughter. At last it was time for mother and child to come home. In honor of this occasion, Joseph borrowed Augie's car—not only for comfort and safety, but also because he had something to discuss with Catherine—something too private to mention in a cab, too urgent to wait till they got back to the apartment.

HOUSEHOLD SAINTS

Catherine was nervous with the baby. When Joseph opened the car door for her, she hesitated, as if he were asking her to jump down a well.

"Slide in," he said.

Joseph drove in silence till they stopped at a long red light. Then, staring straight ahead, he said, "Listen, about that pinochle game."

"What pinochle game?"

"You know. Before we got married. The one Nicky was talking about, the night he came over to eat."

Catherine looked confused.

"*You* remember. The one where Lino was supposed to have bet you."

"Oh, *that* pinochle game. What about it?"

"What I want to say is . . . I would have married you anyhow, even if I didn't win you in that game."

"Thanks." Catherine wondered how this could be true. Then she said, "Did you cheat?"

"Sure. While the others were sucking in that cold air, I was palming extra hearts from the deck."

Catherine laughed. The baby was sleeping against her chest, and she could feel its warm breath through her dress.

"Isn't that always the way?" she said. "You win your husband in a card game."

"Is it? I didn't know it was such a common thing."

"It is. One way or another."

"I feel better," said Joseph. "Somehow I feel better." He smiled at his family, at Catherine and the soft little package wrapped in the yellow blanket from Union Square.

"Look what I won in that card game," he said. "An angel."

The baby was an angel, and the winter light, streaming into the nursery and bouncing off the plastic bassinette, surrounded her with a halo-like glow. Poking through the lacy covers, her tiny fingers grabbed at the sun motes, and Catherine couldn't look at her without thinking that her existence was a miracle. Overwhelmed by her beauty, and by love, Catherine channeled these unruly passions into the most mundane and uninspiring tasks of motherhood.

Sometimes it seemed to Catherine that the biggest change in her life was the staggering volume of Theresa's baby laundry. She recalled Mrs. Santangelo telling her that when Augie and Joseph were born—even before their cords were cut—she'd sent Zio out for *cornuti* to hang around their necks. But what Catherine sent Joseph out to buy was a washing machine.

Brand new, shiny, and big as an oven, the washer was installed in the kitchen. On clear days, Catherine strung Theresa's clothes on a line and sailed them out across the alley. Catherine had always thought of laundry as a torture, like one of those eternal frustrations sinners suffer in hell: You roll a stone up the hill, it rolls down. You wash a shirt and the next day it's dirty again. Yet now she was filled with joy by the sight of baby nightgowns flapping in the wind, and calmed by the very repetitiousness of the work: You wash a diaper, it gets dirty, you wash it again. Dirty laundry means the child is alive and growing. The diapers will stop, the baby clothes will get bigger. Life goes on. . . .

Catherine felt the urge to knock on wood. But this urge disappeared gradually, along with the wood, as Mrs. Santangelo's oak furniture was replaced, piece by piece, by vinyl, formica, and chrome. For Catherine was bent on modeling herself after those women in the *Good Housekeeping* ads, those smiling, competent American housewives, their consciences as clear as their glassware. It was obvious to her that the search for newer and stronger detergents was part of the same blessed science which had arranged Theresa's safe arrival into the world, equally obvious that America and its science had already served the Santangelos better than any old country saints. She felt that Theresa was a gift—and a provisional one; she wasn't so much worried that the gift would be taken back (though that was part of it) as convinced that it had come with certain inviolable conditions. Mrs. Santangelo, with her spitting three times and making the sign of the horns, was no more fervent and ritualistic than Catherine with her one-cup-per-load of Ivory Snow.

She consulted *The Mother's Medical Encyclopedia* regularly, and every other month took Theresa to St. Vincent's for check-ups, blood tests, vaccinations. On the doctors' advice, she fed her bottles of formula, then jars of processed baby food, and Theresa grew so fast that Catherine—sewing and crocheting according to the instructions in her women's magazines—wore out stacks of back issues. With their help, Catherine struggled to keep Theresa's wardrobe up to date, her baby smocks shirred like Ukrainian christening gowns, her felt skirts appliqued with woolly poodles in rhinestone collars.

By Theresa's second birthday, Catherine's cuddly angel had turned into a devil. But her deviltry was classic, the same spaghetti-dumped-over-the-head which every mother who came into the shop described, and the women reassured each other: It was only temporary. So Catherine sponged up the spaghetti and watched Theresa destroy her pretty nursery, for the mothers had promised: At three, the devil would vanish as suddenly as it had appeared, and the child's true nature would begin to emerge.

So it happened with Theresa; to celebrate, Catherine redecorated her room. Occasionally she caught herself wishing that her mother-in-law were alive to witness the transformation; it amused her to imagine Mrs. Santangelo's ghost revisiting her old haunts. Catherine scraped the half-peeled lambs off the wall and plastered it over with huge decals of Mickey and Minnie Mouse, dancing. In this room, the Holy Family was Popeye, Olive Oyl, and Swee'Pea. Mrs. Santangelo's bed was unrecognizable beneath its canopy of candy-striped chintz, its ruffled valances and eyelet-covered bolsters. Enthroned like pashas, plush animals surveyed a kingdom of milk glass and mirrored vanities, jars of hand cream and vinyl jewel boxes lined with velveteen: A magazine-perfect little girl's dream room.

Yet even then, Catherine was beginning to realize that Theresa's dreams were taking place in some imaginary recreation of Mrs. Santangelo's old room.

One morning, Catherine took Theresa to Woolworth's to buy a plant. By that time, the plants had taken over every available space, but Catherine kept buying them, for Theresa's sake. Inspired by countless articles on family togetherness, she intended these trips to the five-and-dime as ceremonies of mother-daughter closeness for Theresa to remember all her life. But they always seemed to bore her, and that morning she wandered off while Catherine was paying for some new kind of cactus which had caught her eye—a dry, gray lump, more like a pebble than a plant.

Catherine searched the store, then notified the manager, who set the saleswomen looking: Theresa was gone.

Often, in Joseph's shop, mothers told stories of the time the baby took off and turned up, here or there; to illustrate their panic and subsequent relief, the women would put their hands to their hearts and sag at the knees. Now Catherine felt that tightness in her chest, that weakening in her legs, and in addition heard a ringing in her ears, as if all the sirens and burglar alarms in the city were sounding at once. In this state, she ran home and back. None of the old women on the doorsteps recalled a stocky, big-eyed, dark-haired girl in a shirtwaist dress printed with chickadees in night shirts and pointed sleeping caps. But all of them had stories about the time their children vanished and reappeared unharmed.

First Catherine searched alone, then others joined in, and finally someone called from the door of Our Lady of Mount Carmel: She's here! And there she was, perched on a stool by the font, splashing holy water like a sparrow in a birdbath.

It was a week before Catherine could tell this story in the shop, and when she did, she put her hand to her heart, bent her knees, and said, "Elbow-deep in holy water."

"Like my Louise in every puddle," chorused the women. "Like my Sal in the toilet bowl."

Years later, when people began telling stories about Theresa Santangelo, these same women would reminisce about the holy water incident to marvel at this prodigy of devotion. But Catherine could never think of it without remembering how she'd hit Theresa, right there in church. Not counting baby taps, it was the first real smack of Theresa's life, more of a push actually, but a push from behind, hard enough to send her sprawling. And she remembered Theresa's shoulder blades (so fragile they'd brought a lump to her throat whenever she'd bathed her) snapping together like wings when she fell from the stool to the floor.

This memory disturbed Catherine so that she asked Joseph to ask Frank if Theresa could start attending Sunday mass with the Manzones. She herself hadn't been to church since Theresa's baptism, and it seemed wrong to her to treat church like the circus—someplace you'd never be except for your child. Every Sunday morning, Theresa trooped off with the Manzones, leaving Joseph and Catherine with the first time they'd had in years to drink an extra cup of coffee and go back to bed: A blessing.

Two years passed so quickly that the mothers agreed: It seemed like yesterday that their Sal was splashing in the toilet, and now they were telling horror stories about his first day at school. This one's Vincent got punched by a second-grader; that one's Mary Kay threw up every morning; this one spent weeks making Jimmy's turkey costume for the Thanksgiving pageant, and when Jimmy tried it on and looked in the mirror, he screamed and screamed.

"That's nothing," said Catherine. "Five mornings in a row, I take Theresa to the public school. And every morning, by the time I get home, Joseph's had a call from the sisters at St. Boniface: Theresa's sitting there in the first grade class. All week I take her to the public and she runs away to the parochial. Where does she get it from?"

Overhearing, the old women rolled their eyes. It was obvious to them that Theresa got it from Joseph's mother, just as it was obvious that generations could live on apple pie and American cheese and still have pasta in the blood. But the younger mothers, who could hardly remember back past their own children's births, had another explanation: "They come into the world, they're people. What can you do? They've got minds of their own."

"Since when has a five-year-old girl got a mind of her own?" Joseph was not really asking, but rather, boasting about his little daughter's independent mind, and the women were so charmed by this adoring and exasperated father that once again they forgave him for tipping the scales.

Neither Joseph nor Catherine could imagine anyone choosing parochial school. But they'd survived it, and if that was what Theresa wanted . . . Judging from what the mothers said, they were lucky that she wanted to go to school at all.

Rather than argue, Catherine put her energy into counteracting the damage done by St. Boniface. If Theresa went a little overboard at the holidays, Catherine made sure that they were celebrated in the safest, healthiest, most American way. At the Santangelo home, Easter had nothing to do with death and resurrection, but rather with dyed eggs, marshmallow bunnies, fluffy chicks in baskets of shredded green cellophane. During Christmas week, they stood on line at Macy's for hours so Theresa could meet Santa. The official photo showed a pudgy Theresa, out-twinkling Santa. He was asking her what she wanted him to bring her, and she was telling him, a scapular. The ugliest and biggest scapular he had.

"A scapular?" said Santa, in such a way that Theresa knew, he wouldn't be bringing her one for Christmas.

What Santa did bring her that year was a pair of needlework panels which Catherine had stitched and framed from directions in the *Ladies' Home Journal*.

"Yay." Theresa cheered half-heartedly. "Snow White and Prince Charming."

The pictures went up on Theresa's wall. By New Year's, when Catherine went in to straighten up, they were gone, replaced by a big black crucifix and a plaque of the Holy Family. Catherine recognized Mrs. Santangelo's things from the box in the hall closet. Her first thought was how pleased her mother-in-law would be to see her holy pictures side by side like comfortable old friends. Next it occurred to her that Theresa hadn't just borrowed these objects at random, but had picked and chosen. San Gennaro (what did a New York City girl know about volcanoes?) was still packed away. But Baby Jesus was everywhere.

That weekend, Catherine began taking Theresa to the movies. From then on, on Saturday afternoons, they walked up to Eighth Street or across to Delancey, wherever there were children's matinees—Porky Pig festivals, old Koko the Clowns, an occasional feature-length Disney cartoon. The second time they saw *Bambi,* Catherine was crying by the end of the opening credits—but Theresa showed no emotion. Nor was she visibly moved when Danny Kaye as Hans Christian Andersen sang, "There once was an ugly duckling," to that poor bald boy. When *Robin Hood* played the Essex, they went every Saturday for seven weeks; each time, Catherine searched her daughter's face for some sign of recognition that romance in Sherwood Forest was a lot more exciting than making your first communion.

And then one afternoon when Theresa was eight, she came home and told her mother: They were showing a movie in school that weekend. It was something *she* wanted to see.

"In school?" Catherine imagined some short about the art treasures of the Vatican, a documentary about missionaries in Bolivia. "What kind of movie?"

"A Hollywood movie," said Theresa. *"Miracle of Fatima."*

That Saturday afternoon, the parish hall basement was almost unrecognizable as the place in which Joseph and Catherine were married. It was lined with folding chairs, buzzing with children, smelling not of flowers and champagne, but of sneakers and contraband bubble gum. Catherine and Theresa had just found two chairs in a back row when the lights went out and an image appeared on the folding screen.

Years later, Catherine would wish that she had watched the movie more closely; it was information she should have had. But at the time, she was too busy watching Theresa. Ten minutes into the film, Theresa had inched forward to the edge of her seat and was staring with her mouth open, her chin tilted up. An hour later, Catherine had to touch her to make sure she was still breathing. Watching her, Catherine had the strange sensation that Theresa was a character in a film which had reached that moment, near the end, when the camera pulls away, and the person gets smaller and smaller, sailing backward through space.

4

LITTLE FLOWERS OF JESUS

ON A WARM MAY MORNING IN 1917, three Portuguese children were tending their parents' flocks in a meadow near Fatima. As the sheep grazed, the children—running in circles, alternately flapping their arms and blowing trumpets of grass stalks stretched between their fingers—played angels at the Last Judgment.

Suddenly the sky grew dark and lightning struck so near that they felt the charge in their hair. The children were terrified, as children are at those moments when their games of pretend threaten to turn real. Hearing a woman's voice behind them, they spun around to see what looked at first like a white bird hovering over a cypress. As the bird swooped toward them, they saw that it was a beautiful woman: Our Lady. The children tried to look at her, as if it were a contest to see who could stare longest at the sun, but her radiance hurt their eyes.

Speaking softly, so slowly that even the youngest could follow, Our Lady predicted another world war, the insidious growth of international Communism, and—after much suffering and the martyrdom of many Christians—the eventual conversion of Russia. She made them repeat her words several times to make sure they got it right. Finally she told them a secret—far more important than any of these revelations.

Ten years later, the eldest of the children—by then a nun—wrote this secret in a letter which she sealed and gave to the Bishop of Fatima with instructions that it be handed on to the Pope. It was Our Lady's wish that this letter be opened in 1960, on the anniversary of her first appearance at Fatima.

In 1960, the girls in Theresa Santangelo's fourth grade class began dividing into groups they thought of as "good" and "bad." After school, the bad girls walked two blocks, safe beyond the sisters' X-ray eyes, then rolled the waistbands of their pleated skirts till the hem was twice the regulation three inches above their knee socks. The good girls left their hems alone and lingered in the classrooms, asking their teachers if they could help. And the very best, like Theresa, not only stayed on washing blackboards and clapping erasers, but practiced walking home on the balls of their feet, like nuns.

Yet all of them, good and bad, spent that year waiting for Our Lady's message.

Oddly enough, the sisters didn't seem to know about the letter, and the information that it would be opened that May had come from one of the worst girls, Cindy Zagarella, who'd read about it in her mother's *National Enquirer.* Nearly all of them had seen the Fatima movie when it had been shown years before in the parish hall; now, with Cindy's news, the memory tugged at them like a dream they'd forgotten, like the chorus of a jumping rhyme which had gone out of style.

Partly, it was something to talk about; partly, curiosity. They were dying to know what the letter said. Most of the good girls expected a perfect and infallible program for universal peace; the more bloody-minded predicted that Our Lady would issue a call for repentance and set a specific date for the end of the world.

The bad girls, too, were of different opinions. Some claimed that the letter would contain something powerful enough to make Nikita Khrushchev drop dead; the girls with skeptical fathers said that it didn't matter what the letter said, the Pope would never tell.

Only Theresa had no desire to speculate. Because for her the letter was not a matter for conversation or curiosity, but rather, pure emotion—the excitement a child might feel on hearing that there is buried treasure in the backyard. For Theresa, the letter was a kind of heavenly alarm clock. Already, unopened, it had rung for her. Wake up. Wake up.

Later, Theresa would tell herself that she should have known better and followed the example of the nuns, who actively discouraged all discussion of the letter and turned it into a heresy of recess and after school. But at the time, Theresa could hardly sleep for counting the hours till this mystery would be revealed.

By Easter, the tension was nearly unbearable. Dressed in her pastel finery, she was all set to accompany her parents to the Fifth Avenue parade, when she was overcome with dread: Suppose the letter were being read and opened while she was off beholding the latest in little girls' straw bonnets? Faking a stomachache, she sent her mother and father on without her.

Finally the morning came, dawning, Theresa imagined, as bright as the sun on the meadow near Fatima. She awoke at five and put on her best clothes—white socks, a yellow angora sweater stitched with seed pearls and a tartan skirt with accordion pleats which her mother had set by hand. Later she would have to change into her school uniform, but she wanted to start this special day off right. She buckled her patent leather Mary Janes, then sat on the edge of the bed with her ankles crossed and her hands folded in her lap. She heard her mother in the kitchen, but stayed where she was.

"If I don't move a muscle for five minutes," she thought, "maybe the message from Our Lady will be good news."

Smelling coffee, she ventured out to find her mother at the stove. Catherine bent to kiss her forehead, but Theresa squirmed out of her embrace.

"I'm going out," she said. "I'll be back in two seconds."

"Out?" said Catherine. "Out where, in your party clothes at six in the morning?"

"To get the paper." After a stop in her room to empty her piggy bank, Theresa hurried out the door. At the corner of Elizabeth and Hester, the blind man was just rolling back the shutters on his stand. Theresa waited (God was watching, she had to be patient) while he cut the strings on the stacked papers. Then she took one from each pile—*The Times, The News, The Post, The Enquirer, The Herald Tribune, Il Progresso,* and even a Chinese paper, just in case.

Before she got home, she'd already read the front pages. *The Times* featured photos of President Eisenhower and Sherman Adams, *The News* bannered a triple suicide-murder in the Bronx, while *The Enquirer* proclaimed in bold letters: MAN BECOMES WOMAN AND DIES IN CHILDBIRTH. Theresa couldn't understand why none of these papers considered the Virgin's message front page news.

She spread the papers out on the kitchen table, where her father was drinking his coffee. Joseph looked them over.

"You investing in the stock market? Or maybe it's the daily double at Belmont?"

"Daddy," said Theresa, in her primmest, don't-tease-me tone. She picked *The News* first, because it had the most pictures and the largest print. Licking her thumb, she leafed through it, searching for a sign, a word, an artist's rendering of Our Lady, or even (who knew what miracles might have happened) an actual photo. But after she had passed the entertainment pages, the want ads, the sports news, and still found nothing, she pushed *The News* aside and opened *The Post.*

"That's last night's," said Joseph.

"Oh." Theresa reached for *The Tribune.*

"What are you looking for?"

"The letter."

"What letter?" asked Catherine.

"The letter with the secret message from Our Lady of Fatima. The Pope's supposed to open it today."

"Check the Dear Abby." Joseph and Catherine exchanged smiles over Theresa's bowed head. But when the difficulty of handling *The Tribune's* unwieldy pages brought tears to Theresa's eyes, Joseph stopped teasing her.

"I bet the Pope won't tell," he said. "Seriously. I mean, the guy's got to be pretty smart to get elected Pope. And if he's that smart, he'll keep that kind of information private. Six months from now, he'll come up with the big secret, pretending like he's thought of it himself."

"He's got to tell," said Theresa. But he certainly hadn't told the papers. She read each one twice, even searching the Chinese paper and *Il Progresso* for some kind of hint, and would have read them all again if Catherine hadn't ordered her to change for school.

She dressed very slowly, like an amnesia victim trying to remember which clothes go on top of which. It was a miracle that she got to school. Twenty minutes late, she walked in on the middle of a history lesson.

"When was the conversion of Constantine?" asked Sister John Xavier.

"Three hundred and twenty-four years after the birth of Our Blessed Lord Jesus," the girls chanted in unison.

Theresa wondered: If the Virgin's message had just been revealed to the world, would they still be going on with these same lessons? But there was no way to ask till lunch, when the girls unwrapped their sandwiches and were permitted to whisper.

"Psst." Theresa hissed so loud that Sister Jerome threatened to suspend her whispering privileges. "What about the letter?"

She could tell from the way that everyone looked at Cindy Zagarella, they'd discussed this thoroughly before school.

"He's opening the letter today." Cindy fancied herself an authority on everything because her mother bought *The Enquirer*. "It won't hit the papers till tomorrow."

This sounded so reasonable that Theresa felt nearly faint with relief.

Again the next morning, she went out for the papers, though this time she skipped *Il Progresso,* the Chinese paper, and *The Times*. Again she spread them out on the kitchen table, searched for a revelation, and was late for school.

Cindy's new explanation for the Pope's mysterious silence was less convincing than the day before's: "There's a time difference, dummy. In Rome, it's yesterday morning, and the Pope's still sleeping."

"Oh," said Theresa. "That's right."

A long night, another morning, and still no word from the Vatican. Even Cindy Zagarella was at a loss, and the girls were so fidgety that Sister John Xavier threatened them all with a week's detention unless they told her what was going on.

"It's the letter from Our Lady of Fatima," said Cindy. "The Pope was supposed to read it three days ago, but he hasn't said a word."

Sister John Xavier thought for several minutes before coming up with an answer which, it was later agreed, made even less sense than Cindy's: "If that's what the Pope decides, the Pope knows best."

At lunch, dozens of sandwiches were unwrapped and immediately stuffed into the wastepaper basket with prayers for forgiveness for the sin of wasting food. That night, countless plates were pushed aside, and mothers knew better than to nag their daughters about eating.

"What's wrong with her appetite?" asked Joseph.

Catherine knew exactly what was wrong, but let it pass till after the meal, when she and Theresa were doing the dishes. Then she nodded at the pile of creased newspapers on the floor near the garbage and said, "No letter, sweetheart?"

"No." Theresa rubbed vigorously at a plate which was already dry.

"Theresa, when I was a little girl, much younger than you, I heard a story about the Virgin and the Angel Gabriel."

Theresa put down the dish towel and stared. Since when did her mother know stories like that?

"It was just after the Annunciation," said Catherine. "Gabriel had finished his speech, 'Fear not, the Lord art with thee, et cetera et cetera.' He was just about to fly out the window when Mary grabbed the tip of his wing and held him back.

"'Sir,' Mary said. 'Can you tell me something? This thing that's happening to me—is this what you would call a miracle?'

"'I would,' said the angel.

"'And the baby's birth? Will that be a miracle too?'

"'That is always a miracle. But this birth will be the greatest one of all.'

"'And the child's life?'

"'That too. Miracle after miracle.' Again the angel turned and shook his wings to fly off. But now he stopped on his own, and looked at Mary. And you know what he said?" Catherine was stalling till she was sure she had the punchline right.

"What?"

"'Madonna,' he said, 'there are plenty of miracles in this world. But life is too short to sit around waiting for them.'"

Theresa studied her mother, who, as far as she knew, had never cared about anything but the sew-it-yourself patterns in *Family Circle*. What did she know about angels and miracles?

"What's that got to do with the letter?" she said.

"Maybe there was no letter," said Catherine. "Maybe the souvenir shop owners at Fatima concocted the whole thing to keep the pilgrims coming. Maybe there was nothing *in* the letter, maybe it was written on cheap paper and fell apart after thirty years. Or maybe the Virgin was trying to teach you girls the lesson she learned from the Angel Gabriel, that life is too short to waste expecting miracles."

Theresa considered her mother's explanation for as long as it took to dry the dishes. Then she dismissed it. For already she had come to her own conclusions, answers which seemed more logical—more probable—than any she had heard.

It turned out that no one had ever promised that the letter's contents would be revealed—only that the letter would be opened. It turned out that the Pope had read the letter and decided, for the good of the world, to keep Our Lady's message a secret.

By the time this news filtered down to the classrooms of St. Boniface, Theresa was convinced that the whole thing was her fault. With the monumental egotism of an eight-year-old, she had come to believe that God, the Virgin, the Pope, and even the children of Fatima had engineered the entire incident to remind her of her sins.

One night, when her disappointment was still fresh and almost constant, Theresa closed her eyes and begged God for a sign. When she opened them, the first thing she noticed was a spelling paper from school, more red pencil than black, topped with an angry-looking C-minus. Next she saw the zebra plant which her mother had given her and which, in her anxiety over the letter, she'd neglected and nearly killed.

Signs, evidence, positive proof—and all of it pointing to her. It stood to reason that the Virgin might hesitate to squander the key to salvation on a world full of sinners too lazy to water a plant. Theresa had always dreamed of becoming a nun, but now she asked herself: Why would God want a bride who couldn't spell?

She couldn't remember a time when she hadn't wanted to join the convent. It was as if she were born with her vocation, the way other children came into the world with a fear of dogs, an allergy to watermelon. But it was stronger than any allergy or fear. Once, when she was very small, her father had shown her how to raise the hair on her head with a comb rubbed along

122

her sweater; that pull on her scalp was the closest thing she'd ever felt to her attraction for the cloister. She'd longed for it, even before she knew what it was, the way children who have never been to the circus long to run away and join one; in school, she discovered that the life which the sisters described was what she'd been longing for. At meals, while Joseph and Catherine talked butcher shop gossip, Theresa imagined the refectory with its noiseless chewing, its silent forks and spoons. Saturdays, at the movies, she watched Robin Hood marry Maid Marian and thought of taking her final vows in a wedding gown which would make Maid Marian's look plain as a housedress. At night, she lulled herself to sleep by conjuring up a convent choir singing the Te Deum in high, clear harmonies.

Only now, with the silence from the Vatican in her ears, did she realize how this dream had already removed her from the world—not to any higher, more contemplative plane, but down into sloth and pride. Vain in her calling, she did poorly in school; drifting away from her fantasy-refectory, she left her mother to clear the dishes alone; off in her imaginary convent, she had let the zebra plant die.

That night, Theresa vowed to spend the rest of her life repenting and, like so many eight-year-old penitents, decided to begin with her homework. From that night on, she studied with the zeal of a fanatic. No medieval monk transcribing the Holy Writ could have taken his job more seriously than Theresa recopying her math problems till the columns hung straight as plumb lines, Theresa drafting a wall-sized map of Italy with colored pencil on the regional boundaries, a little green star for Rome and a big gold one for the Vatican.

Meanwhile she asked herself: Is this enough? Is this enough? She told no one that she was doing her schoolwork to atone for the confusion over Fatima, but in confession, agonized over every spelling mistake. Though the priests could find no penance to assign her, they recognized that she was headed for trouble and warned her about scruples. Yet these well-meant lectures only added doubts to her scruples. Uncertain of ever finding the way, she could only keep on going, while praying for God to turn her in the right direction.

At the end of the term, she coaxed copies of next year's lesson plans from the sisters and spent the summer preparing for fifth-grade math. Three summers later, while the girls on her block were stuffing tissues in the tops of their bathing suits and working on their suntans at Coney Island, Theresa was working ahead on the eighth-grade essay, "Why Communism is the Anti-Christ," six pages of narrow-ruled looseleaf covered with her neat round print. Her theme was that the Russian people, cut off from the church, were like infants snatched from their mothers' breasts; her style was so eloquent that she couldn't believe she had written it.

The nuns couldn't either, but they knew Theresa too well to suspect her of plagiarism, and voted unanimously to award her first prize in the St. Boniface Middle School Essay Competition. In a ceremony held in the auditorium for the entire school, Theresa was presented with a copy of St. Therese of Lisieux's autobiography, *The Story of a Soul,* specially bound in white vinyl with gold-tooled letters.

Much later, Theresa's former schoolmates would tell of having seen her take this prize and press it to her chest, as if hoping that the words inside it might somehow skip her eyes and brain and pass directly through her clothes to her heart. But the truth was that Theresa didn't open the book till later that evening, when she'd finished her homework; and even then, she approached it from a certain distance.

The first book she'd ever read was a life of St. Francis, in simple sentences with big round print and color illustrations of birds. Since then, she'd read dozens of saints' lives, preferring the ones who traveled and had adventures, like St. Helena, and the ones with the grisliest martyrdoms; she'd reread St. Lucy's blinding till she could hardly stand it. Most of all, though, she loved the saints who did crazy things, like St. Simon, perched atop a pillar in the desert for twenty years. But she could never connect these stories with her own life, and she wondered: Where would St. Simon perch today? A rooftop TV antenna? Nor could she picture St. Theresa of Avila riding her donkey down Mulberry Street.

Yet now, in the introduction to *The Story of a Soul,* Theresa learned that St. Therese was born Therese Martin, in France, a country without deserts, in 1873, a time without knights in castles—not Mulberry Street, exactly, but more like Theresa's own world. And besides, as the monsignor who wrote the introduction kept emphasizing: except for one thing—the intensity of her devotion—Therese Martin, "The Little Flower of Jesus," was in no way extraordinary, but rather, the simplest of simple girls.

By the time Theresa finished the first paragraph of the autobiography itself, she had opened her notebook and was copying down whole sentences with the dreamy absorption of a bride copying recipes from a magazine. And indeed no cookbook could have seemed easier to follow than the Little Flower's Little Way. Her whole life was a testimony to modesty, humility, vocation. Service to God in the most mundane and menial tasks.

"To ecstasy," wrote St. Therese, "I prefer the monotony of daily toil."

When Theresa read that line, she understood that her prayers had been answered. She had asked God to show her the way, and He had not only taken her by the shoulders and turned her around, but given her step-by-step directions, impossible to miss: Theresa, go here. Do this. Turn there. Stop when you see Me.

The painting-on-metal of St. Therese (which Theresa bought at the same store where her mother had purchased the St. Anna medallion) showed a pink-cheeked girl with the eyes of a cocker spaniel: The Little Flower was prettier than Theresa, sweeter than the sweetest girls in her class, and dressed like a nun, in brown. Still, she looked like a pretty nun you might see on the street. And she wasn't carrying her head on a plate like St. John, or her eyes like St. Lucy, but rather an armful of roses and a crucifix.

Certainly the Little Flower had suffered; as the introduction said, she had packed a lifetime of suffering into her short span. But her specific martyrdom could have happened to any sickly, unlucky girl on Mulberry Street. By the age of four, she had lost four siblings and watched her mother die horribly, of cancer. Later, she would see her beloved Papa crumble away—insanity, paralysis, another slow death. She herself nearly died at nine, suffering fever and hallucinations so violent that the nails in the wall appeared to her as the stumps of charred fingers. And she departed this world at twenty-four, of the virulent consumption which, she confided, felt "like fire, like sitting on a bed of nails."

Yet through all this, she kept faith. Her first near-fatal illness was cured when a statue of Our Lady—perhaps the same one Theresa had in her room—seemed to smile and shed radiance on the ailing girl. On recovering, Therese sought admission to the convent—a request denied, because of her youth, until she was sixteen. Then she was taken into the Carmelite order to live out a few brief years of service and humility till her final agony began.

Shortly before she died, the Little Flower was sent a bouquet of roses. When the petals dropped, she asked the sisters to save them, and predicted: Someday, someone would find the petals "pleasurable." After her death, there would fall "a shower of roses." This shower, as the introduction pointed out, was symbolic. For the petals which rained on the world were the copies of her "little book," *The Story of a Soul,* the spiritual autobiography completed in the last weeks of her life. Promoted by the church, translated into fifteen languages, the book became an instant best-seller—its influence not merely inspirational, but miraculous. Slowly at first, then faster, the reports came in: A poor Lyons family prayed to Therese and, while gardening, unearthed a sock stuffed with a million francs. A modest Saint-Malo shipbuilder received, with Therese's intercession, a government contract. An Auvergne boy, mute from birth, spontaneously began to read aloud from *The Story of a Soul*. A Lisieux man recovered from terminal cancer after swallowing a petal from the Little Flower's last bouquet. Documented cures, recorded in a ledger at the Lisieux convent, soon filled an entire library. Her birthplace became an unofficial shrine. Three miracle cures were chosen as substantial proof of Therese's beatitude; canonization followed shortly thereafter. And the whole church welcomed this paragon of modern saintliness, of holiness achieved not through heroic mortification, but through ordinary domestic chores; this unassuming girl who moved sainthood out of its medieval castle and into modern life.

"I am only a very little soul," wrote the Little Flower, "who can serve God only in very little ways." Young women were exhorted to follow her Little Way, and the good ones, like Theresa Santangelo, were rewarded with copies of her "little book." All over the world, girls like Theresa reread their copies so often that the bindings disintegrated, and the pages had to be tied with string and rubber bands; not that it mattered, for they knew the book by heart and could recite their favorite passages like prayers. Countless bedrooms like Theresa's sheltered private altars: candles, plaster Virgins, saucers to catch the dripping wax, paintings of St. Therese, embroidered cards and, invariably, a certain holy card—the best known photo of the saint. Grainy, out of focus, the picture showed a skinny girl on her hands and knees, scrubbing the floor with a brush. "To ecstasy," said the caption, "I prefer the monotony of daily toil."

Every night, some little girl like Theresa read *The Story of a Soul* and felt that she had been graced with revelation: The answer was love. The way was serving God in the simplest acts, in the dirty dishes, the laundry. And every morning, some girl would wake to discover the difficulty of following this Little Way through one single hour. Each day, these girls would reaffirm that old cliché, the truth which the church and even the Little Flower identified as one of the biggest stumbling blocks in the spiritual path: That is, you can take a million vows in the middle of the night, but things look different in the morning.

The next morning, Theresa insisted on doing the breakfast dishes. The warm water and the flowery smell of detergent were pleasant, and Theresa reminded herself, over every plate, that she was scouring it for God. But when she found a smear of egg yolk on her clean white cuff, her first impulse was to throw a dish at the wall. Determined to love everyone, she smiled at the people she passed on the way to school; but by second period, she was hating Sister Angelica, the Latin teacher, for getting all teary-eyed and quivery over Cicero's *Oration Against Catiline*.

That afternoon, Theresa offered to cook dinner. Catherine was delighted, partly because she wanted so badly to see it as a sign that Theresa was changing; as far as she knew, nuns didn't go in for cooking. Besides, she had read in her magazines that girls of Theresa's age showed an inclination—sometimes a positive genius—for imitating their mothers. But whom was Theresa imitating, to imagine that normal people ate omelettes and raw vegetables for dinner? Never suspecting that these were among the few foods which the Little Flower was documented to have eaten, Catherine reassured herself with the magazine-advice that girls should start with something simple: Eggs. Salad. English muffin pizza.

Later, Theresa would never understand exactly how she burned the omelette, but would think of it as a lesson which most of the great female saints must have learned, and which even the Little Flower had taught her Carmelite sisters: That is, the kitchen is no place for ecstasy. All Theresa knew was that she had the eggs in the pan and was cutting the carrots in perfect julienne strips, contemplating every cross-section with its thin green ribbon, its grain like orange and yellow wood. . . .

Suddenly the kitchen filled with smoke, and Catherine, who'd been studiously keeping her distance, rushed in, shut off the burner and opened the window. She flipped the omelette onto a plate, sliced the blackened crust off the top, cut the remaining egg into three parts and called downstairs to Joseph.

"Don't worry," she told Theresa. "Some days, everything goes wrong in the kitchen."

The apartment was still smoky when they sat down to eat; everything tasted of charcoal. But Joseph and Catherine were so charmed by their daughter's effort at domesticity that they crunched their carrots and ate their scorched egg with genuine pleasure; already they were prepared to look back on this bit of family history with irony and warmth, like the dinner Catherine ruined at her father's house.

"Always," said Joseph, "there's something delicious. With your mother, it was the antipasto. And tonight . . . the carrots."

But Catherine would never have laughed so happily if she'd known that Theresa, like Mrs. Santangelo, saw the hand of God in every cooking mistake; the difference was that Theresa didn't see it working the family destiny, but only her own.

No sooner had Theresa taken her first mouthful of egg than she remembered: The Little Flower hadn't just eaten an omelette—but a burned one. As a test of humility, Therese had taken the charred part which none of the other Carmelites would touch. With this in mind, Theresa could have eaten burned omelette for the rest of her life. But as she watched her parents, cheerfully and determinedly chewing the bitter eggs, she decided that mortification was worthless unless it was freely chosen. If burned eggs were all you were served, it didn't count. Right then, Theresa resolved to become a good cook and pay attention, because if you're cooking for God, you might as well cook something which people might like to eat.

Theresa became an excellent cook, and such a competent housekeeper that the cockroaches (which had long preceded the Santangelos and survived two generations of constant attack) fled the apartment. A dirty dish never touched the sink, a crumb never lingered on the breadboard. Bed sheets, bath towels, even dishcloths were ironed; the beds were made up with hospital corners. Worn socks disappeared from the hamper and came back clean, darned, soft as kittens.

After school, when the bad girls rolled their skirts and the good ones clapped their erasers, Theresa rushed home to reline the silverware drawers. Too busy for friends, she had no time to envy the others with their giggling, their autograph books and slumber parties. At rare lonely moments, she reminded herself that the Little Flower had endured worse torments than loneliness, and consoled herself with dreams of another world, some lost Atlantis where everyone was exactly like her. In the convent, she imagined, her sisters would know why it took her two hours to line each drawer, and would treasure the perfect rectangles of butcher paper.

The only one she really envied was the Little Flower. Sainthood had come naturally to her; as a child, she'd seen her name written in the stars. She hadn't had to follow anyone's example, but had only to lead her own life—in another place, another time, when it was so much easier to be saintly. True, she'd suffered slights and insults; she'd had to contend with doubts, aridity, even the pride which made her rage at some sisters who quoted her without naming their source.

Yet the Little Flower had so much help—family and friends to love and guide her on her Little Way. While Theresa had no one but Joseph and Catherine—two stubborn parents who seemed to have locked arms and planted themselves in their daughter's path.

•   •   •

It was during this time that Joseph came home from the shop with a brand-new eighteen-inch television. Winking at Catherine, he announced that it had fallen off the back of a truck.

"It's a miracle it didn't break," said Theresa.

Joseph turned on her with such a stunned look that Theresa felt she had robbed him of his pleasure in his new possession, and vowed again to watch how she talked at home, guarding even casual references to miracles and blessings. Then Joseph laughed.

"Fell off a truck," he repeated. "It's only an expression."

After promising Catherine that the set would be hidden away when Lino came to visit, Joseph installed it in the living room. All three of them watched through the Sunrise Sermon and "The Star-Spangled Banner," as they did the next night and the next. But on Saturday night, Theresa got up in the middle of Perry Como and went off to do her Monday homework. Within a month, Joseph and Catherine were turning the television off by nine, and gradually it fell into disuse, much like the radio which Joseph had never bothered asking his father-in-law to repair.

Yet every afternoon, when Joseph was down in the shop and Theresa away at school, Catherine tuned in her favorite program, "The Millionaire." Counting reruns, she'd seen each segment twice, but she never tired of watching lives disrupted and almost ruined by the anonymous gift of a million dollars with no conditions except secrecy about how it came. For unlike the movies, these modest stories confirmed what Catherine had learned from life, from living with Theresa.

From the outside, it looked like a blessing, a million-dollar daughter whose only desire was to help around the house. But like the recipients of those anonymous gifts, Catherine knew that every blessing had its drawbacks. In the shop, when she complained of how hard it was to make sausage with Theresa snatching the grinder away to wash it before she was even done, the mothers asked: Was she boasting or complaining?

The answer was: Both. Catherine loved her daughter; she was proud of her sweet nature, and of the beauty which was growing more obvious each day despite the St. Boniface uniform's considerable skill at hiding it. Still, Theresa made her nervous. She went too far. It was hard enough stuffing eighty pounds of sausage a week without someone breathing down your neck, nearly tripping you. A day was long enough without the extra work of contending with a daughter who'd turned, overnight, into a picky eater.

Theresa wasn't skinny, thank God; but she didn't eat like a normal person. She pushed stuffed artichokes, scallopini Marsala, fettuccine with cheese and butter around on her plate, and preferred the spinach, meatloaf, and reheated leftovers which (Catherine knew from her magazines) other children wouldn't go near. For a while, till Joseph put a stop to it, Theresa ate with a towel pinned from her collar to the tablecloth, like a sling. Why? Because the Carmelites believed in catching and eating every crumb. She refused to touch meat on Fridays, no matter what the Pope said, and asked to be allowed to eat standing, or kneeling at the stove.

"You want to eat?" said Joseph. "You can sit at the table like a human being."

Catherine never told him about the times she caught Theresa doctoring her food—salting her zabaglione, adding mustard to her cocoa, watering her stew. Catherine didn't have to be an expert on theology to recognize that Theresa was trying to mortify her sense of taste. She wondered how such a child had been born to her and Joseph, and joked with the mothers about babies switched in the cradle. The women only laughed: For Theresa, with her mother's dark coloring and her father's sturdy build, was a perfect cross between her parents—and her nature was pure Mrs. Santangelo.

Catherine admitted that Theresa had inherited her grandmother's talent for padding around the apartment and appearing over your shoulder, like Judith Anderson in *Rebecca*. She had all the old lady's pride, the arrogance of true believers who act as if the world will stop turning without their candles and novenas. And Mrs. Santangelo's zeal for her family and her saints seemed almost mild in comparison with Theresa's passion for the convent.

Yet Catherine, like mothers of troublesome children everywhere, convinced herself that everything would be all right. One day, the holy pictures in Theresa's room would yield to Elvis and Frankie Avalon. One night, the phone would ring, and a boy would ask for Theresa. Imagining this, Catherine felt time rush by, and so much love for Theresa that she was ashamed of her impatience with her daughter's eagerness to help. How could she complain about this blessing, this million-dollar gift, this girl who asked nothing but permission to polish the meat grinder and do the laundry?

Children went through phases—particularly little girls. For some it was horses; for others, ballerinas or dogs. She herself had had her movie magazines, and dozens of plants had survived as mementoes of her first love. Time had changed her; it would change Theresa.

Later, Catherine would claim that she never believed this, that she had always known that her daughter would never be normal and had spent Theresa's whole life waiting for the other shoe to drop.

Catherine wasn't alone in listening for the sound of the other shoe, of uneasy premonitions confirmed. Even Lino, with his hereditary lack of foresight, predicted trouble; but in his view, the trouble was Nicky. Falconettis were known for their reserve, yet even Lino knew—to survive, to stay human, a man had to talk, if only a few sentences now and then: Nice weather we're having, how's the family? But Nicky never said a word.

For months, Lino waited for Nicky to come out of his fog; finally he had come to accept it as Nicky's permanent weather. He'd always been quiet, withdrawn, a peculiar duck. But Lino knew: This was different. Nicky grunted and mumbled, ate and slept, went through the motions of living. Yet for all the life in him, Lino could have been sharing his meals and his work place with a corpse.

Over the years, Nicky had grown accustomed to his own detachment, that sense of observing his life from a distance. But this was something new. Ever since returning home, Nicky felt as if he were a shadow, a dim reflection of what he should have been. He felt like a newly brokenhearted lover: Everything reminded him of his loss. He couldn't take a shower without thinking of the geisha who should have been scrubbing his back, couldn't drink coffee without wishing for green tea, couldn't pick up a fork without hearing the gentle click-click of chopsticks, couldn't pass the kitchen table without picturing a bowl of formally arranged chrysanthemums, each one perfect as a miniature autumn sun. Every meal his father cooked made him long for incense to cover up the smell, and even his pleasure in the radio was diminished; now, he couldn't listen to Milton Cross's plot summaries without mentally translating them into sign language and simple English for his imaginary Japanese bride.

Yet unlike a brokenhearted lover, Nicky was unable to take comfort in conjuring up his sweetheart's imperfections, blemishes, her irritating mannerisms. Because Nicky's Madame Butterfly had never existed outside his imagination—and it had never occurred to him to imagine her with defects.

As if to convince himself that hope was still possible, he began taking occasional meals in Chinatown, praying that he and his geisha would find each other—Hollywood-style—across a crowded restaurant. But the waiters were all male, the girls accompanied by families and fiancés. He took his wash to the Chinese laundry, but the Chinaman's daughter didn't look up from her trouser press when her father did business with Nicky.

Clutching his neatly wrapped, pressed shirts, stung because the girl in the steamy back room hadn't noticed him, Nicky was forced to admit that his life would never be opera or tragedy or even high drama, but only the pathetic story of an ordinary GI who couldn't find an Oriental girl to marry him. He saw his past as a private hell, a circle of sausage and pinochle, and now he had sunk to an even lower region, in which he couldn't find a pinochle player on Mulberry Street willing to deal him into a game.

The neighborhood watched him sink. Nicky had been drinking heavily since he was fourteen, but now disappointment drove him beyond Frank Manzone's wine and straight to the Gordon's gin. Now that the last holdouts had bought televisions, there wasn't much business in Lino's shop—which was just as well. Because Nicky couldn't be counted on to do much of anything except stumble from the house to the liquor store and back.

Watching him pass, the old women nodded at this sad example of what happens when you stray from the trodden paths and seek to marry outside your kind, clucked their tongues at this drama of misdirected longing, and shook their heads—just as they might have done at the final act of an opera.

Of all of them, Theresa had the most compassion for her Uncle Nicky. Without knowing half the details, she recognized the terrible strain of transforming your life into something else—the plot of an opera, the autobiography of a saint. She prayed for Nicky, but went out of her way to avoid him. For whenever she saw her uncle weaving down the street, she felt instinctively that her story would never be any more like the Little Flower's than his was like Madame Butterfly's.

Each day confronted Theresa with the near-impossibility of leading a consecrated life in New York City, in 1964. Though the good girls (whose number was dwindling) still observed the name days, the feast days, the seasonal devotions, by far the most popular saints at St. Boniface were Paul, John, George, and Ringo. Each day she rededicated herself to the Little Way, only to lose it when she couldn't find the oregano; she asked

God for the patience which deserted her when the sink clogged, and the aging washing machine shredded her father's shirts.

She could only remind herself that her real life had not yet begun. Her present existence was like shaking someone's hand through a thick glove, and she lived for her high school graduation, when she would enter the convent and take off this glove. But she had learned to conceal these hopes at home, to behave as if she had no future, as if the Last Judgment were scheduled, conveniently, for graduation day.

By now, her favorite part of *The Story of a Soul* was the Little Flower's long and precocious struggle for admission to the convent. Burdened with a preternatural foreknowledge of her own early death, Therese first sought to take the veil as a child of nine. No one would permit this—not the Monsignor, the Bishop, nor even the Pope to whom Therese traveled in order to petition in Rome.

Then one day, as if by some miracle, Therese got lost and was picked up by a carriage transporting a church official who heard her pleas and was charmed into acquiescence. Rereading this chapter, Theresa prayed for a similar miracle to aid her in her time of need.

That time arrived near the start of Theresa's senior year, heralded by a postcard inviting the Santangelos to a meeting with the St. Boniface college counsellor.

"College?" In the face of all evidence to the contrary, Joseph had somehow assumed that Theresa would marry soon after high school and spare them the necessity of arranging her future.

"I'm not going to college," said Theresa. "I'm joining the Carmelites."

Catherine was setting a platter of polenta on the table when Theresa made this announcement so casually, she might have been asking for the serving spoon. Later, Catherine would say that this was the first of many times she would think: The other shoe. Bracing herself, she wondered if Joseph hadn't been expecting it too. How else could he have ignited so quickly?

"Over my dead body!" He slammed his fist down so hard that the silverware jumped. "You'll see me buried before any daughter of mine works like a dog, twenty-four hours a day, to line the Pope's pockets."

"It's not for the Pope," said Theresa. "It's for God."

"For God?" mimicked Joseph. "You show me where God says some poor old lady has to freeze her ass off in the vestibule at Macy's, shaking that little tray of coins at the Christmas shoppers."

"Joseph," said Catherine. "Your language."

"Theresa, when you work as a butcher nearly thirty years, you get to know women. You know what makes them so beautiful, you know why you love them. And the reason is: They want something. Maybe it's a pound of sausage, or a compliment on their new dress. Sometimes they want a tender roast and sometimes"—he winked at Catherine—"they want the butcher. It doesn't matter. The wanting is what makes their eyes shine, and when you cheat them a bit, they just shine brighter. But the thing about nuns is: They don't want anything. They come in for an order of veal and you don't have veal, they never blink, they never miss a beat. You can practically see them thinking: It's God's will, I'll have chicken. And their eyes look like this." He fished in his pocket for a handful of change, sifted through the pennies, then shrugged. "I can't find one dull enough."

"They *do* want something," said Theresa. "God."

"If they want Him so bad, maybe they've already got Him. They should leave it alone, get married. Nuns are sick women, Theresa. And my daughter isn't sick."

Theresa almost wished she were sick; perhaps illness might give her the sense of urgency she needed. Back in her room, she unfocused her eyes, sucked in her cheeks, stared into the mirror. The depressing evidence confronted her: a big, healthy girl, more rosy-cheeked than those idealized portraits of St. Therese. Perhaps if she had galloping consumption, a taste of doom, a deadline to meet—some debilitating illness which might, paradoxically, give her the strength to ignore her father and take her case to the Pope. But nowadays, no one died of consumption. No matter how Theresa starved, she could never get below a size fourteen; she went without a scarf all year and never caught more than one cold each winter. How easy it would be to suffer for God, to spit out your lungs and die for Him. How hard it was to imagine climbing over your father's corpse and up the steps to the Carmelites' door.

A death sentence would have been kinder—at least she would be going straight to God. But a life outside the convent was a life in prison, and Theresa knew that she had received this sentence as punishment for her sins. Worried about pride, she asked forgiveness for feeling superior to her classmates. Worried about gluttony, she brooded over the sinfulness of second helpings. Yet no matter how she agonized over envy, she couldn't stop envying the Little Flower for her unshakeable vocation, her poor health, and especially for the many small miracles which had lifted her over the obstacles in her saintly path.

Like any prisoner with an incommutable life sentence, Theresa prayed for a miracle to deliver her from jail. In December, it came—not a miracle, exactly, but inspiration enough for Theresa to reopen her case. And unlike those convicts with their registered letters and dog-eared law texts, Theresa found a means of petition which was not merely simple, but effortless; not merely effortless, but involuntary: One morning, she didn't want breakfast. That evening, she had no appetite for dinner.

Joseph and Catherine ignored it till the third night. Then, with studied casualness, Catherine asked Theresa what she'd eaten for lunch.

"Nothing. I wasn't hungry."

"Are you sick?"

"I'm fine."

"Take something. A slice of bread."

The way Theresa picked at the soft center of the bread so

reminded Joseph of his mother that he could almost hear her saying, "At my age, who's got teeth for crust?"

"For Christ's sake," he muttered. "Eat."

"When you let me join the Carmelites," said Theresa, "that's when I'll eat."

Theresa looked startled, even more so than Joseph and Catherine. She hadn't planned on saying that. My vocation, she thought, speaking through me.

"Then starve," said Joseph.

Later that evening, Catherine warmed up a plate of brasciole, dished out a bowl of ice cream and brought it on a tray to Theresa's room. But Theresa refused, and Catherine ate the ice cream herself, thinking: At last, the other shoe.

Later, when Joseph and Catherine came to regret the consequences of their stubbornness, they recalled, with melancholy irony, that those few weeks marked the height of Catherine's cooking career. Shrimp fra diavolo, tortellini with ham, peas and cream, sponge cake soaked in rum and Amaretto—the Santangelo kitchen had never seen the likes of the meals she made to tempt Theresa. But there was no pleasure in the cooking. Catherine couldn't light the oven without thinking of *Mildred Pierce*—Joan Crawford baking and sewing and scheming for a daughter whose only desire was to be someplace else. And Theresa wasn't even tempted.

That year, mothers were beginning to come into the shop with horrifying stories—the flask they'd found in Sal's jacket pocket, the cigarettes in Mary Kay's purse. But Catherine couldn't bring herself to mention the tension at home, which had grown until she and Joseph ate almost as little as Theresa. Leftovers crowded the refrigerator; Catherine scraped full plates into the garbage, then turned to Joseph and said, "Give in. She'll change her mind."

"Wait," said Joseph. "She'll get hungry."

But each passing day made it easier for Theresa to hold out. After a week, the dull ache in her stomach disappeared and she felt a peculiar giddiness, as if an angel were fluttering inside her head; then came euphoria, and the increasing certainty of victory. Like an impatient bride-to-be, marking off her calendar, Theresa believed that each uneaten bowl of tortellini was bringing her one step closer to her wedding day.

And then one night she awoke from a dreamless sleep and smelled sausage. She looked at the clock, listened for sounds from the kitchen. Why would her mother be frying sausage at three A.M.? Suddenly Theresa realized that she was having an hallucination, and thought of all the convincing deceptions which the devil showed Jesus and the saints. Positive now that this smell had been sent to test her, she tried to tell herself that it was as foul as sulphur and brimstone. But the truth was that the delicious aroma was making her crave sausage more than anything on God's earth.

She started out of bed, then checked herself (as the priests advised), not with interdictions but with questions. Did she want this sausage enough to go back on her vow? Did she want it as much as a world in which everyone understood her, a life of peace broken only by ringing hymns? Did she want it more than a lifelong marriage with God?

The answer, at that moment, was yes. Though fully awake, Theresa felt like a sleepwalker; nothing could have stopped her but a tap on the shoulder from God. And no one touched her as she moved toward the kitchen, no one stirred till the sausage was sizzling in the pan, and the smell woke Catherine. With a mother's instinctive awareness of where her children are (in the dark, the night), Catherine knew that Theresa was in the kitchen and thought: Thank God. She's eating. It never occurred to her to rouse Joseph, or to leave Theresa alone.

Can I get you something? were the words on her lips. Can I help? But when she reached the kitchen, these questions caught in her throat and she leaned against the doorpost.

For the set of Theresa's back so resembled Mrs. Santangelo's that Catherine was reminded of her first day of marriage, when she left Joseph's bed to find her mother-in-law at the stove. She looked at Theresa, saw Mrs. Santangelo, and grabbed for the robe she'd forgotten to put on. And yet her confusion was only sensory; her instinct, unaffected, was not a daughter-in-law's, but a mother's.

"Sausage on an empty stomach?" she cried. "Sweetheart, start with something easier to digest. A glass of milk. A peach."

Theresa never remembered how much sausage she ate, nor who cleaned up the kitchen, nor how she got back to bed. She woke the next morning with the taste of meat and garlic in her mouth, and a fullness in her stomach which suggested she'd had plenty. The taste disappeared when she brushed her teeth, but the heaviness stayed with her through a breakfast of juice, eggs, toast, and milk. She felt weighed-down, sleepy, as if at every moment she'd just finished a ten-course meal.

God didn't want her; otherwise, He'd have helped her keep her vow. Like any rejected lover, she walked around with a knot in her chest—which only Theresa could have mistaken for undigested sausage. Too tired to consider the future, she tried to forget convent life. It was as if her vocation were a suitor who'd come seeking her father's permission; refused, he'd never dreamed of asking her to elope, but had simply shrugged and walked away.

Months went by; the lassitude remained. Theresa was dimly aware that plans were being made for her, decisions she was too full and exhausted to protest. Yes, she kept saying, yes. And only later would she understand how easily she could have dissolved that lump in her chest if only she had seen the grace of God in that plate of sausage and all those unhappy yesses.

That spring, an old woman came into Joseph's shop for a half-pound of veal scallopine. Pale, white-haired, dressed in white gloves, white shoes, and a white dress printed with lilacs, the woman seemed to have been dusted from head to foot with talcum powder. Unaccountably moved by her fragility, Joseph took special care with the veal, as if to cut slices delicate and pale as the woman herself. The thought of cheating her never crossed his mind.

She inspected her order, smiled, told Joseph that she was a feature writer for *The Daily News,* and asked if she might look around the store. Holding his breath, uneasy lest something drip on those immaculate shoes, Joseph produced his best stock for her appraisal. The woman moved her lips as if she were tasting everything she saw. On her way out, she smiled again and said, "Look in this weekend's *News,*" just as the good witch in a fairy tale might say, "Look under that toadstool in Grandmother's garden." And Joseph was so bewitched that he didn't even realize she'd left without paying him.

That week, it was Joseph's turn to get up early and run to the newsstand before the blind man opened, to spread the paper on the breakfast table and search every column. But he was luckier than Theresa, or perhaps it was just that the old lady's promise was easier to keep than Our Lady of Fatima's.

On Saturday, Joseph spotted a story about the neighborhood, followed by a list of stores. Right beneath Pollicini's Bakery was Santangelo's Sausage Shop: "Spectacular Sausage. First-rate meats cut to order at reasonable prices."

"Catherine," said Joseph. "Look at this."

Joseph underlined the sentence, mounted the article in plastic and taped it inside the window of his shop. But after a few days, he took it down because the story didn't mention Frank Manzone's vegetable stand and Joseph didn't want Frank reminded every time he passed.

According to rumor, the old lady had breezed into Manzone's and breezed right out. It was no wonder, the way Frank's luck had been going. All summer, his brother hadn't been able to grow a radish; his crops had fallen prey to every pest and blight to come through New Jersey. Forced to negotiate with the big California growers, Frank had signed contracts which were little better than suicide notes. His prices were the highest in the area,

142

his store empty except for his oldest customers—who were not simply loyal, but also too infirm to walk around the corner to another stand. How much did such people buy? Joseph remembered his mother telling him about some saint, the patron of grocers, who could restore inferior produce to freshness; even if he'd remembered the saint's name, he could never have brought himself to tell Frank to pray.

Frank's family life suffered. His wife looked pinched, his eldest boy got divorced the same week his youngest dropped out of school. His daughters ran with the "bad" St. Boniface girls who rolled their uniforms and spent all afternoon smoking Newports on the corner of Elizabeth and Spring.

Yet no one knew how bad the situation was until November, when it was Frank's annual custom to bring around the first of his new wine for the neighborhood men to sample.

"Is it that time again?" Joseph got out the two snifters which he kept in his shop, reserved for this ceremonial purpose.

"It's that time." Frank smiled happily as he filled both glasses to the top.

"To your health." Joseph drained his glass.

Seconds later, he felt a burning in his throat. He forced himself to swallow, then choked, coughing so hard that Frank ran around behind the counter and smacked him on the back.

"What's the trouble?" said Frank. "Too strong for an old man like you? Can't take it anymore?"

"It's great." Joseph raised his glass, as if in another toast, and grinned at his former pinochle partner. But there was no use pretending.

It was vinegar. Wine vinegar. And both of them knew that the neighborhood men had been choking on it all morning. Up and down the block, they'd stared at Frank, just as Joseph was staring at him now. Then they'd looked away, embarrassed and vaguely guilty, as if somehow it were their fault that Frank Manzone's luck had run out. That day, no one got drunk, and the women knew there would be no bargains.

By May, when Joseph removed the newspaper clipping from his window, Frank's hair had turned white and his skin was as pale and flaky as pie crust. He was selling the storefront for practically nothing to a firm which planned to open a string of espresso places for tourists. As Frank walked by on his way to the pharmacy, Joseph was glad he'd taken down the clipping. Fate was unpredictable, luck took strange turns. As his mother used to say: Why advertise?

Joseph knocked on wood and thanked God that his own luck was holding. Except for the baby's death and that bad time with Catherine right afterwards, his life had turned out better than he'd expected.

His father, rest in peace, would be proud. Even without the clipping in the window, customers came from all five boroughs. Each week, Catherine's sausage sold out, as did the seasonal Thanksgiving turkeys and Easter lambs. And Joseph took pride in his work. In an age of supermarket processors and plastic wrap, craftsmen like himself were rare, and people still knew the difference: His scallopini made supermarket veal look like chuck steak. So what if he cheated a few pennies? No one counted pennies, it was that much less to report on his taxes, and the IRS was no better at catching him than his customers were. The women still loved it, and Joseph gloried in the fact that business was so good, he didn't have to cheat. No longer a matter of profit, it became even more of an avocation, an art.

In his home life, Joseph felt equally lucky. Catherine was a good wife and mother, an excellent cook except on those rare occasions when she went overboard with "Chinese" concoctions of canned soup and undercooked vegetables, like something his crazy sister-in-law would make. The apartment looked nice with her houseplants suspended in the hangers she knotted from instructions in her magazines. Obviously, she was no longer the sly little alley cat he married. But what would he—with his thickening middle—do with an alley cat now? Peace at home, strong coffee, tasty food on the table every night—that was sufficient. At Saturday dinner, they had wine—not home-made, but Chianti in straw bottles from the liquor store. On Sundays and holidays, there was pastry from the Roma.

Of course, he would have liked a son, but it hadn't worked out that way. He was thankful for his daughter, and if she leaned a little too far on the saintly side, it was better than Frank Man-zone's girls, draped around the lampposts with their Newports. Joseph had seen plenty of girls go through holy phases. For years they had one foot in the convent, and the next thing you knew they walked into the shop with a baby in a stroller and another on the way. The healthy ones grew out of it, and Theresa, knock on wood, was healthy enough; the proof was that she'd started eating again after that stupid hunger strike. Besides, she was good-looking, smart. Before too long, she'd find a husband to take care of her, and that would be the end of her saintliness. If Joseph's luck held, a line of boyfriends would be forming around the block by the time Theresa finished high school, and the light—that glow of desire which Joseph loved in women—would return to her eyes.

Graduation neared, but still there was no line of boyfriends, and Theresa's eyes were as cool as a nun's. Yet Joseph wasn't dis-couraged. After several long talks with Augie (whose Stacey was in her second year at Marymount), he'd decided: This wasn't Italy, where you married your baby daughter off in diapers; this wasn't twenty years ago, when you staked her in a card game. This was the 1960s, in America, where you could send her to a respectable Catholic teacher's college, a girls' school where she couldn't get into trouble and where (at a properly chaperoned social) she could meet some nice Italian law student, a future doctor or high school principal—a better class of boy than she could have found in high school. If the right boy didn't turn up in college, Theresa would still have her teaching certificate—some-thing to do till she found him. And finally, as Augie assured him, a daughter in college heaped honor on the Santangelo name.

"Like this," Joseph told Catherine, "she won't have to spend *her* life stuffing sausage."

Catherine needed no persuading. She thought it a wonderful idea, as did Sister Madeline Dolorosa, the college counsellor at St. Boniface Hall. At a conference with Joseph and Catherine in her office, Sister Madeline numbered Theresa's virtues as if delivering a eulogy, listed her awards and honors, and concluded by saying that of all the girls in her graduating class, Theresa was by far the best candidate for the holy orders.

"She doesn't want to be a nun," said Joseph. "She wants to be a teacher."

"Is that true?" Sister Madeline asked Theresa. It was not what her teachers said.

"Yes." Theresa nodded. Too numb to argue, she could only hope that God would change His mind if she showed Him that the Little Way could be followed anywhere—even in college.

"She'll make a wonderful teacher, God love her," and Sister Madeline produced a sheaf of applications from her desk.

Theresa shuffled and reshuffled the applications until it was arranged that she would attend St. Angela's Academy, in Brooklyn; it was almost like going to another city, and yet she could live at home. With this resolved, graduation came and went, unremarked except for the cake (huge, white, layered like a wedding cake but with a solitary girl in a mortarboard on top) which Joseph ordered from the Café Roma. And Theresa spent the summer listlessly following her mother around the college sections of the midtown department stores, cringing when the pretty salesgirls in their college buttons approached her, and wondering how the girls from Iona and St. Joseph's and Marymount always knew to zero in on her.

Later, Catherine would think of that summer with nostalgia for the air-conditioned melancholy of department stores on hot afternoons and the intimacy of those dressing rooms. Watching Theresa try on clothes, she could hardly believe that this nearly grown woman's body was once a tangle of limbs under a yellow blanket. Because by the following summer, the other shoe had dropped, and Catherine had learned: There is never just one other shoe but always a rain of them—heavy, inexorable, like the footfalls of an approaching army.

Lino Falconetti had become one of those old men who cannot think of anything which didn't used to be better. Having witnessed the decay of everything from cars to the weather to family life, he could pretend to accept his own decline philosophically. Yet no amount of philosophy could sweeten the bitter fact that everything was better before television, that Lino was a radio man who'd outlived his time.

It wasn't as if he hadn't tried. He'd dissected hundreds of sets, paid meticulous attention. But when he reassembled them, the screens turned into funhouse mirrors, distorting the actors and actresses into Laurels and Hardys. He bought a TV repair manual and followed the instructions, but the misshapen faces only flipped upside down and croaked like frogs.

And so he had come to accept the fact that God had not meant him to fix televisions. Like butchers, radio repairmen were a dying breed; but unlike Joseph, Lino had no cause to exult in his rarity. It shamed him to admit that he would have gone out of business completely if not for the clock radio, and he believed that he was living on borrowed time till some genius thought of wiring an alarm to a television.

With Nicky, too, Lino felt that time was running out. But whereas the business seemed destined for a gentle and predictable demise, Lino sensed that his son was more likely to explode; and like the legendary Falconetti assigned the dreaded job of guarding Garibaldi's powder kegs, he could only sit by and wait for the inevitable spark.

It was equally inevitable that in Nicky's case, this spark would be struck by *Madame Butterfly*. It wasn't the first time it had played since Nicky's return; when Nicky saw it announced in the paper, he bought an extra bottle of gin and prepared for a dismal weekend. For unlike the other operas, which could still lift him partway out of himself, *Madame Butterfly* depressed him and pushed him back into the dead center of his life. Hearing it made him feel as if he were looking at an old photo of himself and trying to recall what the person in that picture was thinking.

That afternoon, Nicky drank through the first two acts and wept through the third. Just as Butterfly was bidding farewell to her baby, Nicky dozed off. When he awoke, it was dark outside his window, but it seemed to him that the opera was still in progress, and that Milton Cross was speaking Japanese.

That was the start of Nicky's hallucinations. From then on, he heard music though none was playing, selections from his favorite operas set with new words—lyrics referring to him, mocking commentaries on his situation.

By far the most troublesome of Nicky's delusions was his conviction that every Oriental in the city was personally responsible for his misery. At least once a month, he'd fire himself up on gin and go down to the laundry to harangue the Chinaman and his daughter in vile language which they wisely pretended not to understand. Eventually he'd charge off—uptown to a Korean greengrocer on Sixth Avenue, in and out of restaurants and finally into a Pell Street dumpling shop in which he made a particularly ugly scene on a busy Saturday night. Sunday morning, a chauffeured limousine pulled up in front of Lino's shop, discharging two Chinese men in business suits who spoke to the Falconettis so convincingly that Nicky's campaign of harassing Orientals stopped.

But still he prolonged his drama through two final acts— both of which took place on a single Saturday afternoon.

More than ever, Lino had come to hate Nicky's opera broadcasts; whenever possible, he left the house. But that day, it was raining, there was nowhere to go. So he sat in the living room, reading the paper, his ears stuffed with cotton balls through which he could still hear every note; he noticed immediately when the music ended.

The door opened, and Nicky walked through the room with the radio on his shoulder. It was heavy, Lino knew, but not enough to make Nicky stagger beneath its weight like Jesus dragging the cross up Calvary. Lino's first thought was that radio was broken; Nicky was taking it down to the shop. He doubted that Nicky could fix it in his present state, but for the sake of conversation said, "Something wrong with the set?"

"Yeah," said Nicky, but he didn't take it to the shop. Still stumbling on bent knees, he lugged it four blocks through the rain, down Grand Street to the Chinese laundry.

The laundry was closed, but Nicky pounded on the door and rattled the windows till the Chinaman and his daughter appeared at the back of the shop. Edging forward, they seemed not so much frightened as deeply uncomfortable lest someone overhear the commotion and blame it on them. Finally they unbolted the door.

"Here!" Nicky lowered the radio and shoved one corner of it through the half-open door. "Take it!"

The old man nodded and reached out his thin arms, but Nicky brushed past him and set the radio on the counter between two piles of brown paper parcels. Nicky waved the cord in the air till the young woman took it from him and plugged it into a socket at the end of a tube light.

"*Carmen,*" said Nicky. "Sixteen hundred on the dial."

The Chinaman gave Nicky a fleeting, embarrassed smile, then reached between him and the radio, and turned the knob. Beneath his fingers, the dial moved swiftly and surely, flew past the figures, way beyond sixteen hundred, and stopped in some polar region of the dial which Nicky had never explored. Nicky heard the plucking of stringed instruments, then an ear-splitting female voice, wailing like a cat.

"*Chinese* opera," explained the daughter.

Suddenly Nicky felt himself turn to wood, with rigid limbs manipulated from above by some powerful puppeteer; he thought how lucky it was that this puppeteer knew what was supposed to happen next. The invisible strings jerked Nicky out of the laundry, down the street and back to the apartment, where he went straight to his room and shut the door.

"What happened?" Lino called after him. "Couldn't fix it? I'll see about it tomorrow. . . ."

But Nicky didn't answer, and it was then that Lino heard him singing. Until that moment, he had never heard Nicky do a musical thing in his life except turn on the radio; he'd never heard him hum, or even whistle. Now, his singing made Lino nervous, and this uneasiness increased as he realized that it was opera—a terrible burlesque of opera, a fake falsetto trilling off-key arias, cracking and dying as it strained toward the high notes.

The music ended abruptly. Lino ran to Nicky's room and opened the door.

Nicky was lying on the floor with a samurai sword protruding from his chest. His knees were folded beneath him, as if he'd been kneeling and had fallen backwards. A dark stain was spreading on the carpet.

Even so, Nicky looked so cheerful, so radiant, and the whole situation was so operatic and absurd that Lino had to bend over and touch his son before he was sure that Nicky wasn't joking.

Had Theresa been a saint, she might have been able to intercede directly on her Uncle Nicky's behalf. As it was, she could only pray to St. Therese to intervene in his favor. Theresa sympathized with him—sentenced to perpetual torment, exiled to that section of hell reserved for suicides. By then, she too was in exile, off in another world—if not as dismal as Nicky's, then certainly as different from any she had ever known.

Each day, Theresa took the A train to Brooklyn, transferred to the Myrtle Avenue El and got off at Vanderbilt Avenue, then walked three blocks past brownstones, used furniture shops, and Spanish groceries to reach St. Angela's. If she'd joined the convent, she kept thinking, she would never have had to take the subway; but it comforted her to realize that no convent could have tried a novice's patience more than the teacher's college was testing hers. Eight hours praying on your knees on a cold stone floor would have passed like a flash compared to one of Sister Philomena's beginning curriculum lectures. No Mother Superior could have been more demanding, nasty and capricious than Professor Kemper, who taught Catholic education theory. And the most antiquated and arbitrary rules of convent life could not have been more pointless than the college's German requirement.

Theresa was determined to experience every trying minute of it, to receive her education as if it were a gift from God. At home, she copied German vocabulary words on three-by-five cards and puzzled over her philosophy texts, attempting to follow a dozen different proofs for the existence of God. She kept the radio on for company, ignoring the static, forgetting to listen till "The Star-Spangled Banner" signalled that the station was signing off for the night. Then she would panic, thinking that she'd fallen asleep, and had to reassure herself with the notes she'd taken, the lesson plans she'd copied. At such moments, she examined the smudged photo of St. Therese and felt certain that the saint was smiling, because another "little soul" had finally succeeded in bending itself to God's will.

So be it, she thought. If she couldn't be a captain in His army, she would settle for being one of His common soldiers. For this, she believed, the teacher's college was a kind of basic training, and like any good recruit, Theresa was ready to take orders from anyone who claimed the authority to give them.

In this spirit, she studied her German unquestioningly, though she knew she would never be called upon to use it. She gave up trying to understand the proofs of God's existence and accepted them on faith. And she told herself that if God wished her to take the subway twice a day, she would do it without complaint. If He wished His future teachers to attend after-school programs and weekend retreats, she would do that too.

151

And so it happened that a young man named Leonard Villanova came to join the ranks of Theresa's "superiors."

On alternate Saturdays, the League of Catholic University Students sponsored what they called retreats. Unlike the retreats Theresa remembered from St. Boniface—week-long meditations at idyllic Staten Island estates—these retreats were coed, one-day sessions held at colleges in the city, at which students from the boroughs could socialize while discussing such topics as "Jesus, The Church, and Communism" and "Teachers in a Doubting World."

One Saturday afternoon, riding the subway uptown for a forum on "Television and the Future of Catholic Education," Theresa couldn't stop wondering what she would say if, God forbid, she were called on to speak. Could she talk about television ruining her grandfather's life, her mother watching "The Millionaire"? Could she mention that she herself had watched TV constantly when it first came into the house and then—in a fit of penitence—had given it up completely. At the start, keeping this vow had demanded a certain vigilance, but gradually she almost forgot they had a television; in the end, she was gratified by her abstinence, for she imagined that none of the saints would have achieved beatitude if they'd watched a lot of TV.

But what did any of this have to do with the future of Catholic education? And how could she tell a roomful of college students that she had sworn off television because the contents of the Fatima letter were never revealed?

Distracted by these questions, Theresa couldn't concentrate on the opening panel and didn't begin to relax till the audience broke up into small discussion groups and it became clear that the leader of Theresa's group—a young man who smoothly introduced himself as Leonard Villanova, a second-year law student at St. John's—planned to do all the talking.

Leonard Villanova was an expert talker. He spoke like the former Loyola High debating team captain he was, like the

Jesuit he was in his secret heart. In one sentence, he could propose theories, suggest alternatives, weigh their merits, and ask pertinent questions which he answered with dozens of appropriate examples. Leonard had the facts at his command—statistics, percentages, television sets per capita, television hours per family per week. To hear Leonard talk, you would have thought that there was nothing in the world but television.

Theresa was happy to listen to him; she certainly had nothing to say. And though she was impressed by his eloquence and knowledge, she was not nearly so impressed by Leonard. A gangly boy with tortoiseshell glasses and a greased-up brush of dark hair, he was wearing a button-down shirt, a frayed crewneck sweater, khaki chinos too short by at least an inch. Watching him, Theresa thought it a pity that Leonard didn't know as much about personal grooming as he knew about television. His face was pocked with shallow pits, his cheeks covered with a faint oily down, as if they were still too tender from a recent bout with acne for Leonard to risk shaving.

Ashamed to be entertaining such unworthy thoughts about someone who was putting himself to so much trouble, Theresa forced herself to stare straight at Leonard with the open steady gaze which she could envision St. Therese bestowing on a loyal and treasured brother.

Theresa's stare attracted Leonard's attention, but he failed to identify it as a saintly look and thought that she was trying to pick him up.

As soon as the discussion group ended, Leonard approached Theresa, reached behind her and rather clumsily helped her into her coat. Faking a boldness which he did not feel but imagined he saw on Theresa's face, he asked if she would like to join him for a cup of coffee at the Automat.

Right away, Theresa recognized Leonard as an expert at taking girls for coffee at the cafeteria—an expert at door-holding, at plucking a tray off the stack in such a way that she knew not to bother getting one for herself, at guiding her through the line, asking how she took her coffee and paying before she could reach into her purse. Not only did he steer her expertly through the cavernous restaurant, but his expertise seemed to come naturally. For when Theresa asked him if he went there often, he shook his head and said, "Of course not."

And yet for all that, Theresa was unimpressed by his worldliness, unmoved when he smiled conspiratorially and called the other students at the retreat a bunch of idiots who deserved to spend their lives teaching Catholic school. She was not even stirred by the one thing which—given her own belief in the importance of a conscious life-plan—should have impressed her most: Within the first five minutes of their conversation, Leonard had outlined an elaborate plan for the rest of his life. This scheme included a St. John's law degree, a Lincoln Continental, a family, a town-house in the East Eighties, a summer place in the Hamptons, membership in a dozen clubs which had never admitted Italians, and a brilliant career in the new and wide-open field of television law.

"You mean like Perry Mason?" Theresa knew that this was not what Leonard meant, but it was all she could think of to say.

Leonard laughed—a tight, strained chuckle, high in his throat.

"That's good. Very good. But not quite what I had in mind. I'd be strictly behind the scenes."

"Behind the scenes?"

"Behind a big fancy desk on the top floor of Rockefeller Center." After a moment, Leonard said, "And you? No doubt you have plans of your own?"

"No. Not me."

"Come on now. It's a lawyer's business to read human nature, and the minute I saw you at that discussion group, I thought, 'There's a girl who knows what she wants and knows how to get it.'"

"Me?" Theresa was shocked. "I wish I did."

"I'm sure you do." Leonard leaned across the table. Theresa couldn't look at him.

"I guess what I want . . ." She stopped. "What I really wanted was to go into the convent."

There was a long silence, and suddenly Theresa was afraid that Leonard was regretting the money he'd spent on her coffee. This possibility so dismayed her that she would have said anything. What she did say was, "I just wanted to serve God the best way I could. Ever since I read about St. Therese—"

"Ah ha! The Little Flower! So you're one of those!"

"One of whiches?" Were there others like her?

"The Little Flowers. Half the girls in my neighborhood wanted to grow up to be the Little Flower."

"Is that true?" Theresa was encouraged to learn she had so much company. "Well," she rambled on, "you can see why. Everything the Little Flower did, she did for God. And she didn't do anything, really, didn't live out on the desert or get shot full of arrows. She just washed the floors and the dishes and said her prayers. . . ." Theresa froze. She'd never told anyone this before. Out loud, it sounded like something a five-year-old might say.

But Leonard seemed intrigued.

"Theresa," he said, in the cagey tone of a lawyer beginning what he thinks will be a brilliant cross-examination. "Why shut yourself off from life? Didn't it ever occur to you that a woman can serve God and her family at the same time? All those things you mention—the floors, the dishes—you can do them in a home of your own, for a family of your own, and God will be just as pleased."

He won't be, Theresa wanted to say. There won't be enough left over for Him. It seemed too easy to cook for the husband, kiss the baby, and forget about God. . . . Or maybe it was just *her* insufficiency; *she* didn't have enough for both. In her mind, Theresa rehearsed all the inner debates, the arguments with her father, the struggle which ended so ignominiously with a plate of sausage in the middle of the night. Until finally

155

it dawned on her that Leonard had taken her hand and was awaiting a reply.

Theresa turned away and gazed out the picture window at Fifty-seventh Street. It had been a crisp December afternoon, lit by that early winter sun which makes every surface seem to glitter with promise. All the little boys were carrying hockey sticks or clarinet cases, and the girls swung past in threes and fours, ice skates dangling from laces around their necks. Lovely women clicked by on high heels, clasping bunches of shopping bags like bouquets; down the block, couples waved to each other, met, kissed, then disappeared into movie theaters and taxis.

It was growing chilly, and the light was beginning to fade. Everyone seemed to be in a hurry, as if they had plans for an evening so magical that they couldn't wait for it to come. As Theresa watched them, a certainty came over her; she felt, as at no other time, that those beautiful women were clicking their way toward God, that God was helping the lovers into their cabs. Perhaps it was the general excitement, the light, or simply the effect of the coffee which Theresa rarely drank. Whatever the cause, Theresa knew beyond any doubt that God was present everywhere—even in Leonard Villanova's sweaty hand.

"Ahem." Leonard made a show of clearing his throat. "If you're not busy next Saturday, we might get together again. . . ."

Theresa smiled, so transfixed and exhilarated that Leonard misunderstood the source of her radiance and imagined that he alone had caused her to shine.

No one doubted that Leonard Villanova would make an excellent lawyer. Already he could recite whole pages from his property texts by rote. After his father, an accountant, chanced to mention television law, Leonard read every word ever printed on this topic; he liked to think of his mind as a bloodhound, sniffing out the finest details.

Something of an expert on public affairs, he conscientiously followed the papers and news magazines. Since junior high, he had subscribed to *The National Review* and considered William Buckley the greatest thinker of the decade. A practicing Catholic, Leonard was versed in scripture and doctrine, and kept up to date with the Vatican's latest pronouncements on key issues.

Yet even experts have their limits, and so it was with Leonard. It was one thing to know the history of the church's stand on birth control; it was quite another to practice it. When it came to sex, Leonard was by no means the expert he pretended to be. When it came to women, he was as pure as a saint.

One Saturday afternoon, after a long and tedious retreat on "Ecumenicism and the Catholic Teacher," Leonard walked Theresa to the subway. As she started down the stairs, he grabbed her arm, yanked her back and kissed her.

Theresa waited till he was through, then turned and went down the stairs as if nothing had happened. Leonard took a deep breath. The incident was over so fast, there had been no time to consider the fine points of technique he'd been agonizing over all week. Not counting his mother and sister, Theresa was the first girl Leonard had ever kissed.

The next week, they met at the Metropolitan Museum to look at the religious paintings. As Leonard enlightened Theresa with a running lecture on Renaissance art, she allowed him to hold her hand. The museum was full of lovers, arm in arm, and each time they passed such a couple, Leonard felt honored and proud.

Once again, at the subway entrance, Theresa let him kiss her. This time Leonard was less nervous and more aware. It was discouraging that Theresa didn't kiss him back. But there was something about the way she stood there with her eyes closed, submitting patiently, which made Leonard think that she might let him do anything he wanted.

At the start of the fall term, Leonard had moved from his parents' Bay Ridge home to an apartment on Montague Street which he shared with Vince Migliore and Al DeMeo—boys who came from good families like Leonard's and acted as if they were already partners in some prestigious and conservative law firm. Soon afterwards, the three of them chipped in on a two-year subscription to *Playboy*.

"Even the Pope gets *Playboy*," said Al.

They kept the back issues stacked neatly in the living room, borrowing and returning them with the same care they would have shown crucial reference books from the office library. And that—as reference—was chiefly how they used them. Though none of them were music lovers, Al bought a stereo, which Leonard and Vince stocked with records mentioned in the *Playboy* music column. Occasional beer drinkers, they splurged on a bottle of good Scotch which they placed on a round tray with some highball glasses and cocktail napkins, near the stereo. In the optimism of that gentle Indian summer, it was understood that this set-up would be used for entertaining girls. And yet, throughout that fall, the only female to grace the apartment was the Miss October whom someone—no one admitted having put her there, nor did anyone volunteer to take her down—tacked to the inside of the bathroom door.

Having read the step-by-step instructions, Leonard knew that you invited girls home to listen to your sound system, to admire the view from your terrace, to sample your twelve-year-old Chivas Regal. But instinct told him that these ploys would never work on Theresa Santangelo. Theresa would never go home with him to be entertained or served. *She* would have to do the serving.

One afternoon they met by previous arrangement at Borough Hall. By now, Leonard had persuaded Theresa that the retreats were a waste of her time; he had promised her a tour of Brooklyn Heights. As they walked along the Promenade, Leonard recounted the history of the construction of the Brooklyn Bridge. Suddenly he stopped in mid-sentence and said,

"Would you do me a favor?"

"Sure.

"It's these curtains. . . . My mother sent them to me for my room. For days now, I've been trying to figure out . . . Being a male, I'm not exactly an expert at hanging—"

"I'll put them up for you," said Theresa. "I'd be glad to."

It was so simple, Leonard couldn't believe it had worked, not even when Theresa was actually sitting beside him on the living room couch, with *Bitch's Brew* playing on the stereo. Though he knew that such scenes took place every day, it didn't seem possible that he would be personally involved in one. Other men, maybe, but not Leonard—who had never had much luck with girls beyond a few uncomfortable college coffee dates. And now that it was really happening, now that he was clinking the ice cubes in his Chivas Regal (which, he discovered, he didn't much like), he felt a peculiar detachment, as if he were somewhere else, far away, looking at a Chivas Regal ad in a magazine.

He reached out and took Theresa's hand. As he ran his fingers over her palm, his detachment gave way to anxiety. What in the name of God was he supposed to do next?

Leonard knew, from his reading, how other girls reacted at this critical juncture: They swished across the room to check out the view from your terrace. They asked you to freshen their drink. They pointed out that the record on the turntable had run out. But Theresa did none of these things. She said, "The curtains?"

"Right," said Leonard. "The curtains."

He recognized this as the crucial point in a seduction—certainly no time to give up or get discouraged. Yet still he could not get it through his head that seduction was humanly possible.

"Come on," he said. "They're in the bedroom."

Astonishingly, Theresa followed him into his room. After much searching, he found the dark blue fiberglass drapes in a box at the back of the closet. It was obvious that they were not the urgent problem he'd claimed to be facing, but Theresa didn't seem to care.

"Anything to hang them on?" she said.

Leonard located a neatly stapled package of collapsible rods and pins. He pictured his mother buying them at A&S, barraging the salesgirls with nervous questions. . . . The last thing he wanted to be thinking about now was his mother.

Theresa sat on a chair by the bed and began slipping the hooks beneath the pre-sewn pleats, her fingers working so nimbly that Leonard was moved, and felt that he was witnessing some age-old—even primal—female activity. She stood on the chair to hang them, and Leonard was so stirred by the way her blouse tightened over her back that he was ready to risk anything for a look at the flesh beneath that white school-girl's shirt.

And yet when he said, "Take off your clothes" (the words came out so garbled that he had to clear his throat and repeat himself), it was less out of lust than curiosity to see if such a thing could happen.

Acting as if she hadn't heard, Theresa drew the curtains, got down off the chair and stepped back to admire her work. The afternoon light shone blue into the room. She had heard him, but it hadn't sounded like Leonard. For the voice which had ordered her to take off her clothes was so commanding, its authority so plainly derived from some secret knowledge of her own destiny, that it never occurred to her to disobey.

Theresa turned to face Leonard. Then very slowly, looking straight at him, she undressed and lay on top of the bed, staring up at the ceiling.

In the blue light, she looked like a drowned woman, floating, pale and lovely, miraculously uncorrupted by the water. It was a sight so beautiful—so wondrous, so unexpected in his room— that Leonard began to pray.

"Blessed Lord Jesus," he whispered. "Get me through this and I promise you, I'll never do it again."

But it couldn't have been Jesus who showed him how to undress and lie down beside Theresa so quietly that she wasn't even startled. How would Jesus have known how to hold her and kiss her, how to enter a virgin so slowly that it didn't hurt? It couldn't have been Jesus who told him to wait and let Theresa catch her breath, then gave him the go-ahead to move—slowly at first, then faster, like the expert Leonard knew in his soul he wasn't.

And so, because it was not Jesus who had gotten him through, Leonard felt no obligation to keep the solemn vow he had made Him, and he and Theresa did it again and again and again.

As Leonard and Theresa piled sin upon sin, Theresa wasn't thinking of anything so abstract as sinning. At the time, her mind was empty, but later, while Leonard slept and Theresa lay watching the light change from blue to black, she had plenty of time to think. And what she thought was: Her mind had not been empty so much as absent altogether.

Someone else had done those things in bed with Leonard.

The possibility of winding up in Leonard Villanova's bed had honestly never occurred to her. Over the past months, she had come to think of him as a brother, a friend. And if he sometimes held her hand and kissed her . . . She knew boys liked such things. She herself had felt nothing impure. What was the harm?

Even as she undressed and lay naked on the blankets, she had felt an overwhelming sense of freedom. The saints spoke of floating out of your body, and that was how it was for her. She was not in bed with Leonard of her own free will. She was following someone else's orders.

Now she wondered: Whose?

Obviously, Leonard was the one who'd told her to take off her clothes—but she'd never felt as if she were obeying Leonard. Traditionally, it was the devil who tempted and wheedled and dragged you into sin—but she hadn't felt the devil's presence in the room.

That left God. But why would God lead her into bed with Leonard Villanova?

Suddenly she remembered all the saints who had fornicated, lied and stolen, all the pickpockets and con-men and whores.

Augustine, Magdalene, Mary of Egypt—Theresa made a mental list. She thought of the robber crucified with Jesus and saved, the great sinners plucked from the midst of their evil lives and sanctified. For a moment, she thought: Maybe St. Therese's Little Way wasn't the only one; maybe that was why God had brought her to Leonard Villanova's dark bedroom.

She put her hand on Leonard's bare chest, felt his measured breathing and experienced a rush of tenderness and awe. It was as if she were touching God there, in Leonard Villanova's skinny chest.

Leonard stirred.

"Jesus," he mumbled. A long time later, he said, "What time is it?"

Turning, Theresa saw a luminous plastic clock on the night table. It scared her, as if its dial were a human face which had been watching them all afternoon.

"Nine."

"Won't your folks be worried?"

"No," said Theresa, doubly guilty for the lie and for the fact that her parents were probably very worried. Two sins, she thought. She felt confused, and heard that old refrain in her mind: What would the Little Flower do now? Even St. Therese had made her family worry. But she had never done the things which Theresa had done that day with Leonard.

"Mea culpa," she mumbled under her breath, pretending to cough so Leonard wouldn't wonder why she was hitting herself in the chest. Then she lay very still. This is it, she thought. I'm going to hell. She waited for a chill of fear, but all that came was a vague nostalgia and a not-unfamiliar disappointment. She felt as if she were remembering herself as a little girl and thinking of all the childish wishes which hadn't come true: I wanted to become a nun, but I didn't. I wanted to go to heaven, but I went to hell.

"Are you okay?" said Leonard.

"I'm fine. I just better get going."

It was pitch-black, and warm enough, but Theresa dressed with her elbows drawn in and her arms across her breasts for protection. She thought of a painting Leonard had shown her at the museum: Adam and Eve after the Fall, so ashamed that they walked bent over, like old people. The painting had embarrassed her—Adam in his fig leaf looked a million times more naked than Jesus in a loincloth. But it was nothing compared to the embarrassment she felt now.

"It's true," she thought. "Afterwards, you walk different."

Dressed, she switched on the night-light. The first thing she noticed was the brownish bloodstain on Leonard's sheet, and her impulse was to cover it with both hands. For though she was still disoriented enough to think that she must have gotten her period, she never doubted that the blood was hers.

Without getting out of bed, Leonard eased her hands away and pulled up the blanket.

"Forget it. It's nothing."

"I'll wash it for you," said Theresa, her tone too urgent to be offering a casual favor.

"I'll take care of it." Now Leonard too was embarrassed, for nowhere in his *Playboys* had he seen this problem discussed. In all his fantasies about this first time in his room, he had never imagined a girl insisting on washing the blood off the bed linen. He understood that such things were important to women, and wondered if Theresa meant to take the sheet home and keep it, substituting another. Leonard felt a wave of possessiveness: It was *his* sheet, and now it was just as much his memento as hers. He pictured himself taking it to the laundromat with the secret satisfaction of knowing that his wash concealed the blood of a virgin. And besides, he was hardly about to jump up and hop into his clothes while Theresa stripped the bed.

"I want to," said Theresa.

"I *said*, 'I'll take care of it.'" Leonard's tone was sharp.

Theresa dove for the corner of the sheet with such determination that Leonard knew: There was no way to stop her short of physical violence. It took him less than a second to weigh the evidence and decide: No dirty sheet on earth was worth using violence on the first girl he'd ever gone to bed with. If she wanted it so badly, how could he deny her?

So he got up and grabbed for his clothes while Theresa unmade the bed, folded the dirty sheets, then remade it with some clean ones he found for her in a drawer. Normally Leonard considered himself a gentleman. But as he watched Theresa fluff the pillows, he felt such pride, such a sense of accomplishment that he was taken out of his normal self and moved to think something which would never have crossed a gentleman's mind.

"One afternoon in the sack with me," thought Leonard, "and she's begging to do my laundry."

From then on, Leonard had only to say, "Let's put up some curtains," for Theresa to follow him into his room. After a while (when it became clear that Theresa didn't particularly want them) Leonard dispensed with the preliminaries which *Playboy* claimed all women want. The love-making took only a few minutes which, Theresa told herself, were no more significant than any others in her day. Except that often, as Leonard finished, he would cry, "God!" And Theresa understood instinctively that it was not a blasphemy, but a prayer.

Then she would jump up and get to work. When Leonard's room was spotless, she turned her attention to the rest of the apartment. The kitchen was a typical bachelor mess, and Theresa spent hours scrubbing jelly rings off the cupboard shelves. At first she blushed when Al and Vince came in to find her cleaning, but they treated her so politely that she overcame her shyness. And why should she be shy? She was doing it for them. Mercifully, she had no idea that they called her "the cleaning lady" behind her back. But perhaps she might not have cared. For already she was moving beyond the point of caring what people called her. A cleaning lady worked for money. A housewife worked for her family, her home, her husband—and by extension herself. But this wasn't Theresa's apartment, Leonard wasn't her husband, and her service was pure, benefiting no one but Leonard, his roommates, and God.

Ever since that first afternoon in Leonard's bed, she had decided that God could be served through Leonard Villanova. It was not yet a certainty—but she would never know for certain unless she tried. Meanwhile she enjoyed transforming the messy kitchen and took special delight in preparing complicated dishes—hot antipasto, mussels oreganata, tagliatelle, pasta with fresh pesto—with its rudimentary equipment. She served Leonard on trays in his room, and it pleased her to see the gratitude on his face. Clearly, Leonard was growing to love her, and she knew that loving another human being was one step closer to loving God. If nothing else, she was helping Leonard on his way.

Leonard *was* grateful, at least enough to endure his roommates' teasing without ever making the kind of crude remark he'd heard in his mind that first afternoon. For even the most callous men never said such things about women they truly loved. And slowly, in his own fashion, Leonard was falling in love with Theresa. It was not just the thrill of going to bed with her, or the gratification of talking to her and seeing her suitably impressed by his expertise, but also the gentler contentment of watching her smile and hum to herself as she washed his coffee cups and sorted his socks. He loved the meals, the trays adorned with fresh flowers and linen napkins she'd borrowed from home. And as she set them in front of him, he couldn't help thinking how much lovelier she was than Miss October.

His roommates' opinion was that Theresa was one of those girls who go to college for their M.R.S. degree, and Leonard admitted the possibility that Theresa was trying to show him what a good wife she would make. Nevertheless, he assured them: The subject of marriage had never come up. If Theresa became pregnant, God forbid, he would do his duty as a Catholic and marry her. But Leonard had his heart set on a different sort of wife—a leggy blonde Grace Kelly-type whose idea of housework was a list of instructions for the maid. He imagined that you worked your way up to such a woman; along with the important business contacts came the wife to entertain them. And his passion for Theresa never grew much stronger than the love he felt for his education and would feel for his first job: She was someplace to start.

Nor was Theresa thinking of marriage—or not, at least, to Leonard. More and more, she saw her life with him as a test. Despite what she let him do to her, she still felt no more for him than sincere friendship; she'd seen enough movies to know that it wasn't love. And if she could give herself totally to this boy she didn't love, if she could make this dingy bachelor apartment her life's work, these acts of devotion and sacrifice might reach all the way to God, and something would happen.

She could not imagine (nor was it hers to guess) what this something would be. Perhaps she would hear another call to the convent, stronger this time and accompanied by a more effective strategy. Perhaps God's will would circumvent her entirely and work a miracle. Overnight, her parents would change their mind, they would take her out of college and escort her to the Carmelites' door. Maybe He would show her the truth in a vision, a ray of light beamed on the dish suds. Or perhaps He meant to reconcile her to housework, to so addict her to the pleasures of a tidy kitchen that she gave up and married someone like Leonard.

Open to any kind of revelation, she believed that the intensity of her devotion to Leonard was a way of forcing God's hand, and that God had put it into her mind to force things this way. She felt this so strongly that she stopped going to confession for fear that the priests might try to talk her out of it. She refused to bother herself with the illogicality of it, or wonder: Why would God reward her for serving Leonard when—after all those years of helping her own mother—He hadn't even given her the strength to resist a plate of sausage? Instead, she defrosted Leonard's refrigerator and rinsed the shelves with boiling water, all in the euphoric state induced by that rare intoxicant—the belief that her work had a purpose, that the smallest acts were part of a larger plan. Engrossed in the vegetable bins, she felt a calm come over her, soothing as the hot lemon and honey her mother used to brew her when she had a cold. She wondered if this were all she would ever feel, and thought that it was almost—but not quite—enough.

Inevitably, her daily visits to Leonard's cut into her school time. But she was convinced that cleaning his apartment would teach her more and bring faster, more permanent results than any college. Still, she tried to keep to her former hours and carried her texts with her—mostly for show, but also to skim on the subway back from Leonard's. In the evenings, Joseph and Catherine would look at her, their faces full of love, and ask what she was learning in school. Praying for forgiveness for misleading them, Theresa would summarize the pages she'd read on the way home. The truth—that this subway cramming was the only studying she did—would only have hurt them more.

Because now, when she went to her room to do her homework, her doubts and fears besieged her, demons so numerous that the room seemed just as crowded and more distracting than a rush hour train. She began sleeping with the night-light on, as if to keep away the dark suspicion that Leonard had been sent by the devil to ensnare her in sin upon sin. Suppose she were wrong, suppose her relations with Leonard weren't God's secret way of saving her soul. Most likely, it happened all the time—misled sinners brought to Judgement, saying, "You, I did it all for You!" only to hear God answer, "Me? You must be mistaken."

It was equally possible that neither God nor the devil were at work but simply, ordinary life. Nothing had happened which wasn't happening to some girl somewhere every minute. She'd found a boyfriend, she'd let him go too far. At worst, she'd get pregnant—Leonard had promised to marry her. But that was all she could hope for: No grace, no vision, no revelation.

She was also afraid of angering God with the arrogance of her challenge. For who was she to say, "Look, I'm scrubbing my knuckles raw for this boy I hardly know. Now show me something"? Who was she to test Him? Lying awake in the dim light, she recalled all the Bible stories in which someone (Lucifer, Adam, the citizens of Babel) called God's hand and lost the game. And finally, she was terrified of the stakes, the penalty for losing—an eternity of hellfire which would burn her to ash so black and fine that a legion of devils couldn't scour it off the grill.

Later, when Catherine wondered how all this could have happened without her suspecting, she would think of a page from *The Mother's Medical Encyclopedia*. In an image so clear that she could see the drawing of a thermometer in the upper right-hand corner, she remembered the section on childhood diseases and in particular the warning against confusing the flush of fever with the glow of health.

In the beginning, Catherine took this admonition so seriously that she was constantly fighting the urge to take Theresa's temperature. But after a few minor illnesses, Catherine learned to read her daughter's color, and developed enough confidence in this ability to take it for granted. When Theresa came down with her annual winter cold, Catherine was warming lemon and honey hours before the first sneeze; for the rest of the year, she could relax.

By the time Theresa was burning with the fever to serve Leonard Villanova, Catherine had forgotten the warning. And besides: After Nicky's death and all that trouble over the convent, Catherine so longed for health and normality that no thermometer could have convinced her otherwise.

Also the symptoms were easy to misinterpret. Theresa left home in time for school and returned promptly for dinner. Perhaps it was the walk from the subway, but she invariably sailed in with good color and bright eyes. She was eating like a normal person—no hunger strikes, no water in the gravy, no slings to catch the crumbs. She helped with the dishes, swept the kitchen, then went to her room to study—and never once mentioned the convent.

The best—and most misleading—sign was the fact that Theresa finally had a boyfriend.

Catherine would have been longer in discovering this if not for the family laundry which Theresa did, as always, on Saturday mornings. Over the years, Catherine had grown so accustomed to Theresa's steady efficient rhythm that she noticed immediately when Theresa began working faster, stuffing clothes into the machine with an awkward, secretive haste. When Catherine was busy in the kitchen, or anywhere near the washer, Theresa hovered over it, making idle conversation. If the cycle ended while Theresa was out of the room, she'd race back, as if to make sure that her mother didn't get there first. She waited to unload the washer till Catherine stepped out; when Catherine wouldn't leave, she pulled the clothes out in a tight little knot which she hid with her body.

In the shop, women were perpetually telling stories about teenagers who acted this way about their rooms, their purses, and mothers who ferreted out caches of marijuana and birth control pills. But what, Catherine wondered, could Theresa be hiding in the laundry?

One morning, Catherine waited in her room till she heard Theresa go into the bathroom, then hurried to the kitchen and opened the washing machine. As the spinning slowed, she saw several pairs of men's socks plastered flat against the drum, white crews striped with blue. Where had Joseph gotten such socks? Then she realized: They weren't Joseph's. First she was embarrassed, then surprised to find herself so moved that tears came to her eyes. It wasn't that she wanted to rush Theresa into a lifetime of washing some boy's dirty socks; she herself had been doing it long enough to know that there was no intrinsic glory in it. Still, those blue stripes, stopped now in their orbit, had made her think: The next round of socks, and soon it's the next set of baby clothes. Life goes on.

She closed the lid and told no one about her discovery. She knew from her magazines that girls wanted privacy in these matters, especially at first. Theresa would mention it when she was ready. Nor did she tell Joseph, for she knew how fathers worry.

Now more than ever, they had cause for alarm. In the afternoons, when Catherine turned on the television for company, a program didn't go by without some reference to teenage sex, drugs, runaways, communes, gurus, innocent children ravaged by LSD and free love. Even in the neighborhood, life had changed. Women announced their daughters' weddings and couldn't look at you; but when the grandchildren came six months later, they dared you to look away. There had always been such babies, but now no one bothered pretending they were premature. Now the mothers said: "You think when the children are grown, you can stop worrying. But the worrying never stops."

Yet Catherine wasn't worried. She knew that Theresa would never turn into one of those commune girls with their frizzy hair, their beads and empty eyes. Theresa was the kind who had the wedding ring at least nine months before the baby. And even if she were doing more for this boy than washing his socks . . . Catherine knocked on wood and told herself that a slightly "premature" grandchild was better than a daughter in a convent.

Weeks passed, and Theresa remained so reticent about her boyfriend that Catherine had to reassure herself of his continued existence by examining the laundry. One Saturday, she found a T-shirt with a name tag—"Leonard Villanova"—carefully stitched on.

Later, remembering this, Catherine felt a chill—the shiver which, she imagined, would come over you on first hearing the name of someone who will eventually do you harm. But at the time, she thought: Thank God. An Italian boy with a mama who loves him.

Later, Catherine would recall all this to explain her misreading of the color in Theresa's cheeks. And Joseph would comfort her, saying: How could they have known? Even if they had recognized the flush, they could never have diagnosed the disease. For how could they have suspected that Theresa's flame for Leonard burned low beside her fever for those T-shirts and socks?

No one told Joseph and Catherine that Theresa had stopped going to school. No one noticed. She was not the kind of girl whose presence would be missed in a large lecture hall, nor had she ever been one to seek out her professors' personal attention.

Each day, she stayed longer at Leonard's apartment—dusting, straightening, intercepting discarded shirts on their way to the hamper. Salt stains were not permitted to accumulate on Leonard's boots, nor was Leonard allowed to sleep on the same pillowcase twice. He couldn't pick up a sugar spoon without her swiping beneath it to wipe the table. And yet, for all these intimate attentions, she seemed progressively less interested in going to bed with him. Often, in the midst of it, he'd catch her eyeing the clock, and it would turn out that she had put the spaghetti water on to boil before coming to his room.

She arrived in the morning to hand him his orange juice and coffee, to hold his jacket and knot his tie. Most days, when Leonard left for classes, Theresa was just getting busy in the kitchen.

"Go ahead." She'd glance up at him from a sink full of dishes or a sudsy floor. "I'll let myself out when I'm through."

But she never seemed to finish. At lunch, Leonard and his roommates would come home to find her kneeling by the stove; the harsh smell of oven cleaner clung to their clothes and followed them to their rooms.

Though Al and Vince gladly shared the leftover delicacies and teased Leonard about loaning Theresa out to make their beds, they were just as glad that Leonard wasn't about to loan her. They didn't want anyone staring at them with that doggy look she gave Leonard. They suspected her of manufacturing work; it was a small apartment, there wasn't that much to clean. They knew that girls went to extraordinary lengths to catch husbands. But Theresa was going too far.

One afternoon, Al walked into the kitchen to discover Theresa scouring the inside of the toaster with a toothbrush. Intent, nearly cross-eyed with concentration, she didn't look up, didn't even hear him. That evening, when Theresa went home, Al and Vince knocked on Leonard's door.

"Al and I," began Vince, in the hushed tone which he supposed a lawyer might use in approaching a partner on a personal and highly delicate matter, "we know you and Theresa are pretty close. We think the world of her, I swear. But what we've been thinking is, maybe you're *too* close. What we mean is . . . Al and I've been noticing . . . It's not normal how she knocks herself out around here. There's neat people, there's clean people, there's good housekeepers . . . But Theresa's not normal. Maybe it's the strain—first year of college, papers, exams, you remember. Maybe she should talk to somebody."

"I've talked to her," said Leonard. "Believe me. Last week I found her dusting the radiators with a ripped-up handkerchief she'd fished out of the garbage. And the next day, she must have had second thoughts, she was darning the damn handkerchief. She scrubs the inside of the juice bottles before she'll throw them in the trash, she'd brush my teeth if I let her. . . ."

Leonard stopped. Al and Vince were staring at him. Misinterpreting, he imagined that the question in their minds was, "What's a smart guy like Leonard doing with a crazy female like that?"

"I don't know," he said. "I really don't. She wasn't always like this. She's a nice girl, it seemed like we had a lot in common. She was so sweet, she couldn't do enough for me. How was I supposed to know? And *now* what? If I tell her I don't want to see her anymore, God knows what she'll do. I wouldn't want to take the responsibility."

"We're not saying stop seeing her," said Vince.

"Then what? You tell me."

"You talked to her?" said Al.

"Twice a day. I tell her, 'Look, Theresa, you don't have to wash my socks. My own mother won't do that anymore, I'm a grown man, I can go to the laundromat.' But she just gives me that terrible scarey smile and says, 'Please let me. I want to.'"

"Maybe you'd *better* tell somebody," said Vince.

"Who?"

"Her family."

"That's all we need. Her father's a butcher. He'll be over here with a meat cleaver in five minutes flat."

"Isn't there a guidance counsellor at her school . . .?"

Leonard wouldn't dignify this with an answer.

"Then okay, a doctor. A psychiatrist." Al looked to Vince for support. Vince nodded. "Leonard, it looks to us like she's having some kind of nervous breakdown."

The truth was that Theresa's behavior over the past weeks had so alarmed Leonard that he'd checked out every psychiatry text from the law school library.

"Listen," he said. "Backward schizophrenics don't cook gourmet meals. No, Theresa's just going through a mild, pretty textbook manic-depressive episode. Overwork, mood swings, cycles . . . Sometimes these things blow over on their own, especially if there's no previous history. Let's wait. Ride it out. Spring's coming, I'll make her go easy on the housework, get out more. She'll get better." Winded from the effort of sounding like an expert, Leonard took a deep breath and thought of how, in a few short months, Theresa had shaken his confidence in expertise.

Theresa got worse.

Two weeks later, she arrived very early on a rainy morning. When Leonard left for school at eight, Theresa had just set up the ironing board in his room and was starting to press a red and white checked shirt.

At four, he came home to find her ironing the same shirt.

"You were ironing that shirt when I left," he said.

"No," said Theresa. "It's not the same one."

"Theresa, I only have one red and white checked shirt."

"You did this morning. But now you have thousands."

As she gazed up at him, Leonard saw that her face was shining—or perhaps merely flushed from all those hours over the ironing board.

"How's that?" he said.

"Look." Theresa opened Leonard's closet and, with a sweeping gesture, indicated his clothes—neatly creased chinos, a dozen white, off-white, and pale blue shirts. "Thousands of red and white checked shirts. Aren't they lovely?" Theresa turned back to him and sighed.

"Oh, Leonard. This is how it must have looked—the loaves and fishes! The wine for the wedding at Cana!"

Leonard took the iron out of her hand and rested it, point up, on the metal plate.

"Sit down," he said.

He went into the kitchen and dialed Theresa's home number. A woman answered.

"Mrs. Santangelo?" For the first time, Leonard wished that he had met Theresa's family. "This is Leonard Villanova."

"Leonard," said the woman, as if she knew him, and suddenly Leonard was afraid that the mother might be as crazy as the daughter.

"I'm a friend of Theresa's," was all he could think of to say. And then, for lack of anything else, added, "She's been up here alone all day. She's been ironing the same shirt since eight o'clock this morning."

Somehow he spelled out his address and hung up. When he went in to check on Theresa, she was perched on the bed, staring rapturously at the open closet. She turned toward him, and though there was no extension in the bedroom, Leonard had the distinct impression that she'd overheard every word.

"Leonard," she said. "You were wrong. I wasn't alone."

"I wasn't alone," she repeated. "Jesus was with me all day."

"Up here?" Leonard tapped the side of his head.

"Sure, here." Theresa tapped her own head. "But also h*ere.*" She pointed at the floor. "As real as you're standing there now."

"Jesus? In my room?"

"Not three feet from this ironing board. He got here the minute you left."

"Oh," said Leonard.

"You know, my whole life, I used to wonder: What would I do if I really had a vision. How would I act if I actually saw God's face? Would I fall on the floor and start foaming at the mouth like Saint Paul? It could happen anywhere, I used to think. What if you were on the subway and started bleeding from your ankles and wrists? If Jesus came, would you have the sense to look around for a soft place to fall?"

"That's what you've been worrying about. All your life?"

Theresa nodded.

"Once I saw a boy have an epileptic fit in Washington Square Park. Before anybody knew what was happening, his guitar crashed to the pavement, and the boy fell on top of it. And I thought: That's how it would look if Jesus came to you in Washington Square. You'd sink like a stone, with fifty people watching you sit on your own guitar.

"But this morning, when Jesus walked into the room . . . I wasn't thinking about it. Of course I had Him in mind somewhere, just like I always try to keep Him in mind when I'm doing something around the house. But you know how it is. You get to ironing, you're trying to make a collar lay flat . . . You're not expecting to see Jesus.

"I didn't even see Him walk in. I was turning the shirt around so I could get under the buttons, I glance up . . . And

FRANCINE PROSE

there He was. I jumped. I'd have jumped to see anyone there. The first thing I noticed was His eyes—big, dark, calm. You wouldn't believe that anyone would look at you so steady. He was smiling.

"'Don't let me interrupt you,' He said.

"I couldn't look at Him. I looked down at the ironing board. So this is what it's like, I thought. You don't faint dead away, leaving Jesus to make sure that the shirt doesn't burn. You don't have to worry about stigmata dripping blood on Leonard's carpet. You just feel shy, a little embarrassed. You try to get on with your ironing, but you can't.

"I made myself look up. He had long curly brown hair and a beard, like in His pictures. To tell the truth, I would have thought it was some hippie wandered in off the street if it hadn't been for that halo around Him. Like Christmas lights strung around a house front. Like a make-up mirror. He was wearing a filthy white robe—a rag, really, a rag with armholes and a neck—ripped, greasy, streaked with mud. He wasn't particularly tall—not nearly so tall as you, Leonard. But He carried Himself like a king.

"'Go ahead,' He said. He was still smiling and pointing at your shirt. 'I don't want to disturb you.'

"'Then why did you come?' I said. I thought: What kind of way is that to talk to Jesus? But somehow I didn't hesitate to say exactly what was on my mind.

"'I came to keep you company,' He said.

"'Thanks,' I said. I mean, no one ever offered to keep me company before. Not that . . . I never needed . . ."

"Forget it," said Leonard. "Go on."

"I started back on the buttons. My hands were shaking so bad, the only thing that saved me was that I'd done it so many times, it was automatic. I could do it with Jesus right there. When I was done, I hung it on a hanger and held it up for Him to see.

"I don't know what I expected Him to say. Since when do

you ask Jesus to admire your ironing? But what He said was, 'Thank you.'

"'For what?' I said.

"'For grooming one of my lambs.'"

"For grooming one of my lambs?" Leonard suppressed a giggle.

"That's what He said." Theresa was absolutely serious. "Then after a while He sighed, and I swear, the light around Him dimmed. I could see a shadow pass over His face, and I knew it was the shadow of the cross.

"'If only there was someone to do as much for me,' He said. I couldn't imagine what He meant. He touched His robe.

"'I was buried in this.'

"'I thought they had your shroud at Turin,' I said.

"'How could it be?' He said. 'I've been wearing this without respite for two thousand years. Can you imagine what that's like?'

"'No,' I said. 'I can't.' Then I thought a minute, and it didn't make sense. 'What about your crown? Your golden raiments?'

"'That's what I wear in the paintings,' He said. 'In the artists' minds. But this is what I wear on God's right hand.'

"'But He's your father. Why would He want you to dress like that?' I should have realized: If He'd let His son die on the cross, anything was possible. But I wasn't thinking.

"'For the angels' sake,' Jesus said. 'Just as men need to see me on the cross, to be reminded of my suffering for their salvation, so the angels need to see me in my shroud. It reminds them of the wear and tear of death, the strain of resurrection. It keeps them from getting sentimental for their lives on earth.'"

"I never thought of that," said Leonard.

"Me neither," said Theresa.

"I hung your shirt in the closet. Then with my back still turned to Jesus, I said, "'Lord, let me do it. There's plenty of time. I know Leonard wouldn't mind. I could wash and iron it for you in two seconds flat. I'd take good care of it. And there'd be no problem. . . . Look, I'll leave the room. You can put on one of Leonard's robes.'

"He didn't answer. I turned around to see if He would take me up on it.

"He was laughing. His face was so bright, it hurt my eyes to look.

"Then I noticed. There was another red and white checked shirt, exactly like the one I'd just finished. It was clean, freshly sprinkled—just waiting to be ironed.

"Leonard, the room was full of checked shirts—everywhere, covering every surface. It looked like a picnic, a circus, a red and white checked wedding tent. . . .

"I've been ironing them all day, and Jesus has been here to keep me company."

"Theresa," said Leonard. "Do me a favor."

"What's that?"

"When your folks get here, tell them what you just told me."

Theresa tried, but no matter how many times she retold her story—stopping to explain, adding details she'd forgotten to give Leonard—Joseph merely stared at her and Catherine said, "Theresa, honey, there's only one checked shirt."

"I only have one," Leonard kept repeating.

"We heard you the first time," said Joseph.

In the forty-five minutes which had elapsed since Leonard's phone call, Joseph had taken charge. As soon as Catherine told him that Theresa was in some kind of trouble, he'd closed up the shop and bundled Catherine straight into a cab, which was waiting now, downstairs.

During that time, Leonard had prepared a full explanation, rich with jargon from his psychology texts.

"It appears to me like some sort of psychotic break. Hallucinations, visions, they're often brought on by . . ."

"Right," said Joseph. "The meter's running. Let's go."

"I understand," said Leonard.

"You don't." Theresa spoke up for the first time since finishing her story.

"I'll get her stuff," said Leonard.

It was awkward enough, retrieving Theresa's coat from the bedroom closet. But what bothered Leonard more was that it was a schoolgirl's coat—her St. Boniface coat, navy blue wool, princess style. Just holding it made Leonard feel like a child molester, and he blamed himself for having been so unobservant. Right from the start, that coat should have told him the whole story.

He held it in front of Theresa, who didn't move. He stood there like a bullfighter without a bull, then handed it to Catherine, who stuffed Theresa's arms into the sleeves.

"Christ," said Joseph. "It's like dressing a baby."

"Help her," said Catherine. Joseph put one hand under Theresa's collar and steered her out of the room. In the hall, he passed Al and Vince without acknowledgment and didn't stop moving till Theresa was wedged between him and Catherine in the back seat of the cab.

No one spoke. Even if they'd known where to begin, the cab driver's presence would have inhibited them. How could they discuss family business in front of a stranger?

They drove past blocks of brownstones. Lights were going on in the windows, and Catherine saw families eating dinner and watching TV. She sought out the mothers in their kitchens, at their tables, relaxing in their favorite chairs. And she wondered: Did their daughters see Jesus and spend eight hours ironing one of their boyfriend's shirts?

Turning onto Jay Street, they passed the municipal buildings. Most of the offices were dark. As they sped by, a few fluorescent-lit windows seemed to pop like flashbulbs. Catherine thought of all the stories she'd read in movie magazines, harrowing tales of breakdowns, straightjackets, snake pits. They never tell you about the other person, she thought—not the crazy one, but the one who takes care of things, cleans up, makes arrangements, the person who sits in the taxi and watches the lights go by.

They got caught in a traffic jam at the entrance to the bridge. Overhead lights illuminated the interior of the cab, and Joseph looked over at his family. Catherine was gazing out the window. Theresa was staring straight ahead, seeing God knows what in the headlights of the oncoming lane.

Just one car, he caught himself thinking, just one car jumping over the center divider could settle their problems for good. He crossed himself, looked around for some wood to knock on, and thought how little it takes to turn your life around. One minute, you're sitting on four aces. Your wife's upstairs cooking, your daughter's off at college, you're making good money in the shop. The next minute, you've got a handful of deuces and threes, and you're stuck in a cab coming back from a Brooklyn apartment where your daughter's been shacking up with her pimply boyfriend and losing her mind.

"Jesus Christ," he muttered.

Theresa smiled.

Joseph swallowed. There was a bad taste in his mouth. His mother, rest in peace, had been right all along: How could his life taste more like that first awful meal?

As soon as the apartment door shut behind them, Catherine said, "Hungry?"

"No thanks." Theresa went off to her room.

"Will she be okay in there?" asked Joseph. "I wouldn't want Jesus telling her to fly out the window."

"Jesus won't tell her that," said Catherine. "Want some coffee?"

The coffee, when it came, tasted watery and flat, but out of habit, Joseph said, "Hits the spot." After a while he said, "How come you didn't know what was going on? You're her mother, she's supposed to talk to you."

Catherine thought of that page from *The Mother's Medical Encyclopedia,* but all she said was, "She doesn't talk to me. She's a Falconetti that way. I assumed she was going to college. If it hadn't been for what happened this afternoon, I'd think she was doing her homework right now."

"Didn't you ever find anything in her room? I mean, she had a boyfriend all this time. You didn't know?"

"Oh, that. I knew. Joseph, she used to do his laundry. I'd find his socks and T-shirts in our wash. And I thought it was sweet. Because all those years, I'd prayed to find something like that—a boy's sweater in her closet, a photo on her night table, some little valentine stuck in her drawer. But it was always like a convent in there. No matter what I did, it looked like your mother's old room. So when I found those T-shirts, I thought: Thank God. How was I supposed to know that she was taking them back to his place and ironing them?"

"How *could* you know?" Joseph shook his head.

"Listen. She's got the radio on."

Joseph listened. A man's voice—some kind of talk show.

"Did you get a look at that Leonard?" said Joseph. "Did you see that skin on that guy?"

"His skin was the least of it. He could have had two heads and twice as many pimples and it wouldn't have made any difference. Remember what they said at our wedding, Joseph? 'You win your husband in a card game.'"

"So?"

"So Theresa won Leonard."

"Then she lost. If anyone ever had the Evil Eye, it's that Leonard."

"The Evil Eye. You sound like your mother."

"My mother again."

"Your mother used to see things, too. Things that weren't there. Your father's ghost, who knows what else. Maybe that *is* where Theresa gets it from—"

"Would you stop harping on my mother? My mother never ironed the same shirt for eight hours straight."

There was a silence. Then Catherine said, "We were wrong. We should have let her join the convent. If she had to do all that, she could be doing it for God like she wanted. Giving it to someone besides Leonard. You know what Jesus came to tell her today? Thank you. That's all she wanted, Joseph. Thank you. She's not so different from anyone else."

"Jesus isn't the only one who knows how to say thank you. A two-year-old kid can say thank you, people say it all the time. Why did she have to hear it from Jesus?"

"It's never enough. Look what happened to your mother. She worked all her life for a thank you which just isn't possible. Because the only way your husband can thank you like that is to live forever, the only way your children can thank you is to never leave your breast. It drove your mother crazy, it turned her into a wild Indian. But Jesus? Jesus will outlive you. He never leaves. That's why they go into the convent. He keeps on saying it—"

"Thank you!" said Joseph. "Thank you, thank you! I've been saying it all my life."

"I know it," said Catherine.

They listened to the radio from Theresa's room. Finally Joseph said, "Want to hear something funny?"

"I don't know. I've heard enough funny things for one day."

"No, listen. I never told anyone this. But that card game, that pinochle game when Lino bet you . . . I *didn't* cheat. The truth was, I actually pulled a handful of high hearts from the deck."

"No kidding."

"And after that, a day didn't go by without my thinking, God can always deal the wild card. You think you can tell how the game is going, but you can never tell. He can deal you the wild card any time, and now He's dealt us a daughter who sees Jesus at the ironing board."

"If He dealt it, He'd better tell us how to play it."

"He did before. He told me to put up a blast of cold air."

Despite herself, Catherine laughed, then got up to go check on Theresa. She knocked and, getting no answer, eased open the door.

"Good God," she said.

Theresa was sitting on the bed, straining forward, her back and shoulders tense. The radio was playing so loud that she didn't hear her mother walk in. Nor did she see her, for she was staring at the radio as if it were television.

Catherine rarely thought about her first child. But now she wondered: What if the boy had lived?

"Brothers and sisters," said the voice on the radio. "After Judas betrayed our Blessed Lord Jesus, what did he do? What was the very first thing he did? He kissed Him, brothers! He kissed Him, sisters!" The deep male voice dropped lower and became threatening.

"That was the first Judas kiss, brothers, but not—not by any means—the last. How many of you women out there have kissed your sister and gone out telling tales behind her back? How many of you brothers have kissed your own babies and spent their milk money gambling, drinking, womanizing? How many of you little children have given your mama that Judas kiss, then turned straight around and done the opposite of what she say?"

"Anything you want?" said Catherine.

Theresa pointed at her ears like a deaf person.

"You want anything?"

Theresa shook her head.

An hour later, when Catherine returned with a plate of food, Theresa was sitting in the same position. Now there was gospel music on the radio.

"Thanks, I don't need it." Theresa waved away the food. "Jesus promised He would bring me loaves and fishes."

"Well, if you and Jesus need silverware, feel free to use the kitchen." Catherine closed Theresa's door and burst into tears.

Theresa didn't leave her room for the rest of the night. At three, they heard the national anthem, the bedsprings creak once, then silence.

"What about the bathroom?" said Joseph. "Has she gotten so holy, she doesn't have to go to the bathroom?"

"No." Catherine shut her eyes. "It can't be that bad, she'd forget how to use the bathroom."

It wasn't that bad—but it was bad enough. For three days, Theresa refused to leave her room except to use the bathroom. For three days, she didn't eat, but just sat on her bed, listened to religious programs on the radio and slept.

Finally Catherine said, "This time she'll starve." She was honestly frightened and yet still hopeful that, like the last time, Joseph would say, "Wait. She'll get hungry." But now Joseph looked at her and shrugged.

They both knew that this was different from the last time Theresa stopped eating. It was simpler then, when Catherine could outdo herself cooking because they were both so certain that Theresa wouldn't starve. And all the troubles of the past seemed to shrink into insignificance as they longed for that time before Jesus convinced their daughter to hold out for the loaves and fishes.

It was like falling in love (at that stage when nothing else is important, no conversation of interest unless it concerns the beloved) and discovering an entire radio station devoted exclusively to Him. It was like loving someone who can walk through walls and thus can arrive at any moment, unannounced by the doorbell, the phone. The doorbell might have given her a minute to fix her hair, prepare her face; loving a man who could appear out of nowhere, she had to be ready all the time. It had all the excitement of new love, with none of the anxiety, for Theresa never doubted that Jesus loved her. She hesitated to go out, for fear of missing His visit, and yet she knew that He could find her anywhere. There was no point eating, unless she could share it with Him, no point sleeping except to dream of Him. Yet everything had a point, a purpose, as she waited to see Him or just to find out when they would meet again.

Meanwhile she was vaguely aware of the life around her, of footsteps in the hall, worried faces. Like any young girl in love, she wished that her parents understood, and pitied them for their ignorance. She heard the front door open and close, and knew only that it wasn't Him. Out in the kitchen, people were talking in hushed voices which rose occasionally to shouts. Theresa listened as if from an enormous distance, the way a bride sequestered in her dressing room before the ceremony hears the murmur of arriving guests.

A family council was called: Augie and Evelyn, even Lino Falconetti. Lino was the only one to go see Theresa. Perhaps after so much experience with a lunatic listening to the radio in a back room, he was less intimidated. He watched Theresa from the doorway for several minutes. Back in the kitchen, all he said was, "Christ, that radio of hers sounds like hell."

"Like hell is right," said Joseph.

"She should have let me know." Lino shook his head. "I could have fixed it."

"We should have let her join the convent," said Catherine. "That's what we should have done."

"Catherine." Evelyn spoke in the smooth, assured tone of a toastmaster addressing the guests of honor. "Joseph. Mister Falconetti. The point is not to think of all the things we should have done. The point, as I see it, is to concentrate on now."

"I think we should get her to a doctor," said Catherine. "For the not-eating, if nothing else."

"Catherine, sweetheart," said Evelyn. "The not-eating is the tip of the iceberg. So what you're saying is, you'll take her to a doctor and keep her at home?"

"What should we do?" said Joseph. "Throw her out on the street?"

"On the contrary," said Evelyn. "Correct me if I'm wrong, Joseph, but from what I hear, it's gone too far for her to be home. She's seeing things, hearing voices—there's no telling what a person in that state will do. At the very least, you'll have to watch her twenty-four hours a day. You want to saddle Catherine with that on top of everything else? Catherine, kiss your life good-bye."

"Then what?" said Joseph.

"Joseph," said Augie, "there's places designed to help kids like Theresa."

It took Joseph several minutes to understand what his brother meant. Then he turned his palms out and shook his head as if refusing food.

"No thanks," he said. "We'll manage. We'll work it out. I shouldn't have bothered you folks. . . ."

"Joseph," said Evelyn, "listen to me. I've got some friends on the Island, nice people, I'm not mentioning names. The oldest boy's a junior in the public high school, the top of his class. A handsome kid—friends, dates, everything. One morning, he comes down to breakfast and announces he's Jesus Christ reincarnated. Sure, his folks say, sure you are. That very night, his dad finds him trying to crucify himself on some old rose trellises in the garage.

"I'll spare you the gory details. Things got worse. What could they do? They sent him to Stella Maris, in Glen Cove. It used to be a Franciscan seminary and now it's a hospital—a rest home really, specializing in cases like his. Also priests and nuns who have been working too hard.

"Now it's a year later. Not so long. The kid's home, back in school. Straight As."

"They cured him?" said Joseph.

Augie and Evelyn exchanged glances.

"He's a quiet kid," said Augie. "No way around that. But at least he isn't nailing himself up anymore."

Joseph looked at Augie. Augie smiled—he was always smiling—but now his smile was forced. Who was Augie, thought Joseph, with his trucks, his ranch house, his life like some Italian *Father Knows Best?* Who was Augie to feel sorry for him?

"I just don't know about sending my kid to a nuthouse."

"It's not exactly a nuthouse," said Evelyn.

"Bars on the windows?"

"I've never been there personally. But from what I understand, it's nicer than most Catskill resorts."

"I'll bet it costs like one," said Joseph.

"Joseph, what doesn't cost?"

"It doesn't make sense," Joseph said. "It doesn't make sense that a bunch of strangers could help her better than her own flesh and blood."

"That's just it," said Evelyn. "Sometimes flesh and blood are the *last* ones to help. They're too close. There's no . . . perspective."

"Catherine," said Joseph, "what do you think?"

"I don't know. I don't know if she'd go for it."

But even as she spoke, Catherine knew that Theresa would be happy to go. For Evelyn's nuthouse sounded just like the convent she'd wanted all her life. It seemed possible now that everything might still be turned around if she and Joseph would finally let go, and give Theresa what she wanted.

Joseph took one look at her and knew exactly what she was thinking.

"We could try it," he said. "If it doesn't work, she can always come home."

"I don't know," said Catherine. But she wasn't saying no.

"Joseph, Catherine, I think you're making a wise decision." Evelyn seemed elated, like a scientist who's just been given the go-ahead for a new experiment. "Look, I know it's a difficult time for you. If you want, Augie and I can take care of the details. Augie, you'll call the hospital today. . . ."

After they left, Lino said, "You got a minute?"

"Plenty," said Joseph.

"In private." Lino glanced at Catherine.

Lino put on his coat and Joseph followed him into the hall. Inside, Joseph hadn't really noticed, but here in the dim greenish light, he saw that the old man's skin had that pastry crust look, like Frank Manzone's at the end. Lino made a fist and blew on it.

"I saw them," he said.

"Who's them?" said Joseph.

"Nicky. And Madame Butterfly."

"Where?"

"On television." Lino spat out the word.

"Wait a minute. You don't even have a television."

"I saw it at the San Remo. Last night, I stopped off for a quick one."

"Now I get it."

"You don't get anything. I was soberer than you are, if you want to know the truth. It was late, the place was empty, and the bartender—who knew the guy was such an opera-lover?—had the set tuned to some kind of educational station.

"'Look,' he says to me. '*Madame Butterfly.*'

"And that's when I saw it, Nicky dressed up in a sailor suit, singing. And Madame Butterfly? Jesus, she wasn't even Japanese. Just a big fat Italian mama, all painted with make-up to make her eyes look slanty. And you know what I thought?"

"What?" said Joseph.

"'How silly!' I thought. 'Is this what he wanted? Is this what my kid lived and died for? All this silly braying and mooning and prancing around with daggers and baby American flags? Ridiculous!' I couldn't even follow the story. The only thing was, I did feel a little sorry for that Madame Butterfly at the end? Know why?"

"Why?" Joseph had his eyes closed and was shaking his head: First Theresa, now this.

"Because she married into the Falconetti luck. How was she supposed to know? She was Japanese."

"Don't kid yourself," said Joseph. "There's Falconettis in Japan, Falconettis everywhere. Guys who drink too much and feel sorry for themselves, guys who don't talk and never love anybody, guys with businesses which never fail and never prosper and just limp along. . . ." Joseph stopped. "What am I talking about? Madame Butterfly marrying a Falconetti? I must be going nuts, like you and Nicky and Theresa. . . ."

"Huh?" Lino was too old to afford the luxury of being insulted.

"Never mind."

"The other thing I thought," continued Lino, "was: Isn't it perfect? Isn't it just perfect that a guy with my problems—my history—should see such a thing on television?"

"I don't care what you saw. Or what you think you saw. But one thing's for sure: You didn't see Nicky. Nicky's dead. Maybe that opera singer looked a little like him, or exactly like him—but it wasn't Nicky. So just keep it quiet, okay? Or they'll be shipping you off to the nuthouse with my daughter."

"The only way they'll ship me off is in a wooden box."

"You never know," said Joseph. "You in particular," he thought. Only this time, he was afraid that Lino did know.

"Take it easy," Joseph said, and retreated back into his apartment where he drank three glasses of water in quick succession because the taste in his mouth was as sour as that of Frank Manzone's vinegar-wine.

That year, spring came so late that Catherine began to think that Theresa's lethargy had infected everything. The sun was too tired to shine, the earth too passive to bother warming up. Catherine and Joseph were so resigned that they waited patiently through the week it took Stella Maris to admit Theresa, and did not protest the hospital's suggestion that Augie and Evelyn be the ones to accompany Theresa out and that they themselves refrain from visiting her for at least a month.

The bills started coming immediately, and Joseph was right: It cost like a Catskill resort. The business could sustain the extra expense without much strain. But often, in the shop, it occurred to Joseph that he was working to keep Theresa in a nuthouse. It took the fun out of everything—especially cheating. Gradually Joseph stopped tipping the scales and just raised his prices like everyone else.

It was early March when Joseph and Catherine first took the

Long Island Railroad to Stella Maris. It was a rainy Sunday, and the stuffy train smelled of damp wool overcoats, cigar smoke, wet hair—mysterious odors, of invisible origin, because the car was deserted except for one other family—three small children racing up and down the aisle, a silent father, and a mother who spent the whole trip licking handkerchiefs, dabbing faces, and crying, "Andy! Kevin! Michelle! What will Grandma say when she sees you such a mess?"

Outside the windows, suburban lawns flashed by—neat rectangles of ice, pocked with patches of mud and shrubs which were little more than bunches of twigs. Neither Catherine nor Joseph had anything to say. After a while Joseph took out a packet of cheroots and lit one, enveloping them both in an anise-scented cloud. It was the first time Catherine had ever seen him smoke, but she let it pass without comment.

At Huntington Station, they got out and took a cab over several miles of flooded two-lane road. The cab hit potholes, and sheets of water splashed against the windshield. Then the driver would slam on his brakes and they'd wade through the puddles which rippled out around them like wings. When they reached the gates of Stella Maris, the grounds were shrouded in fog, and the hospital—a brick Victorian fortress—loomed out of the mist.

"Jesus," said Joseph. "Dracula's castle."

"*Rebecca*," said Catherine. "It looks like that house in *Rebecca*."

But the brightly lit lobby comforted them, as it was designed to do. The nursery-yellow walls were decorated with colorful Tuberculosis Society posters and Sister Corita prints. Joseph and Catherine were prepared for wild-eyed, stringy-haired cases in bathrobes and bedroom slippers. But none of the people they saw would have looked out of place in the tidy suburban homes they'd passed on the train. They were encouraged by the number of young people, and by how difficult it was to tell the inmates from their caretakers. On one side of the lobby, patients were entertaining visitors in an airy solarium; nearby, the ones with no company seemed just as content to read the Sunday papers and watch television in a wood-beamed baronial sitting room.

"Look," said Catherine. "Color TV."

"For what we're paying," said Joseph, "they can afford it."

The nun at the reception desk directed them through a door at the end of the lobby. The arched door—heavy oak, with a leaded glass window—swung shut behind them, closing out the twentieth century and admitting them to the medieval monastery which the architect who built Stella Maris had in mind. They followed the damp stone hall past a well-kept, deserted courtyard, then up a circular stone staircase and down another corridor. On both sides of the hall were the patients' rooms—whitewashed cubicles, bare as monks' cells, each furnished with a bed, a desk, a chair, a dresser, a washstand, and a crucifix. It was one of the rules of Stella Maris that residents were not allowed to bring reminders of home.

"They're just like Theresa's room at the apartment." Catherine's voice shook. "I'm sure she feels right at home."

"Catherine," said Joseph. "Relax."

They found Theresa at the end of the corridor, kneeling on the floor. Beside her was a bucket, and she was scrubbing the smooth paving stones with a brush.

"Honey." Catherine knelt to kiss her, then dipped her fingers in the bucket. "You must be freezing. That water's like ice."

Theresa smiled up at them, her eyes so vacant that it was hard to tell if she recognized them.

"I'm fine," she said. "Just let me finish this section, and we can go have a cup of tea."

"Tea?" said Catherine. Since when did her daughter like tea?

Clenching the brush, Theresa's hand swung over the floor like a pendulum, so close to Joseph and Catherine's feet that they had to jump out of the way.

"What's going on here?" cried Joseph. "What in the hell are you doing?"

"Occupational therapy," answered Sister Cupertino, to whose office they were taken when Joseph demanded to see the doctor in charge.

Sister Cupertino was a middle-aged woman, her face as flat and round as a pie, with wire-rimmed spectacles and bright dark eyes like two holes cut out of the crust to let the steam escape. When she stood to shake hands, the Santangelos noticed that she was wearing a mouse-brown ankle-length habit which made her look more like a Brownie leader than a nun.

Nor was her office very nun-like. Framed diplomas hung on the paneled walls. Her wide mahogany desk was littered with documents, stacks of charts, balls of crumpled paper, envelopes. And Sister Cupertino was almost as sloppy as her desk. Catherine had never before seen a nun in a wrinkled veil.

"It's what we call occupational therapy," she said. "In certain cases, it's clearly indicated. When it works." She smiled at them, a twitch of the lips. Catherine smiled back.

"I'll spare you the jargon. But briefly, Theresa's case has been diagnosed as one of acute hallucinatory psychosis, brought on by a particularly difficult and prolonged adolescent psychosexual adjustment, no doubt aggravated by a somewhat obsessional religious nature. What that means in layman's terms is—as I'm sure you know—Theresa has temporarily lost touch with what we call reality."

"Temporarily?" said Catherine. It was what she had always hoped. Overnight, Theresa would change, everything would be normal. . . .

"Often, these states are temporary, though sometimes of course . . . Especially among young people, it's quite common. . . ."

"And all these young people wash the floors?" said Joseph.

"Many of them undertake some form of occupational therapy." Sister Cupertino seemed unfazed by Joseph's nasty tone. "It helps bring them into closer touch with their surroundings. And also, you must understand, the hours do get long here at Stella Maris."

"I'll bet," said Joseph. "But I still don't get it. I mean, what am I paying for? She could be washing floors at home."

"Like Evelyn said," answered Catherine. "Home's not always the best place."

"Since when are you quoting Evelyn?"

Amazed that Joseph would speak to her like that in front of a stranger, Catherine looked down at the rug. There were several blackened matches near her feet.

"Your wife is right, Mr. Santangelo. Here at Stella Maris, we can monitor her condition. She's in intensive analysis, four mornings a week. As an adjunct to therapy, we have her on a low maintenance dose of lithium."

"Lithium?" said Joseph. "What's that?"

"Mr. Santangelo, one question: Does your daughter seem happy here?"

"Happy isn't the word for it."

"Well, then." As far as Sister Cupertino was concerned, the case was closed.

"I guess," said Joseph. "Maybe we should have let her join the convent like she wanted. Anyhow it would have been cheaper."

"Why think about what we should have done?" said Catherine.

"You quoting Evelyn again?" Joseph sank back into his chair. "At least she's safe here from creeps like that Leonard. At least we know where she is at night, which is more than Evelyn can say about her Stacey."

"You see?" said Sister Cupertino.

But Catherine was too tired to see. Her legs ached, as if it were she instead of Theresa who'd spent the day washing floors. She stared down at her hands, chapped and pitted and cracked no matter what detergent she'd used, and she felt the combined effort of all those days in the kitchen, the years which Mrs. Santangelo spent making sausage, the hours Theresa wasted ironing her boyfriend's shirts. Again she had the eerie sensation of spinning back behind a movie camera. Only now she saw that the movie was not a romance, neither *Rebecca* nor Bogart and Bacall, but frame after frame of grimy dishes, balled-up socks. Her life had escaped from her in one continuous moment of chores which would never be done even after she was dead. Twenty years ago, she'd found joy in a line of freshly washed baby clothes. Twenty years later, her baby was washing floors in a nuthouse.

Catherine looked up at Joseph, then over at Sister Cupertino. "What did I do it for?" she said.

Theresa knew how things appeared from the outside: Her family had committed her to a nuthouse. But by then, the only outside that mattered to her was the physical surface of things—the polish of the stone, the clean window pane, the heavy ceramic dishes, so netted with hairline cracks that they'd turned the mottled gray-green of an Oriental brush painting. Pushing the scrub brush over the floor, she thought of how God had created that soap, that water. She saw the miracle in the granite, in the hard bright transparency of glass. The pattern in the netted china was as clear to her as a stenciled rose. She did not have to remind herself of these things, nor did she have to convince herself that Sister Cupertino was extraordinarily beautiful, as dear and familiar to her as her mother and father.

When she walked into Sister Cupertino's office, four mornings a week, the nun's wide face shone at her like the full moon, a flat white disc of light. Sister Cupertino interrogated her with pointless questions—what difference did it make when she had first learned to use the toilet? But always Theresa thought, without trying, of a story she had read: A bishop visits an island on which he finds three hermits. While praying with them, he discovers that the hermits are saying the Lord's Prayer incorrectly and, despite their considerable slowness, finally teaches them to say it right. He bids them good-bye, sails away, and that night sees a light approaching him over the water. As the light grows brighter, he sees that it is the three hermits, skimming toward him, flying hand in hand over the sea.

194

"Father," they beg him, "tell us the Lord's Prayer again, we can't seem to get it right." And the bishop can only say, "Brothers, pray for us."

It was obvious to Theresa that, like the hermits, Sister Cupertino was praising God in her own way, and that all her silly questions comprised some private Lord's Prayer. And so she repeated her own story (not out of any desire to help herself, she didn't need help) but rather as a gift—for Sister Cupertino and, of course, for God. It was a simple story, as Theresa told it: The letter from Fatima. The Little Flower. The Carmelites. College. Leonard. An ironing board, a visit from Jesus, an infinity of red and white checked shirts. Invariably, Sister Cupertino would break in at this point, saying, "Theresa, the laundry is only the laundry."

In an effort to convince Theresa of this, her occupational therapy was shifted to the hospital laundry, where she was put to work folding sheets. When Theresa first touched the heavy institutional cotton (washed smoother than the finest percale), she nearly cried out with joy. She learned to fold each sheet with four swift motions, always the same four, stretching and snapping her arms with such precision and concentration that the sheets came out in identical rectangles—straight edges and perfect corners. Occasionally her rhythm was broken by a torn or stained sheet which had to be sorted out; the rips and spots were as precious to her as the blood on Jesus' shroud.

The laundry was hot and steamy, the smell of detergent intoxicating, and Jesus was there. Theresa felt His warmth in the sheets fresh from the dryer; the soft hospital cotton was the touch of His hand in hers. He was closer to her than the width of Leonard's ironing board, and she was folding the sheets for Him.

What made all this bearable for Joseph and Catherine was their faith that it was only temporary. Convinced that each musty train ride was bringing them closer to the last one they would ever have to take, they almost began to enjoy them. They ordered their weeks around these Sunday trips and prepared for them as if for important journeys. Joseph purchased an accordion grate to pull across the storefront on Saturday nights. Catherine bought him a pair of driving gloves with pigskin palms, and it pleased them both to see these elegant gloves hailing taxis in the rain. Catherine learned to recognize the regulars, other passengers with relatives at Stella Maris. Although they avoided each other's eyes and never spoke, they formed a kind of family—no more distant and no less connected than the Falconettis.

Their visits took place in the solarium, where Theresa served them tea in paper cups and seemed quite fascinated by news of Joseph's business, Catherine's neighborhood gossip. If this were the Carmelite convent, thought Joseph, there would be no gossip, no tea.

Eventually, what they minded most about these trips was the weather. Every Sunday, it rained or sleeted or snowed. The train was always too hot or too cold, so damp and smelly that Catherine felt queasy. Yet even this discomfort came to seem reassuring; even the bad weather was dependable, and this dependability was what they liked about Stella Maris. They knew approximately where they would find Theresa, knew what she would be doing and how she would look. Each Sunday, Catherine took a deep breath and told herself that the other shoe had finally dropped: There were no more surprises.

And so they were doubly surprised when they arrived on a rainy Sunday afternoon in early May and were told that Theresa was resting in her room.

"Something's wrong," said Catherine. "I knew it the minute I got up this morning."

All that was wrong was a slight touch of the flu—nothing serious, according to the nuns who padded in and out on their gum-soled shoes, bringing aspirin and orange juice. Doctor Fontana had been in to check on her that morning and had prescribed an antibiotic. With God's help, she would recover in three or four days.

Theresa didn't even look sick. She was wearing the sort of washed-out white flannel nightgown which can make healthy people look deathly ill; even so, her color was good, almost too good for a girl who'd spent the winter shuttling between an overheated laundry and a cold stone floor. Propped up on pillows, she lay between crisp sheets, her hands folded over the rough green blanket.

"At least it got her out of the laundry," whispered Joseph.

"Shh." Catherine hurried to give Theresa a hug and kiss. Joseph held back.

"You contagious?" he said. "I've got to go to work tomorrow."

"Papa." Theresa patted the edge of the bed. "Come sit by me. I need your help."

"At your service." Joseph took off his driving gloves and rubbed his hands together, blowing into his palms. "What can I do for you?"

"I need some advice."

Joseph looked at Catherine. He couldn't remember Theresa ever asking him for advice. Maybe Stella Maris was doing her good.

"What about?"

"Pinochle," said Theresa.

"Pinochle?" Joseph laughed so hard that he had to sit down. "Is that what you're doing here with my money? Playing pinochle?"

"We don't play for money. Just points."

"That's a relief," said Joseph. "Who do you play with?"

"God the Father and Jesus and St. Therese."

Joseph laughed again, less heartily than before.

"You mean, there's people here who think they're God and Jesus and—"

"I mean God and Jesus and St. Therese."

Joseph glanced at Catherine. She was patting the air: Easy, take it easy. Humor her.

"You folks play often?" he asked.

"Last night was the first time. God had to teach me the rules. Of course they let me have a few practice hands. But you would have been proud of me, Papa. I got the hang of it right away."

"It's in the blood," said Joseph.

Catherine groaned.

"Don't worry, Mama. If God's playing, it's got to be all right."

"This is crazy," said Joseph. "This is the craziest thing I ever heard."

Catherine shot him a warning look.

"You play partners?" he said.

"Girls against boys."

"I should have known," said Joseph.

"We got slaughtered, Papa. We never had a chance. Please don't tell anyone I said so, but the Little Flower wasn't much of a pinochle player. She mumbled so low, you couldn't hear what she bid. God had to make her repeat herself twenty times. It seemed like she passed them every card they needed—it was like she didn't want to win."

"That's a saint for you," said Catherine.

"I guess." Theresa sighed. "I guess I'll never be a saint. I wanted to win, I played hard. But even if I'd been an expert . . . we still didn't have a chance. Because God and Jesus drew nothing but high cards—straights, flushes, the jack of diamonds, the queen of spades. Between them, they controlled every hand. We quit when they had five hundred points and St. Therese and I had zero."

"Honey," said Catherine, "it was God you were playing with. Wouldn't you expect Him to win?"

"You too?" Joseph stared at her.

"I never expected to be playing pinochle with God," said Theresa.

"I know what you mean," admitted Catherine.

"And if I had," continued Theresa, "I would have expected Him to play fair."

"He didn't?"

Theresa looked around the room and out into the hall, as if to make sure that no one was listening.

"If it hadn't been God, I would have sworn He was cheating."

"He probably was," said Joseph.

"He was." Again Theresa checked for eavesdroppers. "After the game was over, God let the others leave before Him. On His way out, He stopped and whispered real low so the others couldn't hear:

"'Theresa,' He told me, 'of all my great miracles, my favorites are tipping the scales and cheating at pinochle.'

"That's what He said. Can you believe it?"

"I can believe it." Joseph looked pale.

No one spoke for a long time. Then Catherine said, "Joseph, what time have you got?"

Joseph looked at his watch.

"The four o'clock train left ten minutes ago. We'd better go, we'll be stuck at the station all night."

"We'll call tomorrow," said Catherine. "You rest up, get better."

"I feel wonderful," said Theresa. "Don't worry."

Catherine touched her forehead.

"You're burning up. I'll send the nurse in when we go."

Joseph and Catherine kissed their daughter's flushed face and left. They were silent in the taxi, but in the train Joseph said, "It's happening again. All that money we paid, and it's happening again."

"Nothing's happening," said Catherine. "She's had a fever. She was delirious."

"That's nothing? Anyhow, I don't believe that's it. What about the last time, at Leonard's? Ninety-eight-point-six."

"This is different. You heard the nurses. In three or four days, she'll be fine."

They watched the landscape rush by, rain pecking holes in the melting snow.

"This has got to be some kind of record," said Joseph. "Snow in May." Then he said, "Listen, how much did she know?"

"About what?"

"You know about what. The pinochle game. Before we got married."

"Maybe she knew, maybe not. *I* didn't tell her. But people talk . . . What difference does it make?"

"It seems like the end of the story," said Joseph. "Twenty years ago, I won my wife in a card game. And now our crazy daughter is playing pinochle with God."

"Take it easy. It's not your fault. No one ever went crazy because her father won her mother in a pinochle game."

"I'm not saying it's my fault. Far from it. I'm saying there's a pattern."

"Patterns. Next you'll be counting potato eyes like your mother."

"Look at that rain," said Joseph, and that was the end of the conversation till the train was pulling into Penn Station. Then Joseph turned to Catherine and said, "It makes you think. I mean, maybe there is a God, and He's the kind of guy who cheats at pinochle. Isn't that what they say, that you make Him in your own image? And like your father says: Isn't it perfect? Isn't it just perfect that a God who cheats at pinochle would end the story this way?"

But it wasn't the end of the story.

There was something which Catherine never told Joseph. Ordinarily she might have mentioned it, but his talk on the train about patterns made her keep it to herself: Every Sunday evening, they had sausage fried with onions and peppers. Easy, quick, delicious, it was by now an integral part of their weekly ritual. But that Sunday, Theresa's illness had so altered their established routine that Catherine couldn't even fry the sausage without feeling that something was different.

She was almost finished cooking when she realized that one

of her cacti had flowered—the one she'd bought at Woolworth's on that morning when Theresa disappeared. In all the years since, it had neither grown nor shrunk, blossomed nor looked any less like a pebble than it did that first day. Still Catherine had gone on watering it, treasuring it as a kind of memento which she could no more throw away than she could Theresa's baby pictures.

Now there was a marble-sized lump on top, covered with downy spines, a dark red tinged with fuchsia, like the center of a rose.

Catherine had always loved flowering plants. But this one terrified her, and she moved it to the back of the shelf where she wouldn't have to see it. This unaccountable dread stayed with her all night and woke her at five in the morning, thinking: There's more. The other shoe.

When the phone rang, she was not even startled, but lay there patiently, waiting for Joseph to answer.

"Mister Santangelo," said the voice on the phone, "this is Sister Cupertino from Stella Maris. I'm sorry to call so early, but I have some bad news for you. Mister Santangelo, your daughter has gone to God."

"Gone where?" Joseph mumbled groggily.

"To heaven."

"No," said Joseph.

"What's wrong?" said Catherine. "What happened?"

"Mister Santangelo, are you still there?"

"I'm here. What happened?"

"God took her."

"I mean how. How did it happen?"

"What?" said Catherine. "Joseph, tell me."

"Fever," said Sister Cupertino. "A sudden high fever. That's all we know. Sister Lucy went in to check on her on her morning rounds at four. She took Theresa's temperature. It was a hundred and six. She went to call Doctor Fontana, and when she got back at four-fifteen, Theresa had passed away—"

"It took her fifteen minutes to make a phone call?"

"Mister Santangelo, it was four in the morning. She got the doctor's answering service. Believe me, it was a great shock to us all."

"We'll be right out." Joseph hung up the phone.

"Theresa's dead," said Catherine.

Joseph put his arms around her and they held each other without speaking until Catherine said, "I feel like a hole's opened up in the world and my life's fallen through."

"I know what you mean," said Joseph. "About the hole."

They got up and got dressed.

"I guess there's no hurry," said Joseph. "We might as well wait for the light to come up." They drank coffee till shortly after dawn, then left.

It was a clear spring morning, so lovely that it seemed a shame to sleep it away, and Mulberry Street was wide awake. Shopkeepers were hosing down the sidewalk in front of their stores. Rainbows shone in the spray, and the asphalt gleamed in the morning sun. Early as it was, the streets were full of people dressed for work—secretaries in the new spring dresses which they'd bought as promises to themselves in the middle of winter.

"Wouldn't you know it?" said Joseph. "Now's when we get a good day for traveling."

Catherine stared at him.

"Some good day," she said.

At the entrance to Penn Station, boys were selling bunches of daffodils.

"You want some flowers?" asked Joseph.

"Daffodils? What for?"

As the train rolled through the suburbs, Joseph and Catherine saw patches of green on every lawn. They passed freshly plowed gardens, and the air carried the smell of manure. Half the trees were surrounded by the reddish aura which immediately precedes the formation of buds; the other half were already in bud.

"You know at the end of 'Red Riding Hood'?" said Catherine. "When they cut the wolf's stomach open and fill it with stones? That's how my stomach feels."

"Red Riding Hood?" murmured Joseph. He pointed out the window. "What's that?"

"I don't know. A hyacinth, maybe."

In the taxi, Catherine said, "In the sunshine, it's a whole different ride."

Stella Maris looked so unfamiliar that Catherine was momentarily afraid that the cab driver had let them off at the wrong place.

"Jesus," said Joseph. "Would you look at that?"

"I'm looking," said Catherine.

The garden was in full bloom. Delicate pink strands hung from the weeping cherries like the fringes of a shawl. The forsythia and early willow were bright yellow, the new grass yellow-green. Beds of daffodils, violets and blue forget-me-nots lined the walkway, and sunlight shone pearly and translucent through drifts of jonquils.

"It's not natural," whispered Joseph.

"What? What are you whispering for?"

"It's not natural. It's not right. Yesterday it was winter and today it's spring."

"Some years it happens like that."

"Not like this. Mud one day, the next a garden. Besides, you saw on the way out—the rest of the Island doesn't look like this."

"They've got good gardeners. The Church always gets the best. There's always some monsignor who'll throw a fit if he sees a dandelion on the lawn."

"The *Pope* couldn't do this. Not overnight."

"What do you know about it? The closest you ever got to nature was Frank Manzone's vegetable stand."

"Enough to know that you don't pull a garden out of a hat."

"Its not out of a hat. There were buds yesterday, the flowers were ready to pop. But it was raining, you didn't notice. . . ."

"Believe me, I would have noticed."

"But you didn't."

"Okay, you're the plant lady. You tell me. Is this natural or not?"

Joseph had stopped beside a bed of daffodils and was looking down at the flowers. They were all the same color: creamy white, with pale yellow centers and saffron stigmata. Joseph wanted to touch the orange stamens, but hesitated. Strangely, he was remembering his wedding night—how scared he'd been to touch Catherine. That night, he'd convinced himself that it was not just permissible—but necessary for life to go on. Yet now, nothing could have persuaded him to touch the inside of those flowers.

"It's those patterns again," he said. "Even the weather's in on it. Remember how hot it was, the night of that pinochle game? And how it rained the next day when you came into the shop? Now for months it rains every Sunday and all of a sudden, the sun . . ."

"Joseph." Catherine spoke very softly. "Theresa's lying out here dead and we're talking about the weather."

"You think I forgot?" said Joseph. "What else should we talk about?"

Catherine had turned her back to him. Her head was bent, her shoulders rounded. Joseph had to remind himself that forty wasn't old, because at that moment the alley cat he had married looked like an old woman.

"I'm sorry," he said, then put his arm around her and kept it there till they reached the lobby.

Sister Cupertino and a priest whom she introduced as Father Dominic were waiting for them. Father Dominic was a thin little man with pointed features, blue-white skin, dark circles under his eyes and a heavy five o'clock shadow. It occurred to Joseph that the priest looked worse than Theresa ever did, and Theresa was dead.

Sister Cupertino took Catherine's hands between her dry

palms and held them. Father Dominic, whose hands were somewhat stickier, did the same to Joseph.

"Good morning." Father Dominic's voice was nearly expres-
sionless, but the solemn look on his face said, God's will be
done.

"That's some garden you got out there," said Joseph.

Sister Cupertino and Father Dominic exchanged knowing
looks. They'd seen it before—so many families needed that
small talk, that buffer before getting down to the tragic business
at hand.

"Isn't it?" said Sister Cupertino. "After all the bad weather
we've been having, it's a miracle."

Joseph gave her a funny look.

"It always comes like that? Overnight?"

"Mister Santangelo, it's practically the middle of May."

Father Dominic ushered them to Theresa's room, then discreetly vanished. Joseph and Catherine hesitated in the doorway.
But when they forced themselves inside, they saw that Theresa
looked almost exactly as she had the day before—only paler,
eyes shut. Her head was still propped up on pillows, her hands
folded over the blanket.

"It's hard to believe," said Catherine.

"What's that smell?" said Joseph.

"What's got into you today?" Catherine sniffed. "I don't
know, some kind of flowers."

"Roses," said Joseph. "It's enough to knock you over."

"So?"

"There's no roses in this room. Do you see roses in this
room?"

"Calm down. Maybe one of the nurses was wearing perfume."

"You know nuns don't wear perfume."

"Then maybe an orderly. Maybe the doctor was wearing
cologne."

"It's not cologne."

"Air freshener, then. How should I know?"
"No air freshener in the world smells like this."
"Maybe it's coming from the outside. From the garden."
Joseph went to the window.
"There's a parking lot out there." Beyond it, he saw green. . . .
"It didn't smell like this *in* the garden."
"So they had flowers in here and took them out."
"Why would they do that? Besides, that smell that sticks around when you take flowers out of a room—it's always kind of stale. And this isn't stale, it's like going up to a rose and sticking your nose right in it."
Joseph approached the bed.
"It's coming from Theresa. Did you ever know her to use perfume?"
"Theresa?" Catherine came closer. "You're right. Maybe it's some kind of soap they use here."
"I know the smell of soap." Joseph shook his head.
Kneeling by the side of the bed, Catherine said a Hail Mary, and an Our Father, then added her personal prayer that Theresa's soul would go straight to heaven. She imagined St. Peter greeting her at the gate, saying, "Theresa! How perfect that you should come today, it's spring cleaning!" And Theresa would enter paradise to find the angels sweeping the clouds with golden brooms, raising puffs of feathery dust.
When Catherine stood, Joseph said, "It's not natural for a healthy young girl to die in one night with no warning."
"I thought they told you it was fever."
"Fever? What do psychiatrists know about fever?"
"So maybe it wasn't fever. Maybe it was her heart. Or some medicine they gave her. She's dead, what can we do now? What do you think, they murdered her? What do you want, revenge?"
"I guess God took her," said Joseph. "Like the lady said."
"Maybe so. We might as well think so."
"It doesn't help. It doesn't help at all."
"I know," said Catherine.

Then Joseph said, "Isn't that what's supposed to happen when a saint dies? Everything starts smelling like flowers?"

Catherine glanced at him. Was he joking? But he was serious when he said, "Suppose she was one."

"A saint? Theresa?"

"Sure, why not? Maybe she got what she wanted."

"Joseph, Theresa was a beautiful girl. A good girl. I'll never love anyone in my life like I loved her. But she was crazy, Joseph. She went crazy ironing shirts in her boyfriend's apartment."

"Saints have done crazier. Look. Look at this." Joseph held up Theresa's hands. Not yet rigid, they bent gracefully at the wrists—both of which were covered with a network of red lines, faintly streaked with blood.

"What's this? Catherine, what's this?"

"What do you think? Stigmata?"

"What then?"

"Mosquito bites. She scratched herself in her sleep."

"Mosquitoes in May?"

"Sure, in May."

"Catherine, remember how much she used to pray? All those times she fasted. Who else acts like that but a saint? Suppose that's what she was?"

"A saint?"

"Who knows? There's been miracles here. First the garden, then that smell in the room, the stigmata, even the way she died . . ."

"You're upset. You're letting it get to you. There haven't been any miracles. Nothing's happened, nothing's *ever* happened to us that couldn't happen normally. The garden was green yesterday—you just didn't notice. Theresa could have started wearing perfume here at the hospital—how would we know? Yesterday she was dying and we didn't even see it. Maybe the burning bush was burning all the time and Moses didn't notice. Maybe the miracle is when you stop and pay attention."

"I don't get it," said Joseph.

"We're not talking about walking on water," said Catherine. "We're talking about ordinary life. Remember when I thought that the dead plants in our place had been resurrected and the truth was, you'd watered them and bought new ones? Remember how your mother thought it was a miracle when that geranium bloomed on the mantelpiece—and all the time I'd known it was going to?"

"It flowered." Joseph was thinking of the daffodil bed. "No matter who knew. Maybe *that* was the miracle."

"Maybe so. But it's not the kind of thing they canonize you for." Again Catherine sniffed the air. The smell was getting stronger. "So what if it is a miracle? What then?"

"Somebody should be told. Someone in the church . . ."

"The church? You must be kidding."

"It's what Theresa would have wanted."

"Okay, that's it." Catherine dusted her palms together. "Forget it, just forget it. There's arrangements to make."

Sister Cupertino—her manner so breezy that she might have been outlining another phase of Theresa's treatment—served them coffee in her office while discussing the funeral arrangements. When at last the Santangelos rose to leave, she put her doughy arms around their shoulders, smiled ruefully and said, "If Theresa had lived in another era, they might have called her a saint."

"If they'd had lithium in Jesus' time," said Joseph, "there wouldn't have been any saints."

"Joseph," said Catherine, "let's go."

"If they'd had mental hospitals, they'd have had John the Baptist on occupational therapy," muttered Joseph, and that was the last that either of them spoke till they were nearly home.

Finally Catherine said, "Joseph, it's not as if *I* believe this. But suppose Theresa was a saint—miracles, stigmata, the works. What if we told somebody and they took us seriously, and the church just happened to need an *American* Little Flower of Jesus? Service and devotion in every little thing—even ironing shirts in a Catholic law student's apartment. Then what? Then poor Theresa, that's what. Would you want her to spend eternity like that, people lighting candles—"

"Who lights candles anymore?"

"There will always be somebody. Telling the saints their problems, begging them for help they can't give. Is that what you want for your daughter? Hasn't she done enough favors?"

"I never thought of it that way," said Joseph.

Catherine waited till they were back in the apartment, then closed and locked the door.

"Joseph," she said, "if you really think that Theresa was a saint, if you think we've seen miracles—think what you want, but keep your mouth shut. For Theresa's sake, Joseph, if you ever loved her—don't tell a soul."

One foot in front of the other: This was what was meant by God's mercy. It seemed to Catherine as if her body were producing its own morphine, stronger than any painkiller a doctor could prescribe. She wasn't expected to do anything, and yet she was so numb that she could help Joseph hang the bunting and accept her neighbors' condolences without bursting into tears. The only trouble with this wonder drug was that it tended to wear off in the middle of the night. And it disappeared completely when she and Joseph walked into the funeral parlor and saw all the roses.

The night after Theresa died had been the first warm evening of spring. The old people had dusted off their folding chairs and come out to take the air, to thank God for the weather and to remark how strange it was that they were alive to enjoy this breeze when a twenty-year-old girl lay dead. At this, the grandmothers had picked at their stockings and waited for their husbands to tease them out of their misery. But their husbands were in no mood for teasing. A young person's death was always a tragedy—but this was like losing a daughter.

It wasn't that they'd felt particularly close to Theresa. She'd kept to herself, they hadn't loved her as they'd loved their children's friends, their grandchildren's friends, the neighbors' kids they'd fed and hugged and practically adopted. But they knew where Theresa came from, and her story was part of them, absorbed into their systems with every sausage they'd eaten in the last thirty years. The old people remembered Mrs. Santangelo and were shocked to realize how long she'd been gone. Middle-aged couples remembered being young and single and dancing at the wedding of the man who'd won his wife at a card game. The women remembered when their children were young and they'd traded stories with Catherine. Now their Mary Kay was married, their Sal had a good job in the garment district, and Theresa was dead.

Her story had marked off their lives, become part of their own life stories—they couldn't stand to know that it was ending this way. Only the good die young, they said so often that they couldn't think of Theresa without conjuring up one of those marble lambs curled up on an infant's tombstone.

Individually and together, the Santangelos' neighbors came to the same conclusion. The only appropriate gesture—the only way to honor such innocence, to sweeten such a bitter end—was to spare no expense and send roses.

And so it happened that Joseph and Catherine walked into Castellano's Funeral Home to find every surface covered with roses—massed on the altar, down the steps, on trestle tables lining the side aisles and spilling from the windowsills so that all four walls were blanketed with roses.

Catherine began to cry. Joseph put his arms around her to support her, and caught himself leaning on her. People were looking at them, trying not to stare, but Joseph and Catherine were alone in that chapel with the roses and Theresa's body. Catherine prayed that Joseph wouldn't start talking about patterns again, because now she was seeing them too, and this one made her angry.

She was remembering her wedding, the feast which—like

these roses—had appeared out of nowhere. Two miracles, two magic tricks, except that both times all Mulberry Street was in on it. Like the wedding guests, the mourners in the lobby looked as if they knew something she didn't, knew that it was more than her wedding, more than her daughter's funeral. And suddenly she felt as if her whole life had been planned this way, without consulting her, contrived to satisfy someone's idea of some old story which had nothing to do with her: First the wedding at Cana and now this shower of roses.

She got angrier each time an old woman filed by and laid a white rosary in the coffin. Nor did it help when Joseph whispered in her ear, "You know who sent those roses? The same guy who stacked that pinochle deck."

All through the wake, the smell of roses grew stronger. By the funeral, their perfume was stale, almost suffocating. Joseph and Catherine barely heard the service; then someone ushered them into a black limousine. As the car swung through a complicated series of turns onto the highway, Joseph looked back and saw that the cortege was so long, every car in the cloverleaf behind them had its lights on.

Later, Catherine would remember nothing about the graveside except her fear that she would never stop crying. When the coffin was lowered, Joseph couldn't watch, and instead looked around and saw that no one could watch.

For the first time that anyone could remember, no one went back to the family's house after the service. Catherine had planned on having her neighbors in, but when she saw all the roses, she'd let it be known that she didn't want company.

By evening, the merciful numbness had returned and Catherine went to bed early. Joseph waited till she was asleep, then went out with Augie to get drunk at the San Remo, where he told his brother the whole story. Perhaps it was the wine, or the will to believe that his daughter's life had had more meaning than a premature death in a nuthouse. Whatever the reason, Joseph heard himself talking as if Theresa were really a saint: "You

FRANCINE PROSE

can tell me they were mosquito bites, but I say no. That hospital room smelled stronger than the funeral parlor this morning. And Augie, I swear to God: We were out there the day before, and that garden was dead. I keep seeing patterns—patterns in everything. Even that hot night, that night I won Catherine at pinochle—God was stacking the deck. God was turning up the heat."

Augie went home and told Evelyn. By noon the next day, the entire neighborhood had heard about the peculiar circumstances surrounding Theresa's death, and everyone was so happy to think that her story might have a different end that they were already beginning to revise it. Now suddenly people remembered that long-ago morning when Theresa got lost and was found splashing in the holy water. Former schoolmates recalled the ceremony in which she'd received *The Story of a Soul.* Except for some rumors about trouble with a boy, no one had much recent knowledge of the shy, standoffish girl, and so it was easy to invent details.

Each teller added new examples of her charity, her obedience, her patience. Somehow the rumor got started that a string of miracles had followed soon upon her death. It was said that all the patients at Stella Maris recovered instantaneously on the day of Theresa's funeral and were discharged to make room for a new generation of residents. It was said that the hospital gardens retained their bloom all summer and were discovered to have healing powers; busloads of schizophrenics were imported from Pilgrim State and cured by touching Theresa's favorite rose trellis. It was said that her bereaved parents gave her radio to her grandfather, and that this radio would play nothing but religious stations, picked up from all over the country. It was said that Lino Falconetti made no attempt to fix the set, though he lived another ten years and died believing himself a lucky man.

Finally it was said that Theresa's holiness could still be partaken of by buying sausage from her father's shop. Following her death, it was rumored, Joseph Santangelo never cheated a customer again. There were many who knew for a fact that this was untrue, and they told it like this: After the mourning period, Joseph reopened his shop and started cheating like never before. And when the women complained, he would flash them his sweetest smile and say, "You know who cheats? God cheats. Go complain to Him."

But by then, the facts of Theresa's life and death were less important than the story and the reasons people told it: At school, the good girls told it as conclusive proof that it was still possible to lead a consecrated life: God knew who thought good thoughts and helped around the house. At night, the men came home from playing cards and retold it, as if to say: You may think we're wasting our time playing cards, but for all you know—we're preparing the way for a saint. And their wives made similar claims whenever they ruined a meal, on those days when everything went wrong in the kitchen.

In the daytime, though, the women told it differently, to each other. The happy women, and the women who still imagined that happiness was attainable, sighed and said, "If only it would happen to me. If only I could see God in the dirty laundry." And the women who looked back on a lifetime of laundry and thought, What did I do it for? said, "Why bother? Look where it gets you—the nuthouse."

"What kind of life did she lead?" they said. "Nothing was accomplished, nothing left behind. She went crazy and died and went into the ground and that was it." Then the others would point out some little girl with a bag of groceries.

"Life goes on," they said, and the women would look at each other, not knowing how to feel.

The only ones who could tell the story with no mixed feelings and nothing to prove were the very old. They told it with reverence, with the same respect they would have shown the life of a saint. They told it as Theresa would have liked it told, as the story of an ordinary life redeemed by extraordinary devotion.

They told it for hope, and its comfort stayed with them even as Theresa's life receded into that time when everything was bigger and better and more extreme.

They saved it for the hottest nights, when the air was so heavy that they couldn't breathe, so still that they could hear the untrustworthy rhythm of their heartbeats. They told it quietly, as if telling a bedtime story to a grandchild. But this was the story they told to reassure themselves, to remind each other: Wait. Such things can happen to anyone, on any hot night—a hot night exactly like this. Hush. Listen to the sound of cards slapping on the table. God is sending us a saint.

ACKNOWLEDGMENT

I would like to thank the National Endowment for the Arts for its support.

ABOUT THE AUTHOR

Francine Prose is the author of sixteen novels, including *A Changed Man*, winner of the Dayton Literary Peace Prize, and *Blue Angel*, a finalist for the National Book Award. Her most recent works of nonfiction include the highly acclaimed *Anne Frank: The Book, the Life, the Afterlife*, and the *New York Times* bestseller *Reading Like a Writer*. A former president of PEN American Center and a member of the American Academy of Arts and Letters, as well as the American Academy of Arts and Sciences, Prose is a highly regarded critic and essayist, and has taught literature and writing for more than twenty years at major universities. She is a distinguished writer in residence at Bard College, and she lives in New York City.

EBOOKS BY FRANCINE PROSE

FROM OPEN ROAD MEDIA

Available wherever ebooks are sold

OPEN ROAD

INTEGRATED MEDIA

OPEN ROAD

INTEGRATED MEDIA

Open Road Integrated Media is a digital publisher and multimedia content company. Open Road creates connections between authors and their audiences by marketing its ebooks through a new proprietary online platform, which uses premium video content and social media.